Praise for

# Touch of Death

"HOLY MEDUSA AND HADES! ... Come along for the greatest ride of a lifetime. You will love the mythology retelling and the cast of characters who will become family to Jodi... I am sure this series will be one people will talk about for years to come."
— Diary Of A Book Addict

"I Hereby Award This Book 5 Wings, but I would gladly award it a thousand times that... It is a MUST read. If you like zombies, necromancers, mythology, gorgeous men and fantastic writing, then you need to add this to your own TBR pile. NOW!"
— Gothic Angel Book Reviews

"I adored this book. Right from the start I found this positively one of the coolest books I've ever read... *Touch of Death* is phenomenal and it completely and utterly took my breath away. I am dying to read more and I cannot wait to find out what happens next. Kelly Hashway is an author to look out for in the future. She is amazing and *Touch of Death* is one book that is not to be missed."
— K-Books

"*Touch of Death* was everything I expected it to be and so much more. It had a gripping story line, young romance, a fierce heroine, evil villains, and a swoon worthy hero. To put it simply, I really loved this book... *Touch of Death* is deadly addictive and I dare you to put it down."
— Readers Live A Thousand Lives

"Devastating truths, compelling characters and a brilliantly unique storyline, *Touch of Death* was unlike anything I've read before and I enjoyed it so, so much. It's going to be Hades waiting to read *Stalked by Death*... I rate *Touch of Death* Five out of Five!!!"
— BookSavvy

Spencer Hill Press

Contact: Spencer Hill Press, PO Box 247, Contoocook, NH 03229, USA

Please visit our website at www.spencerhillpress.com

First Edition: January 2014.

Kelly Hashway
Face of Death : a novel / by Kelly Hashway – 1st ed.
p. cm.
Summary:
A teenaged necromancer must steal another person's body to find closure with her human life and an old love so she can make a final deal with Hades to save her people and the boy she truly loves.

The author acknowledges the copyrighted or trademarked status and trademark owners of the following wordmarks mentioned in this fiction:
BMW, Mack truck, Post-it

Cover design by Kate Kaynak
Interior layout by Marie Romero

ISBN  978-1-937053-92-5 (paperback)
ISBN  978-1-937053-93-2 (e-book)

Printed in the United States of America

# Face of Death

# Kelly Hashway

**SPENCER HILL PRESS**

*To Ayla, with love*

# Chapter 1

I was in Hell. Literally. I choked, coughing up blood, as Victoria, the former head of the Ophi school and my boyfriend's mom—at least, I *thought* Alex was my boyfriend again—made me relive the deaths of every human I'd killed. Even though I was immune to the poison in my own Gorgon blood, I felt it suffocating me. It wasn't real. It wouldn't kill me, but it hurt like hell. I could say that for certain, since I was now living in Hell.

My lungs screamed for air, and my body collapsed on the ground. Hades had enchanted the black abyss of Tartarus to look like whatever it was that would torture us most. We all saw it differently. For me, it looked like my house. The one I'd grown up in. The one I'd been forced to leave when Alex came for me and told me I was part of a branch of necromancers born under the thirteenth sign of the zodiac, Ophiuchus. The one where I'd killed my human boyfriend, Matt, and my own mother, all because my blood was poisonous to humans.

"Aw, what's the matter, Jodi?" Victoria walked in circles around me. "I'm sure the most powerful Ophi in the world, the Chosen One, can handle a little pain."

A little pain, yes. This was excruciating. Hades had wanted us to suffer, me most of all, and he was getting his wish. I didn't want Victoria to see how much she was hurting me, how much I was screaming for the quiet of death, but I was powerless against the agony she inflicted. She was loving every second of it.

"Too tortured to talk?" She laughed and bent down to me. The pain was subsiding—for now. Once each death I relived was over, I had only moments before the next was inflicted upon me. Victoria grabbed my face, squeezing my cheeks and digging her nails into my skin. "You should've joined me when you had the chance." She jerked my head to the right, where Alex writhed in pain on the ground as Troy looked on and smiled. "You did this, Jodi. You caused all of this. How does it feel?"

Before I could answer or think too much about the pain I'd caused everyone when I attempted to take on Hades, Victoria waved her hand over me and a searing pain shot through my hand. It crept up my arm and to my chest. I was reliving the death of Dr. Alvarez when he'd changed the bandage on my finger. I'd bled on him and poisoned his blood. The paramedics thought he'd died of a heart attack, but really, he'd died because he tried to help me.

The agony continued for hours. One death relived after another. Finally, Hades appeared in his usual cloud of swirling black smoke. "Enough!" He motioned for our tormentors to back off.

Victoria and her group of Ophi, whom I'd sentenced to serve Hades for all eternity, stepped away from me and my friends. No matter how much they enjoyed causing us pain, they weren't stupid enough to disobey Hades.

Hades walked over to me, gazing down at my limp body. "Was it worth it, Jodi Marshall? Challenging me? Trying to prove you could take on a god?"

My throat still burned with the effects of the poisoned blood my last victim's death had made me relive. Not that I had an answer for him anyway. Back in the cemetery, I'd done the only thing I thought I could. I tried to raise the souls Hades had taken from us. I tried to rip them out of Tartarus to show Hades we were too powerful to mess with. But Chase had had other plans I hadn't been aware of. He'd made his own deal with Hades to free his mother's soul. He'd been determined to use me to kill all the Ophi, which was what Hades had wanted. The end of the Ophi line. We would stop causing problems for him, and with all our souls under his control, he'd be able to absorb our powers. Only I'd figured out Chase's plan before it was too late, and Medusa had helped me save my friends…had resurrected them before Hades had claimed their souls for good.

A lot of good that had done me. Hades had been furious, and he had taken us all here. We were worse than dead.

"No comment?" Hades smirked. "Maybe I should ask Leticia." He walked over to Leticia, who was cowering on the ground beneath her parents. They were Ophi zombies, thanks to Victoria's botched attempt to raise them. I was the only one who could raise Ophi—another reason why I was on top of Hades' hit list.

"Leave her alone." I pushed myself up to a sitting position. "We can't stop you from torturing us, but we don't have to talk to you." Lamest comeback ever.

Hades laughed. "Suit yourself." He nodded at Leticia's parents, and they picked right up with her punishment. She shook uncontrollably and cried out in pain, screaming louder than I'd thought possible.

"Stop!" I struggled to be heard over Leticia's cries. "Please! I'll do what you want; just please stop hurting her."

Hades held up a hand, and Leticia's body went limp. Her eyes rolled back in her head. Alex immediately reached for her, but Hades blocked his path. "No touching."

Alex's hands clenched, and I rushed over to him. To hell with no touching. I couldn't let him do something stupid like pick a fight with a god. Sure, we were in the underworld already, but we weren't dead. As unimaginable as it was, I knew Hades could make things even worse.

Hades cocked his head to the side and stared at my hand in Alex's. "That's the smartest move you've made, Jodi Marshall. I would've squashed him like a bug."

I squeezed Alex's hand in mine so hard he turned away from Hades and looked at me. I silently pleaded with my eyes. He had to calm down. He had to give me time to come up with some plan to get us out of here. If he did something stupid, and Hades killed him, I knew I wouldn't be able to raise him again. Hades would torture me until Alex's soul had left his body—and since we were already in the underworld, Hades could claim it for himself. Raising Ophi was much harder than raising humans. So far, I hadn't been able to raise an Ophi whose soul had already left their body.

I shook the thought from my head. I couldn't let any negativity in. This place would eat me alive if I did. I had to keep my mind clear so I could talk to Tony and find out if there was any way out of here.

Alex finally returned my squeeze. Time was strange in Tartarus. It seemed to stand still. There were moments when it felt like an eternity had passed, like now. I wondered if it was all really happening in a matter of seconds and my mind was playing tricks on me. Hades smiled as if he was reading my thoughts.

"Can't figure it out, can you?" He walked around my group. They were still on the ground, recovering from the torture they'd been subjected to since we'd arrived. I wondered how Alex was still standing. I had Medusa's blood in my veins. That made me different, stronger. Alex should've been like the others. He should've been unable to move. Maybe years of living with Victoria and Troy had hardened him in ways I couldn't even imagine.

My eyes fell on Chase as Hades stopped in front of him. "Such a disappointment. All that power I gave you, and you let it go to waste."

"Power *you* gave him?" This time Alex squeezed *my* hand to keep me from doing something stupid.

Hades laughed and grabbed Chase by his hair, yanking his head up so I could see his face. I didn't even want to look at him. He'd made me kill all the Ophi at the school. If I hadn't been the Chosen One, they'd all still be dead. Alex would be dead. I'd never forgive Chase for making me use my powers for evil. For the way he controlled me with his touch. For the way he'd almost made me lose Alex for good.

"You didn't really think he could have such an effect on you without a little help from me, did you?" Hades let go of Chase and walked toward me. "Chase *did* have something special, though."

"What was that?" I needed to know the true story—what had really happened.

"Jealousy."

"Everyone gets jealous." My voice was small as I thought of how jealous Alex had been of Chase. Even after I'd convinced Alex I didn't want to be with Chase, when he saw how Chase's power could make me feel…euphoric…Alex couldn't handle it.

"True." Hades stepped inches from my face, and it took all my strength not to back away. The heat radiating from his body was intense.

"Chase, however, was jealous of *you*. Your power. He wanted to be the Chosen One. The funny thing is I probably didn't even need to take his mother. He probably would've gone along with my plan just to get rid of you."

My eyes found Chase, but he turned away from me. It was true. He hated me. Maybe it had been jealousy that started it, but he'd *enjoyed* controlling me, poisoning me with his blood. He was almost as sick and twisted as Hades himself.

I took a step around Hades, afraid he'd stop me, but he simply smiled and moved out of my way. I let go of Alex, and Hades held up a hand to stop him from following me. I shot Alex a pleading look before walking over to Chase. "You never cared about me. You just wanted my power. All that stuff about choosing you—it wasn't because you liked me."

"I liked making out with you." Chase laughed, which caused him to choke. He was still weak.

"What about those rare moments when you were nice to me, almost human?"

"There's nothing human about him," Hades said. "Or any of you, for that matter."

That wasn't entirely true. I'd been half-human until I drank Medusa's blood and killed my human side. I lingered on that thought. My human half. Where was the part of my soul that was human? If I didn't die, and Hades resented me for not giving him my human soul when I drank Medusa's blood, then where was it?

My eyes flew to Tony. I had to talk to him. He was the most knowledgeable Ophi here. If anyone could give me answers, it was him. Except, how could I get him alone? I was sure Hades would let Victoria and the others continue with our punishment the moment he got bored with us.

I faced Hades, set on keeping him talking as long as possible. Leticia and McKenzie, the two youngest Ophi, looked like they couldn't survive any more pain. "So, this is it? This is your plan for us? Keep us here for all eternity? It doesn't make sense. We're still alive. You don't have our souls."

Hades' eyes burned into me. Literally burned with hellfire. I fell to my knees, and Alex reached for me, wrapping his arms around me and blocking me from Hades' view. The fire subsided as soon as Alex broke the connection.

He held my face in his hands. "Jodi? Are you okay?"

I nodded, but I wasn't okay. None of us were.

"There's something to be said for the living," Hades said. Alex and I turned to face him. "I can hurt you so much more than the dead. I have both your souls *and* your bodies to punish."

This was all about payback. He hated us because we had taken souls from him. Now, he was going to make sure we paid for it.

"Well, then." He clapped his hands in front of him, and Victoria and her group advanced on us. Leticia whimpered. McKenzie sobbed. Lexi cowered as her own sister, Abby, moved toward her. The others managed to hold their ground, along with Alex and me. Then, Hades surprised us all. "Shall we get going?"

"Go where?" All I could imagine was a deeper level of Tartarus— someplace darker, hotter, and more painful, if that were possible.

"You'll be moving to the Fields of Asphodel." If his expression wasn't so stone cold serious, I would've sworn he was trying to trick us—lull us into a false sense of security before unleashing some new form of torture ten times worse than the last.

"But why?" Not that I wasn't relieved to get a break from Tartarus, but something was up, and I didn't like not knowing what.

"Your former friends have been doing a commendable job doling out your punishments." He nodded briefly at his new servants. This wasn't at all what I'd intended. Victoria and the others were supposed to be suffering down here in the underworld, not living it up torturing souls. "However," Hades continued, "this kind of torture all the time would kill you, and I'm not ready for you all to die. Yet."

I should've known. He was dragging this out. Keeping us alive for as long as possible, maybe forever. I had to find a way out of here. Hades motioned for us to follow him, and just like when we'd arrived in the underworld, it was like our bodies had minds of their own—or more like they obeyed Hades—because we were following him. Of course, we were all happy to get out of Tartarus, even if it was only for a little while.

Arianna, who had become like a second mom to me—although biologically she was Lexi and Abby's mom—fell in step with me. "We'll figure something out," she whispered.

I nodded and turned to Tony, who was on the other side of Arianna. "We need to talk. I think I have an idea, but I'm going to need your help."

He gave me a weak smile, and I couldn't help thinking he doubted any plan I'd come up with would work. I was never really one for paying attention in class, especially when it came to mythology. I had this thing against Zeus. After finding out that it was Zeus who put Ophiuchus in the heavens to stop him from taking souls from the underworld, well, let's just say he'll never get a Christmas card from me. But Zeus aside, I did remember that only a few people have ever made it out of the underworld alive.

That was the beauty of my plan. I wasn't going to try to get out of the underworld alive. I was going to try to raise my own soul. My human soul. The one I'd killed. I was going to force that soul into the body of another dead person.

I was going to become one of the living dead—and hopefully not the zombie kind.

# Chapter 2

The walk to the Fields of Asphodel was surreal. Mostly because it wasn't a walk at all. Hades sort of floated us there in a cloud of black smoke. It was his preferred method of transportation. As we crossed the Phlegethon, the river of fire, I couldn't help wondering if Hades dipped us closer to the flames; my feet and ankles burned as the flames licked at them.

Finally, we came to rest above the Fields of Asphodel. Hades dropped us—yes, *dropped* us—and we landed in a heap in the middle of fields filled with asphodel flowers. As we got to our feet, I noticed the asphodels were about three and a half feet tall. They looked beautiful with their long stalks and white petals, which had the slightest tint of red down the centers. Not at all what I'd expect to see in a place like this.

McKenzie reached out and touched the white flowers. "They're so strange. They almost look good enough to eat."

"No!" Tony yelled.

Now that Hades was gone, having left in his cloud of black smoke the second he dropped us here, everyone was starting to act more like themselves again.

"What?" McKenzie looked like a puppy that had just been scolded.

"Asphodels are the food of the dead. We're still alive, but if you eat one of these, that could quickly change." Tony looked around the group.

"No one eats them. In fact, no one can eat anything here. If you do, you'll be stuck here forever."

"We're stuck here anyway," Lexi said.

Alex took my hand in his and walked us away from the group. I needed to talk to Tony, to get my plan in motion, but I couldn't resist the urge to be alone with Alex. Part of me was still shocked he didn't hate me.

We sat down, letting the asphodels give us a little privacy. Alex leaned forward and gently brushed my cheek with his fingers. "How are you holding up?"

I shrugged. "We're in Hell."

"I noticed." His lips had a hint of a smile. He was trying to make me feel better. I almost couldn't bear it. He wouldn't be here if it wasn't for me. He'd left the school, left me, but I'd tracked him down and made him come back.

"I'm so sorry you're here." I lowered my eyes, guilt consuming me to the point where I couldn't look at him.

"Hey." He lifted my chin with his finger. "Nowhere I'd rather be."

"Yeah, right." I rolled my eyes. "Seriously, Alex, it's my fault you're here. If I hadn't—"

He leaned forward and kissed me. After all the torture I'd endured, his touch felt like Heaven. My lips tingled. My blood soared through me. I felt alive. I kissed him back, realizing my blood was mixing in my veins. I wanted to do something for Alex, make up for the fact that I'd brought him here. I transferred some of my power to him—a trick I'd learned from Chase, of all people. Alex moaned in response and pulled me onto his lap. The thing about having power transferred to you was that it consumed you. You couldn't think about anything else. Alex was running his hands up the sides of my face, through my hair, and down my back. He pulled me closer to him, deepening the kiss.

I knew I couldn't let this go on. He'd be ripping his shirt off soon if I didn't stop this. I gently pulled back on my power, easing him down from his euphoric state. I pressed my lips against his and held them there. I could feel his shoulders slump when he realized I wasn't giving him any more. I leaned back and stared into his eyes.

"Why'd you stop?"

"Because we're in the middle of the Fields of Asphodel and you were about to…" I couldn't finish the thought. Alex and I had come close to going there on more than one occasion. I was convinced it would've happened already if Chase hadn't interrupted us back at the school, but this wasn't the time or place.

"I guess you wouldn't want the first time to be—"

"In Hell." Saying it brought reality crashing back down around us. I moved off Alex's lap, sitting down beside him.

He reached for my face, and I thought he was going to kiss me again, but instead he said, "I'm glad I came back to the school. I want you to know I don't regret anything that's happened."

"I do."

"What, you want to get rid of me?" He pretended to look hurt.

"Alex, be serious." He was always making jokes to try to lighten the mood and make me feel better. I didn't deserve to feel better right now. "I regret letting Chase come to the school. If he hadn't, none of this would've happened."

Alex shook his head. "Hades set you up. Chase came to the school because Hades wanted him there. There was nothing you could've done to stop it."

"I could've resisted Chase. I could've listened to you. You knew he was trouble before he even got there."

Alex sighed. "No. I was jealous. Chase is…" Why is it that guys can never admit when another guy is attractive? "I knew he'd be into you, and since there's nothing wrong with your eyes, I knew you'd be attracted to him, too." I tried to protest, but Alex put his finger to my lips. "Even if you didn't want to be."

At least he knew I didn't want to have any feelings for Chase. I never had. The entire time Chase was using his powers on me—first to get me to like him and then to control my every move—I wanted Alex. I wanted *only* want Alex. Even with the power boost, even with Hades doing everything he could to split Alex and me up and send me running into Chase's arms, I still wanted Alex.

"I love you." The words were muffled by his finger, which was still pressed against my lips.

He cupped the back of my head with his hand and pulled me to him, kissing me again. This time I didn't transfer any of my power to him. I didn't need to. We were creating a little magic of our own.

"Jodi?" Tony called.

Alex and I pulled apart, both of us out of breath. He leaned his forehead against mine. "Think Hades has any clue what we're doing right now?"

"He'd be here if he did. No way would he let us enjoy ourselves for even a second. You heard what he said. These breaks from Tartarus and the torture are only to make sure we don't die before he can punish us for as long as he wants."

"Or," Alex said, "he does know and he's going to make us pay extra for it later."

I kissed him lightly on the lips. "Totally worth it." I forced a smile.

"Oh, Jodi, there you are." Tony put a hand above his eyes and peered out over the asphodels. "This place is like a maze with no end."

"Sorry." I stood up. "I guess we made it more difficult for you to find us since the asphodels were keeping us hidden." Of course, that *had* been the whole point.

"No problem, but since we don't know how long we'll be here, I think we should discuss your plan."

"Right." I turned to Alex. My plan meant leaving him behind. Leaving all the Ophi behind. A big part of me wanted to abandon the idea completely and look for another way. But if my leaving could give me a chance to find a way to free us all, I had to do it.

Alex was at my side again, sensing my hesitation. "What is it?"

I took a deep breath and turned to Tony, hoping it would be easier to get this out if I wasn't focused on Alex or the look of concern on his face. "This is, like, the hardest place to get in and out of, right?"

"To get out of, yes. In, as you can see, isn't so difficult." Tony's eyes closed like he was trying to block out the image of this place.

"Well, I have this crazy idea. I don't even know if it's possible, but it's all I've come up with so far."

"How crazy are we talking?" Alex reached for my hand, lacing his fingers through mine. I got the impression he was trying to hold on to me, almost as if he knew this plan was going to take me away from him.

"The craziest thing I've ever thought of." I turned back to Tony. "My human half died that night in the cemetery, when I drank the blood from Medusa's bloodstone locket. I went through a transformation, and you all thought I was dead."

Alex squeezed my hand. "Do we have to relive that moment right now?"

"It's important. That's the moment I'm basing my entire plan on."

Tony raised an eyebrow at me. "Jodi, your soul is still inside you. You know that, right?"

I'd figured that out, since my soul wasn't lurking around in the underworld. "Yes. That's what I'm counting on, actually."

Alex squinted at me. "I'm not following. What are you talking about? What does your human soul have to do with anything right now?"

Tony exhaled loudly. Ever since Tony discovered how Chase had been hurting me with his power, he'd been really protective of me. In so many ways, he was becoming a father to me, and judging by the look on his face, he was worried about what my plan might do to me. "She wants to split her soul."

Alex's eyes widened. He stared at me as if I had three heads like Cerberus.

"Am I right?" I could tell Tony wanted me to say no, wanted me to find another way.

I nodded. "If I can raise the part of my soul that was human, I could get out of here. I could find a body to use while I searched for a way to free you all."

"Whoa, wait a second." Alex let go of my hand and started pacing. "You want to split your soul, the human from the Ophi? Am I getting this right?"

"Yes." My voice was small, not at all as confident as I'd hoped I'd sound.

"Is that even possible?" He was looking at Tony now.

Tony held his arms out and let them fall to his sides. "There's never been an Ophi like Jodi. She's the only one who has ever been half-human."

My hopes faded as Tony basically told us he didn't have a clue if my plan would work or how to even move forward with it.

"But…" Tony took me by the shoulders, and I could see the battle going on in his mind between his desire to protect me and his ability to recognize me as his leader. "You're a necromancer. You should be able to feel both parts of your soul. If you can tap into the human part, you should be able to raise it."

"Just like that?" Alex sounded horrified. "What, she's going to rip her own soul out?" He shook his head. "I've never felt any of the souls I've raised, but I've seen what happens to Jodi when she raises one. She feels everything they go through."

"But I can block those feelings now," I said. Tony let go of my shoulders as I turned to Alex. "This is our only chance. No matter how much this hurts me, I have to try."

"No." Alex's mind was made up. "This might kill you. Have you even stopped to think about that? I won't lose you like this. We'll find another way."

Tony stepped back, giving us a little room. It wasn't exactly privacy, but it would have to do.

"Alex, I'm in charge. We may be in the underworld, and Hades might be calling the shots as far as what happens to us here, but I'm still the leader of the Ophi. I'm the Chosen One."

"You fulfilled that prophecy, you and Chase, when you destroyed us all."

Yes, I'd killed them when I kissed Chase and combined our powers, but that wasn't the entire prophecy. That wasn't all I was chosen to do. "Medusa appeared to me when you all died. She told me prophecies are never what they seem. *Chase* was meant to kill you all. I was meant to save you. This is how I'm going to do it."

Alex started to protest, but I stepped forward and took his hands in mine. "I'm going to do this whether you want me to or not, but I'd feel a lot more confident if I had you on my side. Please, Alex."

He closed his eyes. He wouldn't even look at me. For a moment, I thought about transferring some of my power to him. It would've helped him get past these negative feelings, but if I did that to him, I'd be no better than Chase, using my powers to control people and get what I wanted.

"Alex, I need you. Please. I won't try to make you understand. I'm just asking you to trust me."

He opened his eyes. "Where are you going to get a body, and what will happen to this body?"

Tony stepped closer to us again. "I'm only guessing here, but I think Jodi would still have control over both bodies, both parts of her soul. It would be like double vision, almost."

"That will drive you insane," Alex said. "And with Hades torturing this body—" He choked on the words, unable to continue.

"That's why I need you. You have to keep my body safe here. As safe as you can. I can't let Hades know what I'm doing, so someone is going to have to help me, make sure I'm not acting like a walking zombie."

Alex's expression went cold. It was his look of determination. "Tony can watch your body. I'm coming with you."

"What?" My voice was an octave higher than usual. "You can't. You don't have a human soul in you."

"No, but I did die. Twice."

"Sorry, Alex." Tony shook his head. "It doesn't work that way. If it did, Jodi could raise us all right out of here. We've all died. But since we were brought back before our souls had a chance to leave our bodies, we don't have anything for Jodi to raise."

"Are you sure? Shouldn't we at least try?"

"Even if it were somehow possible, Jodi would need to have bodies to put our souls into. We'd end up zombies for the rest of our existence. Our bodies would remain here. Just like Jodi's is going to. Her plan is difficult enough as it is. She's going to have to tune out her soul here in order to function as a human."

While they debated the details, I let my mind wander. If I raised my human soul, would I be human again? Would I get to see my mom? Melodie? I owed her a huge explanation for why I'd suddenly become the worst best friend known to femalekind.

"Hang on," I said over Alex and Tony's bickering. They stopped talking and stared at me. "If I can do this, will I be human in the body I possess?"

Tony looked at Alex first before his eyes rested on me. "You're only raising the human part of your soul, so yes."

# Chapter 3

Human. I'd get a second chance to be human. Tears welled up in my eyes as I realized just how much I missed being human. I wouldn't be a threat to anyone anymore. I really could see my mom—not that she'd recognize me in a different body, but still. I'd get to see her.

Alex stared at me, looking every bit as hurt and rejected as he had when I'd decided to fulfill the prophecy and join my powers with Chase. I knew he was thinking of Matt, my human boyfriend, but that was silly. Matt was dead. I assumed he was in the Elysian Fields where all the good souls went for the afterlife.

"You're really going to do this? You want to be human again?" Alex touched my cheek, brushing away a tear.

"I never got to say goodbye to my old life. I just left after you brought my mom back. I need some sort of closure on that part of me. Killing the human half of my soul didn't kill the feelings I had. They're still buried inside me, and I think if I don't deal with them, I'll never truly be able to lead the Ophi." It hurt to say the words because I knew how much they tore Alex apart inside. He wanted me—all of me, and I'd never be able to give him that. Not until I did this.

He nodded but didn't say a word.

"Thank you. I know it's hard for you to understand." I ran my fingers through his hair, and Tony coughed behind us.

"Sorry to interrupt, but keep in mind that we aren't alone here." Tony turned, and I saw souls wandering aimlessly. It was the first time I'd noticed them. They didn't look like they were suffering. They didn't look like they felt anything. It wasn't a life I could imagine—but then again, it was the afterlife.

"I guess we need to look for a body for you," Alex said.

Tony sighed, still obviously conflicted. "We'll have to wait for a new soul, meet up with her when she arrives. The fresher the body, the easier the transition will be for you, Jodi."

All this talk about fresh bodies to possess was making me queasy. I was going to be doing to myself what I had done to the souls in Tartarus—the ones whose bodies Hades stole, thinking I wouldn't be able to raise them anymore. The ones like my dad.

"Having second thoughts?" Tony asked.

I shook my head and swallowed my fear. "No. I have to do this, no matter how gross it's going to be."

"Gross isn't the word." Alex ran his hands through his hair. "You're going to be torturing your own soul. Do you really think you'll be able to hold on and raise half of your soul when you're in that much pain?"

Great question. There was one way to make sure I pulled it off. That I continued to rip my soul out no matter how much I was suffering.

"Don't even think it." Alex grabbed my arms and looked me square in the eyes. "Chase is not helping you do this. That scumbag would probably kill you the first chance he got."

"What if I can't do it by myself? What if I don't have enough power?" I looked to Tony for help. "Chase may be my only chance."

"I thought I heard my name." Chase walked around the row of asphodels and into view.

Alex was on him quicker than I could blink. He rammed into Chase, knocking him to the ground.

"Alex!" I rushed to them as Alex grabbed an asphodel and brought it down toward Chase's mouth. "No!" I pushed his arm away, throwing myself between him and Chase. I landed face down, inches from Chase's lips.

Chase smiled. "How sweet. You just can't keep your hands off me, can you?" Speaking of hands, I pressed my palms to his chest and jolted him with a dose of pure poisoned blood from the left side of my body. His eyes rolled back into his head, and he passed out.

I pushed myself off him and reached for Alex's hand, pulling him up, too. "We aren't killing anyone. Got that?"

Tony stared at me. "Jodi, I'm glad Chase isn't a threat anymore, but do you really think you should be giving in to your power like that? I do believe this is the sort of thing Hades was talking about. The thing that made Chase turn evil."

"No." I crossed my arms. "Chase was jealous of my power and wanted more to make up for it. I only did what I had to. Yes, I hurt him, but I did it to save his life." I turned to Alex. "And to save *your* soul. Don't let *him*—" I pointed to Chase's limp body, "—turn you into a monster. That's not you, Alex. I get that you're trying to protect me, and I love you for that, but I won't be the reason you become evil. I won't let you turn into your parents."

"I'm going to round up the others," Tony said, motioning over his shoulder. He wasn't one to pry.

"Thanks." I smiled at him as he turned and walked away.

"You don't know what it was like." Alex's voice was small, barely more than a whisper. I knew he was talking about what had happened between Chase and me—how Chase had become a wedge in my relationship with Alex—but I let him get out whatever he'd been holding inside. "I wanted to rip the guy's head off. I've never wanted to kill anyone before, but I wanted him dead. The way he…and the way you…"

I threw myself at him, pressing my lips firmly against his. He couldn't even talk about Chase without going crazy. I'd thought getting that anger out would've been therapeutic, but it was killing him inside. I wanted him to forget about Chase. To forget about everything but me and how much I loved him. He returned the kiss as if it was the last one we'd ever have—and considering we were in the underworld and Hades could very well kill us, maybe it would be.

His arms wrapped around me, pulling me closer. I could feel his heart beating against my chest. Thumping. I wanted to take his pain away, so I allowed my blood to mix and sent some of my power to him through every part of our bodies that were touching. His eyes opened wide in response and then closed as he pressed himself against me. This was what he'd been talking about earlier. This was how Chase used to make me feel. How Chase used to control me. Only I wasn't controlling Alex. I just wanted to make him happy.

"Oh, come on!" Lexi's voice shattered the perfect bubble Alex and I had created for ourselves.

As I pulled away from him, he pouted and tried to find my lips again. "Alex, we have company."

He opened his eyes and looked shocked to see everyone watching us. "What's going on?" He was still dazed from my power.

"Jodi," Arianna said, "I'm not sure that's good for him. Remember, too much power is never a good thing."

"I'm not complaining." Alex had a big dumb grin on his face, and I couldn't help smiling. At least he wasn't angry anymore, or thinking about killing Chase.

"What's it like?" Jared's eyes lingered on me a little too long. If he thought I was going to show him, he was dead wrong.

"Okay, let's talk about my plan before this gets any more awkward." I motioned for the group to huddle up. The other souls in the Fields of Asphodel were pretty oblivious, but I didn't want to take any chances. I wasn't putting it past Hades to send souls to watch over us while he was busy doing who knew what in some other part of the underworld. I tried to sound confident as I filled everyone in on my plan.

Arianna wrapped her arm around my waist. "Honey, I have to tell you that I don't like this idea at all. I'm afraid we might lose you if you try this."

She was sweet to care so much about me. I often wondered if she felt so attached to me because her own daughters weren't exactly the caring type. Abby had gone completely evil and power-crazed, and Lexi was… well, not exactly Miss Congeniality.

"Arianna, I appreciate your concern, but this is our best shot. I know it's risky, and it's going to hurt like hell to rip my soul in half, but if it means saving all of you, I'm doing it. You guys are my family now." Family. I thought of Mom and how, if my plan worked, I'd get to see her again. I held back my tears.

"What can we do?" Carol asked. She owned Serpentarius, the Ophi nightclub, along with her husband Mason, and I was sure she missed him like crazy.

"I'm going to need help from all of you. My body will still be here with half my soul inside, but Tony said I'll have to tune it out. Otherwise, the double vision is going to drive me insane."

Carson, our Ophi doctor, readjusted his glasses and nodded. "You need us to watch over your body, make sure nothing happens to it."

"More than that." I looked around the group. "I need you all to make sure Hades doesn't notice I'm not all here."

"How on earth do we do that?" Leticia asked, already looking defeated.

I wished I had a clue.

Tony put a reassuring hand on Leticia's shoulder. "We talk to her, and if necessary, we pretend she's talking back."

"What about when the others are torturing us?" Lexi asked, and, for once, she actually sounded like she was trying to be helpful. Arianna smiled at her, no doubt proud that her daughter was choosing to do the right thing instead of following in Abby's footsteps. Maybe the fact that Abby had been the one torturing her had finally knocked some sense into her.

"There's nothing you can do about that," I said. "I'm sure my body will respond to the pain, so it will look like I'm suffering just as much as the rest of you." I hoped the torture wouldn't send me rushing back to this body. I had to be strong enough to keep my soul divided and figure out a way to save us all.

Leticia stared at me, and any sign of the fights we'd had in the past—the times when she didn't quite believe I wasn't screwing up on purpose—had all melted away. She was scared for me. "It seems like there's an awful lot that can go wrong with this plan."

"That's because there is." I gave her a weak smile. "Leticia, I told you I never intentionally did anything to harm our group. Yes, I've made mistakes, but I never meant to hurt any of you. If you have any doubt in your mind, I plan to erase it now, by doing this. I'm putting my soul on the line to prove I want to be your leader. I want to be the one to save us all."

She rushed toward me and threw her arms around my neck. "I'm so sorry. I should've believed you. I know you were only trying to do what was best for us."

"Hey, there's no need to apologize."

"Yes, there is. I blamed you. For Randy dying, for my own failures, for everything that happened with Chase. When I saw what he did to you, I realized I was wrong. And now, seeing how you're going to risk everything for us, I have to tell you how sorry I am."

"What's this? Group hug time?" Abby stood with one hand on her hip, glaring at me. She always had been good at sneaking up on me.

Leticia squeezed me even harder, terrified of Abby and the torture she could inflict upon us.

Arianna looked at her daughter with nothing but disappointment in her eyes. "Abigail, this doesn't concern you."

"Mother, didn't you miss me? I asked Hades if I could spend a little extra time with you. You know, to make up for all the time we lost when you shipped me off to the school and dismissed me as Victoria and Troy's problem." Abby was trying to maintain her composure, but I could see her fingers trembling. I remembered how much it hurt her that her own family had abandoned her. But I also knew Arianna had been trying to scare Abby into changing. It was a tough-love kind of situation—a last effort to show her how dangerous it was for her to crave power the way she did. That was the difference between the Ophi at the school and the Ophi at Serpentarius. The ones at the school actively used their powers. The ones at the Serpentarius were Ophi more in theory. They didn't believe in using their blood to raise the dead.

I pulled myself free from Leticia and stepped toward Abby, letting her know I wasn't afraid of her. "What do you want?"

"Hades sent me to get all of you. It's time to return to Tartarus."

How long had we been in the Fields? It hadn't seemed long at all. Definitely not as long as we'd been in Tartarus.

Leticia sobbed. "I can't go back there."

Abby grinned, enjoying this way too much. "You don't have a choice."

"Fine." I crossed my arms in front of me. "We'll go, but not with you."

Abby cocked her head to the side. "I don't think you understand how this works. I have control over you now. This isn't your little school, Jodi."

"No, it's not. It's the underworld, where you're a prisoner, too."

Abby laughed. "Really? Because the last time I checked, I wasn't the one being tortured twenty hours a day."

Twenty hours? That was how long we'd been in Tartarus? Hades was only giving us a four-hour break each day? It struck me for the first time that we hadn't slept since we got here. Apparently, sleep didn't matter in the underworld, because I wasn't tired.

"You're still a prisoner." I managed to find my voice at last. "You aren't free to do whatever you'd like. You're following orders."

"Do you really want to play 'sucks to be you'? I mean, even a simpleton like Leticia can see that you got the short stick."

Now I was really pissed. Leticia was definitely not dumb. She was one of the smartest Ophi I knew. She just didn't like raising souls, and it interfered with her ability to control them. "For your information, Leticia was smarter as a toddler than you'll ever be. And if you think for a second that you have a good thing going on here, you're even stupider than I thought. You're Hades' servant." I got right in her face, knowing she couldn't hurt me right now. At least not the same way she'd tortured us in Tartarus. Not here in the Fields of Asphodel. This wasn't a place of violence. It was a place of indifference. "If you disrupt Hades' balance in this place, you'll be joining us in Tartarus, and not as the one doing the punishing." I had no idea if that was true. Nothing had happened when Alex attacked Chase, but Abby didn't know that.

Leticia took a step toward Abby. "Yeah." It was probably the worst attempt at sounding tough, but I was proud of her anyway. For once, she wasn't cowering or shying away from Abby.

"Now, go find Hades. Tell him if he wants us back in the pit, he can come get us himself." It was a gutsy move, making demands of Hades, but I wasn't about to give Abby the satisfaction of leading us back to Tartarus.

The others stared at Abby, obviously agreeing with me. Tony even waved her on.

Abby glared at me. "Suit yourself, but I'll be seeing you soon, and I *will* make you all pay for this little stunt."

She turned and walked away, leaving us to count the minutes, maybe only seconds, until Hades descended on us and took us back to Tartarus.

# Chapter 4

Hades was a burning pit of rage. His black cloud of smoke swirled around us, scooping us into the air with him and spinning us around until we couldn't breathe. As the smoke swirled faster, it got hotter, transforming into an abyss of fire. My skin bubbled and cracked. He was burning us alive.

After a while, I realized we weren't spinning anymore. We weren't moving at all. I opened my eyes and saw we were back in Tartarus.

Abby's face stared down at me. "Told you I'd see you soon."

I looked around, finding the others not far from me.

Alex stared at his hands and arms. "We were burning."

"Yes." Hades paced in front of us. "I took that one from a page in the Jodi Marshall death register. Can you guess which one?" He stopped in front of me.

I knew who he was talking about. The hiker who had tried to rescue me from Melodie's car after I'd stolen it and crashed it into a tree on my way back to the school.

"He was only trying to help you. Save the poor young girl locked inside a car that was moments from bursting into flame." Hades' voice was overly dramatic as he played up the memory—*my* memory. "If only he knew what he was trying to help. A monster. An abomination. Do you think he would've helped you if he had known the truth? If he had known how many deaths you were responsible for? If he had known you'd soon be the death of him, too?"

"Stop!" Alex got to his feet, but Hades knocked him down again with a simple wave of his hand.

"Boy, don't make me kill you. I have so much more torture planned for you, and if my emotions get the best of me and I get rid of you now, I'll miss out on seeing you suffer."

"Leave him out of this." I stood up, waiting to see if Hades would knock me off my feet too, but he let me stand. "Why are you making them suffer through a death I caused?"

"Because, my dear," he stepped closer, leaning toward me, "I can." His hot breath on my face sent chills running down my body. Hades stepped back. "I think you all should know the kind of person your leader is. She could've sent that hiker away, found a way out of the car without his help."

"I tried!" I screamed. "He wouldn't listen. I made him back off, but I got stuck on the broken glass on the window. It cut my leg, and he rushed over to help me. I tried to tell him not to touch me, but he wouldn't stop." Tears streamed down my face as I recalled the incident in the woods.

"Ah, yes, but it didn't end there, did it?" Hades' voice bellowed through the abyss. "You left his body there to burn when the car exploded in flames. You didn't even try to raise him."

"I couldn't! It happened so fast. He was burned before I could get to him." I couldn't fight off the tears. I sank to my knees.

"Let's see if that was true."

I opened my eyes at Hades' words. What was he talking about?

"Let's rewind. Go back to the moment your blood touched his hand. It was his right hand, if I'm remembering correctly."

At the words, I felt a searing pain in my right hand. Cries of pain rang out all around me. The rest of the group felt it, too. The pain exploded up my arm, shooting through my bloodstream. My heart seized, and I collapsed on the floor. I heard everyone else fall to the ground as well.

"This is my favorite part," Hades said. I felt him leaning over me. "He wasn't dead yet when the car exploded in flames." What? No! "He felt his flesh bubble and burn off him." God, please no! "Tell me, how does it feel?"

I screamed as every inch of me burned. Invisible flames licked at my skin. I knew it wasn't really happening, but the pain was unbearable. My eyes shut, blocking out the sight of my bubbled flesh.

"Amazing how long he remained alive while he burned, isn't it, Jodi Marshall? Or would you rather I ask your friends?" Hades' voice sounded in my ears over the screams of the others.

I choked on the smoke of my own burning flesh. Then, without warning, the pain stopped. The stench of death hung in the air, but everything was silent. I turned my head to the side and saw Alex in the fetal position beside me. I'd never seen him so hurt, and that was saying a lot considering everything I'd put him through over the last few months.

"Well, that was fun." Since Hades' voice was getting farther away, I figured he was moving on from me—choosing the next person whose memories he was going to focus on to torture us all. "Ah, Chase. There are so many to choose from I almost don't know where to start."

"Please." I tried to find the strength to talk. My throat was burning, and my body still felt like it was on fire in some places. "You're killing us." I hoped his desire to keep us alive might outweigh wanting to see us writhe in pain at the moment.

"Aw, come on now. Surely a group of powerful necromancers like yourselves can handle a little more."

"Tapping into Chase's memories and making us relive the deaths he caused would kill us all. You know that." I was trying to keep him talking—put off the torture for as long as I could. Alex reached his hand toward me, and as our fingers touched, my blood rippled. Could I mix my blood to restore my energy? Was that possible?

I looked down at my hand in Alex's and sent him a little life-restoring power. His hand jolted, and his eyes met mine. He shook his head. He was right. Sending only the life-restoring power to Alex would heal him and drain me right now. I was too weak. I needed to mix my blood. I let both sides of my body circulate the blood through my veins. The bubbling sensation felt amazing. Instantly, I began to feel better and from the way Alex squeezed my hand, I knew it was healing him, too.

With my left hand, I reached for Arianna. Her eyes opened at my touch. I watched the color return to her cheeks, and she smiled at me in thanks. If only I could reach the others.

Hades had been silent for too long. He was contemplating his next move. I didn't doubt he was trying to torture us by making us wait for his decision. More torture or let us return to the Fields of Asphodel. I had no idea which way he was leaning.

Alex and Arianna were okay now, so I stopped transferring my power and let go of Arianna's hand. I held on to Alex, though. No matter what happened, we were in this together.

"Very well." Hades stared down at me. I hadn't even realized he'd left Chase and come back this way. I was lost in Alex's eyes, pretending I was anywhere but here. Hades waved his hand, and a cloud of black smoke swirled around us, lifting us in the air. Leticia and McKenzie clutched onto each other, and even Lexi looked scared, reaching for Arianna's hand. Somehow, I knew Hades was returning us to the Fields. He wasn't ready to let us die just yet. He had other plans. I just didn't know what they were.

As we were placed in the asphodels, I thought about how to reach the human part of my soul. I had to find a way to rip it from my body, and I had to find a new body to put it into.

"So, what, do we pretend we're inches from death every time Hades tortures us? Is that the new plan?" Lexi was near hysterics. I was used to her being so sure of herself. She'd once told me Abby was nothing compared to her. That she was the real bitch in the family, but I could see glimpses of what Arianna was holding onto. Lexi wasn't all evil. The power had consumed her, but not to the extent it had consumed Abby.

"We'll figure something out," I said. "For right now, I have to work on tapping into the human half of my soul."

Tony put his hand on my shoulder. "Can you communicate with Medusa from down here? Maybe she can tell you how to do this."

"The last I spoke with her was when we first got here. She said she couldn't help me." I sighed. "We're on our own."

"Okay." Tony nodded. "Then you need to mix your blood. Tap into your powers and try to reach out to your own soul."

Alex stepped closer to me so our shoulders were touching. "No way. Until she has a body to put her soul into, this is too risky. I mean, what if she sends her soul floating into the nearest body? As far as we know, that could be inside Tartarus."

The bodies Hades took from the cemetery at the school. Alex was right.

"All right. New plan. We have to convince Hades to let us serve him. To cut the time we spend in Tartarus down even more and let us help him with the other jobs he has in the underworld."

"Why would he do that?" McKenzie asked.

Leticia was the one to answer this time. "Because he's too busy. He's overseeing this whole place. Judging souls, keeping souls from escaping, punishing souls—that's a lot for one person, even if he *is* a god."

I smiled at her. She may not be great in the actual raising and controlling of souls, but Leticia was smart. I needed that right now.

"Good. We can work with that. I mean, look what he did with Victoria and the others. They were supposed to be suffering down here, but instead they're working for Hades."

"And enjoying it way too much," Lexi said.

I looked back and forth between her, Arianna, Leticia, and Alex. They all had family here. They were all being punished by those family members. I couldn't even imagine how much this was hurting them.

"We didn't cause Hades anywhere near as much trouble as they did." I was grasping at any argument I could use to prove we could be useful, that we deserved a little break from the punishments.

Alex crossed his arms and glared at Chase, who was standing on the outskirts of our group. "That's not entirely true. I'd say *he's* a lot like Victoria and the others." That was saying a lot coming from Alex. Yes, he hated Chase, but those were his parents he was comparing him to.

Chase laughed. "Oh, and Jodi is an angel? You all felt the pain she caused that hiker. Are you going to deny she's done her share of—"

Before Chase could finish the sentence, Alex was on top of him. "Don't you ever talk about her like that. Jodi never would've met that guy if it weren't for you. You started all of this, you son of a bitch." Alex punched Chase in the face and showed no sign of stopping. It took Tony, Carson, and Ethan to pry him off.

I stared at Chase's bloody face, finding it hard to feel sorry for him. Everything Alex had said was true. Chase coming to the school had been the turning point. He'd brought us all down—way down to the underworld. Even Ethan stared at his son like he was to blame. After

Chase had made it clear he was willing to sacrifice his own father, Ethan had turned on him, too. Or maybe he just finally saw Chase's true colors.

Arianna had told me that some Ophi are corrupted by the power in our blood. Her husband, Abby and Lexi's father, had been. Part of me understood why it was so easy to give in to that power and turn off all emotions. We weren't human, after all. Maybe that was why I was so desperate to move forward with my plan and reconnect with the human that once lived inside me.

"What should we do with him?" Ethan asked, surprising us all. I knew he wasn't happy with his son, but I didn't think he'd ask a group of necromancers who hated Chase to decide his fate.

"Leave him. Let him handle things on his own. He's not one of us, and he never will be." I stepped toward Ethan, searching his face for the truth. A sign that he really was abandoning Chase and joining us. "Whether or not you're one of us is yet to be seen. Understand I'm giving you one chance. That's it. The second you blow it, I'm done with you. We're done with you. Got it?"

He nodded.

I motioned for the group to follow me, putting some distance between us and Chase. I could've used the life-restoring power in my blood to heal him in seconds, but I didn't want to. He needed to feel pain. He needed to know he couldn't mess with us. I'd let him control me for too long, and I was done.

We moved through the Fields, walking off the events of the day—or days. I wasn't sure how long we'd been here. I would've killed for a hot shower. It was the only thing that really calmed me down. Since learning I was an Ophi, I'd taken more showers than I probably had my entire life.

Leticia grabbed my arm, bringing me to a sudden stop. "Jodi."

"What?" I looked at her, but her eyes were focused off to my right. "Did you see something?"

I figured it could've been any one of our victims. Someone she'd accidentally killed and now they were roaming these Fields for all eternity. I knew, if I saw the hiker or any of the other poor people I'd killed, I'd need more than a moment to freak out and regroup.

"I'm not sure, but isn't that—?" She pointed to a group of souls, wandering aimlessly. At first I had no idea what she was trying to tell me. There were two women and an older man with them, but none of them looked familiar.

"Leticia, I don't see—" They parted, and I saw who Leticia was talking about.

Matt.

# Chapter 5

No. There had to be a mistake. Matt was a good person. He was perfect. He'd never hurt anyone. If anyone should end up in the Elysian Fields, it was him. I moved toward him, determined to prove my eyes were deceiving me. It had to be someone who looked like Matt. Looked like him but wasn't him. That was the only explanation that made sense to me.

"Jodi." Alex reached for my arm as he followed. "Don't. Please, don't." He gently tugged on my arm, making me turn to him and breaking me from the spell that had taken hold over my body.

"It can't be him." My words shook with the threat of tears. "He was too good to end up here. I have to prove to myself that it's not him."

Alex pulled me to him, wrapping his arms around me. I buried my head in his chest, breathing in the scent I knew so well. Alex. My Alex. He was home to me—even here. When I was with him, everything else seemed to fade away. Nothing else was important. He stroked my hair and kissed the top of my head.

"Don't torture yourself. Hades is doing enough of that. These Fields are supposed to be a break for us. A place where we can rest for a little while."

His words didn't completely register. All I was hearing was that he didn't want me to go to Matt. Not because he was jealous. Not because he worried I still had feelings for him. Alex didn't want me going to

Matt because then I'd see it really *was* him. It wasn't a mistake. Instead of being happy in his afterlife in the Elysian Fields, Matt was living like a zombie, wandering around the asphodels.

I pulled away from Alex, looking him in the eyes. "This is my fault, isn't it?"

"What?" He shook his head. "Jodi, no."

"Yes, it is. Matt's judgment, the one that placed him here, it was based on me—his connection to me. I'm sure of it. Hades is punishing me by punishing him."

"Can he do that?" Leticia asked, coming up behind us with the rest of the group following her.

I looked to Tony, hoping he knew. He shrugged. "He's the god of the underworld. There's nothing he can't do here. I mean, he raised Matt that night in the cemetery, and from what I was told, Matt wasn't anything like the last time you'd seen him."

No, he wasn't. When I'd killed him with my kiss, I'd raised him without knowing what I was doing. I'd brought him back wrong, as a bunny-eating zombie. Hades had brought Matt back human again and very much alive. Until my tears killed him again. Now Matt was here. It had to be my fault.

"Do you think he was in the Elysian Fields when Hades raised him?" I stared at Tony, but he looked away. "Tell me! I need to know if I did this to him."

Tony sighed, and when he raised his eyes to meet mine, they were full of sympathy. "No one can say that for sure. Only Hades knows."

"No, someone else here would know. Victoria, maybe."

Alex rubbed my arms, trying to ease the tension that had worked its way through my entire body. "Victoria and the others are in Tartarus. Believe me, they didn't see Matt."

I turned to Alex for a moment before looking in Matt's direction again. "Abby came here to get us. If she can leave Tartarus, the others probably can, too."

Alex turned my chin back toward him, taking my eyes off Matt. "Abby only came here to get us. Hades sent her. I doubt he does stuff like that often. He hates Abby and the others just as much as he hates us."

"Does he? Because they seem to be having a great old time punishing souls. They don't seem to be in much pain at all." I looked toward Matt again. "He doesn't deserve this."

Alex's shoulders dropped when he realized I wasn't letting this go. "He's not going to be able to talk to you, Jodi. Look at all the souls here. They're completely spaced out. He won't even know who you are. He probably doesn't even know who *he* is."

"Alex is right," Tony said. "Going to Matt is only going to torture you more."

I didn't care. I had to see him. I had to make sure he wasn't suffering here. "I need to do this. I know you don't understand, but I just have to talk to him. Even if he doesn't respond, there are things I need to say. I won't have closure until I do this."

Alex closed his eyes, exhaling loudly and nodding. "Go."

I reached up on my toes and kissed him. "Thank you."

He squeezed my hands. "I deserve serious brownie points for this."

He was right. He deserved credit for a lot of things. I reached up and kissed him again. "Major brownie points. Got it." I let go of Alex and took a deep breath, bracing myself for the worst. Matt wasn't going to recognize me. He might not even acknowledge me.

I forced my feet to move in his direction, which wasn't easy considering Matt was walking in a strange circular pattern. I wasn't sure what to do, how to approach him, so I fell in step with him, making the crazy pattern.

"Matt?" I kept my voice gentle, not wanting to startle him. He didn't respond. "Matt, it's me, Jodi."

At the mention of my name, he stopped. He did remember me! "Can you look at me?"

He was almost in a trance, staring out over the asphodels. I gently reached for his arm, and he jumped at the contact. I pulled away, afraid I'd scared him, but he turned and faced me. His eyes were glazed over, and he seemed to be looking through me rather than at me.

"Matt? Do you know who I am?"

"Jodi." My name was so quiet coming from his lips, like a distant memory, which was all I was to him now.

"Yes, Jodi." I choked back tears. "I was your girlfriend before you came here."

He didn't say a word. His head cocked to the side for a second, like he was trying to understand, but his brain wouldn't process the words. He shook his head in frustration.

"It's okay. You don't have to remember. I just want to tell you that I'm sorry. I never meant to hurt you. I really did care about you, and I think I even could've loved you if we'd had more time together."

"Where?" he mumbled.

"Where what?" I looked around, wondering if he was talking about this place. "Where are we? Is that what you're asking?"

He didn't respond, but I went on anyway. "This place is called the Fields of Asphodel. You're in the afterlife, Matt."

"Gone. Happy. All gone."

My insides twisted at his broken speech. This place was turning him into a mindless soul. It wasn't just his speech that was broken. *He* was broken. A shell of who he once was.

"Warmth. Light."

Was he talking about before he died? Was he wondering why everything was so colorless and cold here? "You aren't alive anymore, Matt. You…died. I'm so sorry."

"Not here. Somewhere else. You." Finally his eyes found mine—really connected. He was seeing me now. "Then gone. Now here."

"Yes, Matt. I'm so sorry. We were in my backyard. You kissed me, and now…this is your afterlife."

"No. Found happiness. Gone now."

Alex had crept up on us, probably because he noticed Matt was actually talking to me—not that I was making any sense of what he was saying. He waved Tony over with a strange look on his face. Did he know what Matt was talking about? The two of them whispered for a moment before Tony approached Matt and placed a gentle hand on his shoulder.

"Matt, my name is Tony. I'm a friend of Jodi's."

"Jodi," Matt said.

"Yes, that's right. Can you tell me if you were somewhere else before you came here? Were you in another afterlife?"

Matt nodded. "Warm. Happy. Not here. Can't find it."

My throat closed. Matt was wandering in circles, looking for the Elysian Fields. I knew it. That was where he'd been when Hades brought him back to the cemetery that night. He'd ripped him out of his own version of Heaven, and when I killed Matt again, Hades had sent him here. It wasn't fair. I had to fix this.

"Matt, I'm going to make this up to you. We'll find your Heaven again. I promise."

Tony shook his head at me. "Jodi, you can't promise that. How do you intend to convince Hades to move Matt to the Elysian Fields? If he's really using Matt to torture you more, he'll never listen to reason."

He was right, and I had no idea how to get to the Elysian Fields anyway. Every time we'd traveled from place to place down here, Hades had us covered in his swirl of black smoke or took control over our bodies, so we only went where he wanted and saw what he wanted. I didn't even know which direction the Elysian Fields were in.

"I'm not leaving him here. I can't. This is too much." My blood boiled under my skin as it mixed in anticipation of using my powers. Only I had nothing to use my powers on. Did I? Then, it hit me. If I wanted Matt to get out of here, I was going to have to do it myself. I was going to have to raise him.

"Jodi, please calm down. I know this isn't what you wanted, but we have enough to deal with right now. Matt isn't hurting here." Alex was trying to reason with me, but he was missing one key thing. Matt *was* hurting.

"He is, Alex. He's in pain because he used to be in Heaven. He used to be happy. Hades took that away from him because of me. If I can't get him back there, then I'll get him out of here."

Alex wrinkled his brow. "You're talking in riddles."

Great, a little trick I'd learned from all the Ophi prophecies about me, no doubt.

"Jodi." Tony was trying to use kid gloves on me, talking slowly and keeping his voice gentle. "This is one thing you are just going to have to accept, to let go."

"No." My mind was made up. I wasn't letting this go. I wasn't going to accept this. Matt deserved better, and I was going to give it to him.

Alex took my face in his hands. "That part of your life is over. I know that hurts sometimes, but you have to move on." His eyes pleaded with me. I knew how this looked to him. Like I was worrying about yet another guy who wasn't him. I didn't want him to feel that way. I loved Alex. He was everything to me. But Matt was in here because of me, and I had the power to do something about it. I couldn't just ignore that to keep Alex from getting his feelings hurt. We were talking about eternity versus a moment of unhappiness. I wouldn't damn Matt to this place for the rest of time to keep Alex from a little discomfort. It wasn't fair.

"Tony, can I have a minute alone with Alex, please?"

He looked back and forth between us and then at Matt, who obviously had gotten tired of standing there and had wandered off again in his circular pattern. "I'll be right over there if you need me." I wasn't sure who he was talking to. Did he think Alex would need help getting me to listen to reason?

As soon as he was out of earshot, I hugged Alex and said, "Do you trust me?"

He pulled away slightly. "Don't make this into a trust thing."

"When you hear what I have in mind, you'll understand what I mean."

"Let me do one thing before you tell me, because I have a feeling I'm going to get royally pissed, and I need to do something first." He leaned down, pressing his lips to mine. My blood tingled throughout my body in response to him. I knew he didn't need it, and I hoped he wouldn't think I was using my blood to sway his opinion at all, but I allowed my power to transfer to him. He instantly deepened the kiss, pulling me closer.

I didn't want him to stop, but I had to talk to him. I had to say this before I lost my nerve. When he kissed me like this, my mind became mush. All I could think about was him, and I could already feel thoughts of Matt slipping away.

I pulled my mouth from his. "Alex." He tried to find my lips again, but I turned away. He found my neck instead, trailing his lips down to my collarbone. I couldn't think straight. I shivered from the chills he was sending down my spine. My lips found his. The more he kissed me, the more power I sent him. It was my body's natural reaction to the pleasure he was causing me.

I was losing this battle of wills. I forgot about Matt. I forgot about my plan to get us out of here. My fingers found Alex's hair, weaving through his unruly and totally sexy dirty-blond locks. His lips found my neck, making me moan. The world stood still. I may have been in the underworld, but I was in Heaven with Alex.

Something bumped into me, and I turned slightly to see Matt. He'd broken his pattern and walked right into me. Alex continued to kiss any part of me his lips could find. I gently pushed him away.

"Alex." He tried to pull me to him. "Alex." I was firmer this time, but he still wasn't stopping.

"Jodi," Matt said. I nearly fainted. He'd said my name, without me talking to him first.

Alex stopped, jolted back to reality by the sound of my name coming from Matt. Alex looked at me, completely confused.

"He walked into us." I felt my cheeks redden. Matt may not have been totally coherent, but having my ex-boyfriend walk into me kissing my new boyfriend still felt awkward as all hell.

"He recognized you again." Alex wasn't happy about this. Part of me wanted to go back to kissing him and make him forget about Matt and the way he held onto my memory. But if Matt was reaching out to me, it meant my plan might actually have a shot.

"I know. It's weird, right? He isn't like the others here. He remembers. I think it's because he's not supposed to be here."

"Please, don't start that again. I was hoping you'd forget whatever it was you were planning after—"

"You kissed me? Was that your plan, to make me forget Matt?" I wasn't really mad at Alex. He was desperate. He'd already lost me once, and he was trying everything he could to keep it from happening again. I pressed my hand to his chest and sighed, letting him know I wasn't angry. "I just wish you'd understand how much I love you."

Alex lowered his eyes. "Loving you isn't that easy. There's always something or someone competing with me for your attention. I just want it to be you and me."

God, I hated being the Chosen One sometimes. Why couldn't I just be a normal girl with a normal boyfriend? No. I knew the answer to that. I wouldn't have Alex. In the end, he was the one I wanted. All of this would be worth it, as long as I had Alex.

"I want that, too. I'm going to do everything I can to make that happen. But first, there's something else I have to do." I took a deep

Kelly Hashway

breath, preparing for Alex's outburst at what I was about to say. "I have to raise Matt. I want to take him with me when I raise my human soul."

# Chapter 6

Alex burst out laughing. I actually had to back up because he doubled over and grabbed his gut. The others rushed over to see what was going on. Exactly what I wanted to know.

"Is he okay?" McKenzie asked.

Lexi's eyes widened as she shook her head at Alex. "He looks hysterical, and I don't mean funny. He looks like he's having a fit or something."

"Alex." I waited for him to stop laughing and explain the joke I'd clearly missed.

"I'm sorry." He was breathing heavily, and his face was bright red.

"What was so funny?" Did he really think I'd been joking?

"Absolutely nothing." He looked at me, and all the warmth left his face. "I just had to laugh because, otherwise, I would've flipped out and attacked poor old zombie-Matt over here."

Matt was still standing by my side. He didn't seem to comprehend anything that was going on around him—not that I did either.

"He's not a zombie. Please, don't call him that."

"I know he's not. I'm not mad at him. He's just the next in a long line of guys who have come between us."

"That's not fair. You know that's not true. The only guys who have come between us are Matt and Chase. And you can't even really include

Matt because he and I were together before you and I were. If anything, you—"

Alex put his hand up to stop me. "Don't. Don't go there. I didn't take you away from him."

"I know. I'm sorry. That was stupid." Ugh, I hated this. Alex wasn't wrong about things coming between us. I got why he was upset, but it wasn't like Matt and I were going to run off and live happily ever after as humans while Alex rotted in the underworld. I'd never do that to him, and he had to know that.

Alex ran his fingers through his hair, tugging the ends in his fists. "I'm so damn tired of this. When do *I* get to have you? Really have you?"

Lexi laughed. "Why am I not surprised Jodi's a prude?"

I glared at her. "That's not what he meant, Lexi." At least I didn't think it was. I knew that was on his mind. We hadn't been together like that yet, but he was talking about more than that, and she was cheapening our relationship.

Lexi held her hands up. "Whatever."

"All right, everyone," Arianna said. "Alex and Jodi don't need an audience. Move along." She ushered them away from us, giving my arm a quick squeeze before she followed.

I moved toward Alex, but he backed away. "Don't do that." I advanced on him again. "Don't push me away. You just said there were too many things coming between us all the time. Don't you be one of them, too." He stopped, and I took his hands in mine. "I'm yours, Alex. All of me."

"No, you're not. You want to raise your human soul and your human boyfriend. What the hell do you think is going to happen when you're both alive again? Together?"

I hadn't thought about it like that. Would my human feelings for Matt come back? "I wasn't planning to raise Matt so we could be together again. I only wanted to get him out of here. I swear. Alex, if I could raise you and bring you with me, I'd do it in a heartbeat. I want you with me. Leaving you is the only thing stopping me from raising my human soul right now."

He pulled me closer to him. "I'm not mad at you. You know that, right? It's just this situation. Ever since Chase came, I've felt like I'm not good enough for you."

"Alex—"

"No, let me finish. You have all this power. You can do things no other Ophi can. And what am I? An average Ophi. Nothing special. I don't deserve you."

"That's not true. I may be the Chosen One, but I chose you."

"Great, so I'm special by extension?"

"That's not what I meant. You're the only guy I've ever loved, Ophi or not. Yes, I had strong feelings for Matt. Yes, I still want Matt to be happy. But I don't love him. I love you. Being with Matt again isn't going to change that."

"Being with him? You mean you aren't just going to raise him? You're going to keep him with you while you find a way to get us out of here?"

Crap, I was making this worse. "I don't want to do this alone. Like I said, if I could take you with me, I would."

"How is Matt going to be of any help to you?" His jaw tightened; he was gritting his teeth. "I hate to say this, but it seems like you just want some extra time with your old boyfriend."

Was he wrong? Was I trying to get more time with Matt? "I'm not going to lie. I do like the thought of getting a second chance with Matt."

Alex let go of my hands and turned away from me. His hands clenched into fists, and he swung at the rows of asphodels, sending white flower petals flying everywhere.

"Alex!" I grabbed him, but he kept swinging. "Not like that! That's not what I meant. Please, if you love me, hear me out."

He stopped, but his whole body shook with rage. He shrugged my hands off his arm.

"Matt was my friend, too. I didn't just care about him as my boyfriend. For most of the time I knew him, he was one of my two best friends. I owe him this. I owe myself the chance to make things right and to say goodbye to him for good. I know I can't keep him in my life. It's too dangerous. But I think I should at least get to say goodbye to him on my own terms, not because he died, not because I have to run away and fulfill my Ophi destiny. I owe him the truth." Now *I* was breathing heavily. I'd blurted all that out, wanting to say everything before Alex got the chance to cut me off.

"You don't still have feelings for him?" He was staring out over the asphodels, unable to look me in the eyes.

"I do still care about him as a friend, but that's all. As a friend." I reached for his arm again, and this time he didn't pull away. "When this is all over, when we're out of here and back at the school, I promise it will just be you and me. No one else. For as long as you want me."

He turned toward me and took my hand. "I'm holding you to that promise."

I smiled, and a tear ran down my cheek. "So, what now?"

"You don't have to ask for my permission. You're the leader, remember?"

"I know, but that doesn't mean I can't ask for your input. You *are* my boyfriend, aren't you?"

"Through bad and worse, apparently."

"Come on, don't say that. Things haven't been all bad." I touched his cheek, and even without me transferring any power to him, he smiled.

"No, definitely not."

I reached up to kiss him, but he stopped me. "We have company, remember?"

I'd kind of forgotten about Matt. "Right. Sorry."

"No need to apologize to me. It's actually nice to see that I can make you forget about everything else."

"You do that to me a lot, you know. I'm sorry if I don't always make you see that."

He kissed the top of my head. "I guess we need to find two bodies for you guys. A guy and a girl. Unless…"

"Don't even think it. I'm not putting Matt into a girl's body." I couldn't help it. I laughed. Poor Alex. He was so desperate not to lose me to Matt he wanted to make Matt a girl. "You are so lucky I love you."

"I know." He smiled, but his tone was completely serious. I leaned forward and kissed him. I knew Matt was watching us, but I didn't care.

"Okay, so how do we find out where the new souls are? I need to find them almost immediately when they arrive."

"I think we need to talk to Tony. He's our expert." Alex took my hand and started toward Tony and the others, but I held him back.

"Hang on." I turned to Matt. "Matt, will you come with us, please?" He stared at me, not understanding.

"Take his hand," Alex said. "He might remember your touch. I would if I were him." Moments like these made me wonder how I'd gotten so lucky. Alex really was amazing. I was staring at him, and I guess he thought I was wondering if it was a trick because he said, "I've seen you hold the guy's hand before. I think I can handle it without flipping out."

"I know. That wasn't it. I was just in awe of you. You're kind of perfect, you know that?" Perfect. It was the word I'd always used for Matt, but it really did apply to Alex, too.

He smiled, and I swear his cheeks got a little red. Still holding Alex's hand, I reached for Matt. He didn't move, so I carefully slipped my hand in his. "Is this okay? Do you mind if I take you to my friends?"

Still nothing, but his fingers curved slightly around mine. That was all the answer I needed. I nodded to Alex, and we walked over to the others. I'm sure we looked like a demented threesome, every bit as awkward as it felt.

The others raised their eyes to us. They obviously had no idea what I was doing. I wasn't really sure I knew either.

I let go of Matt's hand. "Okay, so here's the plan. We need two new souls. I'm bringing Matt with me."

Arianna looked back and forth between Alex and me. I knew she was checking to see how he really felt about me bringing Matt along.

"Alex and I discussed it, and Matt doesn't deserve this kind of afterlife. Hades is only keeping him here to punish me. I have to free him, give him another shot at life."

I couldn't help feeling like they were ignoring me. All eyes were on Alex. I nudged him, encouraging him to say something and make the blank stares go away.

He let them squirm for another moment before he chimed in. "Matt will be human again, and he'll help Jodi. I don't want her to go through this alone. She won't have anyone who knows who she really is since she'll be in a different body."

Lexi raised an eyebrow. "You're sending your girlfriend to shack up with her ex-boyfriend, and they'll both be human? Wow, Alex, I didn't peg you for a complete idiot."

"Enough, Lexi." Arianna gave her daughter a long hard look.

"What? I'm trying to help." She shrugged, and in her own strange way, I think she really was looking out for Alex.

"I trust Jodi." Alex gave me a small smile.

"And we won't be shacking up," I said. "Matt doesn't have to stay with me at all if he doesn't want to. I'll help him get settled, but he's free to live his life however he wants."

"Wait," Leticia said. "You're going to worry about getting him settled before you figure out how to save us? So, like, you two will be getting all cozy in your new lives while we're here being tortured."

"Jodi's body and half her soul will still be here," Alex jumped to my defense. "She'll be suffering right along with us, and it will actually be harder on her because she'll be able to feel both parts of her soul. It's going to be hard for her not to lose it, having to deal with that." He looked around the group, his eyes falling on each Ophi. "So, if anyone wants to question what Jodi's actually going to have to endure while trying to free us, you can take it up with me."

Lexi crossed her arms. "Seriously, I don't know if you are the most romantic guy ever or if you're a total dumbass." I was about to flip on her, but she added, "Either way, Jodi's lucky to have you."

Lexi had definitely changed since we'd come here. Maybe it was seeing her sister again, seeing what Abby had become, but part of me was almost starting to like Lexi. Almost.

"How do we even go about doing this?" Carol asked. "No offense, but I'd really like to get home to Mason. I'm not crazy about having to wait around in Hell while Jodi figures things out."

"I know." I understood how she felt. She missed her husband, and I'm sure seeing Alex stand up for me reminded her of Mason. He'd had no idea that letting Carol come to the school was going to mean losing her to Hades. If I had anything to say about it, they'd be together again soon. "Guys, I know this sucks. I know it's my fault we're all here." Alex opened his mouth to protest, but I shook my head. "I'm the leader. Whatever happens is on my head. I take responsibility. It comes with the job description. But I promise you I *will* get us out of here. All of us." My eyes fell on Carol. "Once we're home, you can go back to Serpentarius and pretend you never met me."

"I don't want to pretend I never met you, Jodi. I just want to be with my family again."

I nodded. "Then let's find some bodies for Matt and me and make that happen as soon as possible."

I looked around the group. Everyone was in agreement. We had to get moving. Scope out new souls. The only problem was that no one knew how to get out of the Fields of Asphodel. Hades had dropped us in the middle of this flower-filled field.

"Any chance Matt knows the way out?" Alex asked. "That weird pattern he was walking, do you think it has anything to do with getting back to the Elysian Fields?"

I pictured Matt walking in his circular route. It had seemed like he was wandering in an unending loop, but what if it was more than that? "We don't really have any other ideas, so let's try it."

I let go of Alex's hand and stood in front of Matt. He had a tendency to get very dazed if he wasn't focused on something specific. I made sure I blocked his view of everything else. "Matt? Do you want to go for a walk? Find that place you were looking for earlier?"

Instead of answering, he turned and wandered away. We all followed, making sure to stay far enough away so he wouldn't bump into us if he changed directions.

"Hey." Alex reached for my elbow. "What if he finds the Elysian Fields? Will you still take him back with you? Raise his soul?"

Let him stay in his own personal Heaven or give him a second chance at life in a different body? It was a tough decision. "I'll let him decide." He deserved to make that choice for himself.

Alex let go of my arm and continued walking alongside me. I couldn't tell if he was upset or just processing everything. As we walked, I kept an eye out for Hades. It seemed like a lot of time had passed since we got here. I hoped Hades wouldn't show up before we were able to follow Matt to wherever it was he was going.

"This is crazy," Lexi said, as Matt curved to the right. "He's not going anywhere. I mean, how can he even know where he's heading? This place looks the same no matter where you are."

"Faith, Lexi," Arianna said. "Sometimes you just have to have faith."

"Faith in a mindless soul? Great."

I couldn't even argue with her.

# Chapter 7

Matt led us in a spiraling pattern that had us backtracking almost as much as we moved forward. We were all losing hope until I saw a gate up ahead.

"Look!" I ran toward it, not waiting for the others. This had to be the way out of the Fields. Matt had done it. He'd found the exit.

"Yes!" McKenzie cheered, running up behind me. "Now, maybe we can find a way out of the underworld all together."

"Don't get ahead of yourself," Tony said as we slowed down. The gate was only a few feet in front of us, and we all stared at it like it was the most beautiful sight. "There are very few ways to get out of here. I'm sure Hades has them all well guarded. He's not going to let us walk out."

"Check it out. Three-Heads is watching us." Lexi pointed to the three-headed dog, Cerberus, standing on the other side of the gate.

"He must have smelled us coming," Tony said.

"That means we aren't going to get past this gate." I looked around. I had no idea how to distract a hellhound.

Matt had finally caught up with us. His spiral pattern had led him to the gate. He looked down at it with his head cocked to the side. Cerberus growled as Matt reached for the latch on the gate.

"Matt, no!" I rushed to him and grabbed his hand. He stared past me at something beyond the gate. I couldn't see it, but I had a feeling the Elysian Fields were in that direction.

Lexi kicked the gate, getting more snarls from Cerberus. "We're stuck. All this way just to get trapped by that thing."

"I'm not giving up." I reached for the gate, slowly releasing the latch.

"Jodi." Alex stopped me. "You aren't going out there. That dog will tear you to shreds."

"I think he guards the souls. Makes sure they stay where they belong. But we don't belong here, and neither does Matt."

"Did someone spike her fruit punch?" Lexi asked. "She's talking crazy again."

"Look, Matt belongs in the Elysian Fields. I think Cerberus knows that."

"Fine, so let him go. See what happens." Lexi raised one shoulder, making it all too clear that she didn't value Matt's soul.

"We don't belong here, either. Hades brought us to Tartarus. That's where Cerberus thinks we should be."

Tony stepped between me and the gate. "What if he tries to bring us back there? He could corner us and make us return to Tartarus. We wouldn't be able to scout out new souls from there. Your plan would—pardon the expression—go to hell."

Alex sighed. "He's right, Jodi. Besides, Matt wouldn't be with us anymore, and you'd have to raise your soul and figure out how to save us on your own. I'm not crazy about you and Matt getting close again, but I'd feel better knowing you had someone to protect you. You won't have your Ophi powers anymore while you're human."

I'd kind of forgotten about that part. I was so focused on not being able to hurt anyone anymore that I hadn't stopped to think about how powerless I'd actually be. Matt was a strong guy. I could use his protection. Especially since we were most likely going to be staying in sleazy motels and riding buses on our way back home.

I stared at Alex, hoping he could see I didn't have a plan. I didn't know how to get us out of here without running into Cerberus.

"What if we strike another deal with Hades?" he said.

I squinted at him, wondering what he was thinking. "Go on."

Lexi scoffed and threw her arms out. "Haven't we had enough deals? I mean, that's what got us all in here in the first place. Jodi making a deal with Hades that she couldn't keep."

"The kind of deal I'm talking about doesn't have consequences," Alex said.

"Then Hades will never go for it," Tony chimed in. "He likes big payouts for winning."

Alex smiled. "That's the beauty of this deal. He's going to win from the start."

"Alex—" Before I could ask him what he meant, I figured it out. The deal I'd made with Hades earlier, when he'd taken Victoria and the others…he'd liked that because it gave him Ophi servants. People to do his dirty work and free up some of his time. "We could offer our services. Help Hades run this place and make his life easier."

Alex nodded. "Exactly. Victoria and the others have Tartarus under control, but Cerberus is left to guard the rest of this place. We never see Hades unless he's making us suffer, so what is he doing?"

"Judging souls, making sure no one escapes, going back to the land of the living." I listed off things I remembered Tony teaching us. "What if he's going after the other Ophi while we're down here?"

"Mason." Carol's voice was small and shaky.

I bit my lip, thinking of how I could approach this. "Okay, Hades obviously needs help down here. We can offer him that. We can help judge the souls. That way we'd know who was coming into the underworld. And when the next couple comes…" I paused, realizing that was a poor word choice on my part. Alex wasn't going to want Matt and me to use the bodies of a couple. It would only make his mind focus on how Matt and I used to be together. "Well, when the next two souls whose bodies Matt and I could use arrive, we can get my plan going."

Arianna and Tony smiled, obviously happy with this idea. Carson, Ethan, and Carol weren't as enthusiastic, but they were willing to try it. Lexi shrugged and gave me a "What the hell? Why not?" Coming from her, that was good. I knew the others wouldn't challenge me. They never had. And since we'd broken off from Chase, it looked like we all could agree on something as a group.

Leticia looked petrified. "Does this mean we have to get Hades' attention? Bring him here to make the deal?"

I took a deep breath before saying, "Yes, it does."

"Any idea how to do that?" Alex asked.

I looked at the gate in front of me. "I'm pretty sure trying to break out of here will get his attention."

Lexi rolled her eyes. "And royally piss him off. He won't make a deal with us if he wants to cause us pain."

"Then I won't let him get angry with all of us." I turned to Alex. "Keep everyone else back. Guard Matt. Don't let him wander off or try to follow me."

He grabbed my arm. "No. You aren't going out there alone."

"I'm not putting anyone else in danger."

"I'm going with you. End of story." He met Tony's eyes. "Watch Matt and the others."

Tony nodded.

This was the best I was going to get. There was no arguing with Alex when he was like this. I kissed him lightly on the lips, just in case my plan backfired and Hades decided to burn me in hellfire instead of making a deal with me. I wanted to make sure I got one last kiss. Then, I unlatched the gate and pushed it open.

Cerberus growled, sending spit flying out of his mouths from the vibration.

"Easy." I held my hand out in front of me. Alex tried to pull me behind him to shield me, but I wasn't having it. I stood my ground. "Can you call Hades?" I asked Cerberus, keeping my voice as steady and non-threatening as possible. "Call your master here. Tell him I need to talk to him."

"Our fearless leader, everyone," Lexi said. "Talking to a three-headed dog from Hell. We're all screwed."

"Can it, Lexi," Alex yelled, and Cerberus snarled at the outburst. He charged at us, and Alex and I lunged to the side. Cerberus rammed into the gate. While he was stunned, I reached for him and shot him with a dose of poisoned blood from the left side of my body. He whimpered and went down.

I removed my hand from his fur and stared at it, unable to believe that had worked.

"You dosed him?" Alex was breathing heavily and staring wide-eyed at Cerberus' still form on the ground.

"I didn't think I could hurt him like that. I just wanted to stun him a little."

"My dog!" Hades' voice boomed from above us as he came swirling down in his black cloud.

Alex rushed to me, ready to face Hades.

"I didn't mean to hurt him," I said. "He attacked us. I just reacted."

Hades' eyes burned into me, but not enough to kill me. He wanted to make me suffer. My eyes watered from the flames, but I wasn't about to cower before him.

"You tried to escape. Of course Cerberus attacked you. He was doing his job."

"No." I held my hands up. "You don't understand. We weren't trying to escape. We were trying to find you. We need to talk to you."

"It's true," Alex said. "Look for yourself." He pointed at the others beyond the gate. "Would we have left them behind if we were looking for a way out of the underworld?"

Of course, my plan *was* to leave everyone behind while I found a way out, but Hades couldn't know that.

Hades looked at the group. Once his eyes were off me, the burning stopped. I stepped closer to him. "We have a deal for you."

He turned back to me and laughed. "What could you possibly have to make a deal with? I have you. You're in my world now. You have nothing to bargain with."

"That's not true. You're swamped down here. We almost never see you because you're too busy running this place. And I'm willing to bet Persephone is around here somewhere, right?" I looked to Tony for confirmation that my mythology was correct. He nodded.

"Leave her out of this." Hades' voice shook the ground, and I grabbed Alex to keep from falling.

"Fine. She's your wife, and actually the deal has nothing to do with her. Not directly, at least. Though it might give you more time to spend with her, if you wanted."

Hades narrowed his eyes at me. "Two minutes. Talk fast."

So, Persephone was his weakness. Good to know. "The other Ophi have a handle on Tartarus for you, but what about everything else you have to do here? You must be going crazy trying to handle it all on your own. Let us help. We could..." I paused, pretending I didn't have this all planned out already. "I don't know…maybe help you judge the souls, place them in the proper afterlives."

"I suppose you want to do this to avoid your own punishments?"

"No. We understand that you won't allow that. We aren't asking to avoid punishment. We are asking to simply cut down on the amount of time we spend in Tartarus each day." I knew the others were cringing at this, but Hades would never entirely release us from punishment. This was the best offer I was going to get us.

"I don't need all of you," Hades said. "I already have three judges."

"Rhadamanthus, Minos, and Aeacus," Tony said.

Damn it, Tony! Couldn't he have told me this earlier? My mind scrambled to find a new job for us, one that would still keep us in contact with the new souls arriving each day.

"They must be very busy, too busy to judge *and* take the souls to the proper places. We could do that. Usher the souls into their afterlives." I looked to Tony, seeing if that sounded reasonable. He nodded.

"That still wouldn't require the services of your entire group," Hades said. "I think your two minutes are up as well. Time to return to Tartarus."

"Wait!" I was desperate. "Just today we found some souls wandering to this gate." I pointed to the gate guarding the Fields of Asphodel. "That's how we found it. The souls remember where it is. They might seem mindless and lost in themselves, but deep down that knowledge is there. We stopped some souls from escaping. I think that proves you could use some of us as guards. Here, as well as at the entrances to the Elysian Fields, and Tartarus even."

Alex raised the corner of his mouth in the tiniest of smiles. I might have just saved us all.

"Who were these souls who tried to escape? Show them to me. They need to be punished." Hades advanced on the gate. Advanced on Matt.

# Chapter 8

Crap! Matt! "No!" I ran to Hades and nodded my head to the side, hoping Arianna would read that as *get Matt away from the gate*. "It's not their fault. The souls don't know they aren't supposed to leave. They aren't sure of anything here."

Hades stopped and faced me again. "You think you know my souls better than I do?" His glare was filled with hatred and the threat of more hellfire coming my way.

"That's not what I'm saying, but you can't deny that necromancers know souls really well. I can see what they're doing, what they're thinking even." Totally not true, but he couldn't prove I was lying. "We could help you control them. They aren't trying to disobey you, and if we can show them how they are supposed to exist here, things would be easier for everyone, especially you."

"I can't help but wonder why this is so important to you." He walked around me, eying me up and down. "Are you trying to save your friends and yourself from torture, or do you have some other endgame, Jodi Marshall?"

I had to be careful what I said next. The wrong thing could blow this plan entirely. "I want something we all can live with. I've seen how Victoria and the others help you. You're more lenient with them, and I can't help wondering why, since they caused you so much trouble. Remember the reason you brought them here?"

"Yes, because you made a deal with me: them for your safety. Only you broke our deal, which made your souls fair game."

"Fine. Well, if we're talking about what's fair, then why aren't you punishing them?"

"Who says I'm not?" Hades smiled and laced his fingers behind his back.

That was it. He *was* punishing Victoria and the others. "We're taking turns. When we come to the Fields of Asphodel, you're busy punishing them. That's where you go!"

"Very good."

This was good. I could use this. "Wouldn't you rather be doing something else? Spending time with Persephone, maybe?"

He stepped forward, getting right in my face. The heat radiating off him burned my skin. I cringed as he practically spit in my face. "I told you not to speak of her!"

"I'm sorry." The mere mention of her name got him worked up. "I thought you'd be happy about that suggestion. I really didn't mean to offend you."

He backed off, and the pain in my face eased. I must have been as red as a cooked lobster.

Alex gently touched my arm. "Are you okay?"

I nodded.

"Honesty is your only chance, Jodi Marshall." Hades stared off in the distance. I remembered Tony saying something about the part of the underworld where Hades lived with Persephone. I didn't doubt that was what he was gazing toward, even if I couldn't see anything.

"What do you want to know?" I hoped he was becoming more open to the idea of another deal.

"What do you get out of this?"

"I thought that was obvious." By the way he glared at me, I knew that was a stupid thing to say. I'd just insulted his intelligence. "What I mean is that I'm not looking for anything more than what you're thinking. I don't want my friends to be tortured twenty hours a day. If I could lighten our sentence by helping you in other ways here, then I want to do it."

We all waited in silence while Hades contemplated my deal. It was killing me to watch him think. He narrowed his brow a few times, which meant he was considering something—whether it was good or bad, I didn't know.

Alex took a step back, pulling me with him. He must have been afraid Hades would turn me down and lash out at us. I was afraid of the same thing.

"I've made my decision." Hades continued to stare off into the distance, avoiding our eyes. It was comforting. I figured if he was about to dismiss my idea, he'd want to see the disappointment on my face. "I'm going to allow this. For now." He finally turned to me. "You and your friends will be stationed at different places throughout the underworld. As it turns out, I like the idea of splitting you all up. There will be no chance for you to conspire against me."

Alex grabbed my hand, and I realized Hades would probably send us to opposite ends of the underworld—if this place *had* ends. Even though I wasn't planning on staying in this body—not fully, anyway—I wanted Alex to be the one to watch over my body while I was gone.

"Here are my conditions." He waved his hand and the gate to the Fields of Asphodel opened. He motioned the others forward. I sighed, realizing I was going to have to find Matt all over again. No way would he stay put with no one watching him.

I pulled myself together. "We're ready. Name them."

Hades snickered. Apparently, he found my comment amusing. "I hadn't realized I needed your permission to continue."

"Sorry. I just wanted you to know we were all listening." Not a great cover, but it would have to do.

"First, when you are on duty, you answer only to me. You may fulfill the judgments made by my three judges and escort souls to their afterlives, but beyond that, you listen to me."

"Done." I'd figured as much.

"Second—and I have a feeling you'll like this one—for four hours each day, you will report to Tartarus to administer punishment to your former Ophi allies."

Punish Victoria and the others? As much as I hated them for everything they'd put us through both at the school and down here, I didn't know if I could put someone through that kind of torture.

"I—I don't know if—"

"Done," Alex said.

I turned to him, wondering how he could go along with this. Victoria and Troy were his parents. Yes, they were awful, and Troy had even killed Alex once, but still. "Alex, no, you can't."

Hades cocked an eyebrow. "Very interesting. I thought you'd jump at the chance to exact vengeance."

"We aren't evil," I said. "Notice Chase isn't with us anymore. He didn't belong. He was consumed by power. We aren't. Alex is only going along with this because he thinks we have to."

One side of Hades' mouth curled up. "Are you sure about that? Maybe your boyfriend has a dark side after all. What's that expression humans love so much? The apple doesn't fall far from the tree, I think it is."

"He's nothing like them!" My blood was mixing in my veins as the anger coursed through me. Alex wasn't a monster like his parents.

"Jodi." Alex kissed the side of my head. "It's okay."

"You're not evil. You never could be. I know why you're doing this, but I can't let you become something you're not just to protect me." Tears spilled down my cheeks.

"How touching." Hades tapped his foot. "Now, do we have an agreement on this term, or should we dismiss the deal right now?"

"We're in agreement," Alex said. His eyes pleaded with me. I knew we had to go along with whatever Hades wanted if we were going to get out of here, but I hated what this might do to Alex.

"Agreed." I tried to keep my voice from shaking too much.

"Good. Then my final condition is that none of you will enter the Elysian Fields or the Fields of Asphodel when you escort souls to their afterlives. You are only permitted to enter the place of judgment, which coincidentally is located in the forecourt of my palace, and of course Tartarus, since you will be both administering and receiving punishment there."

The palace and Tartarus were the only two places we could enter? That meant I couldn't get Matt from the Fields of Asphodel. I'd be raising my human soul alone.

"I'm sensing hesitation," Hades said. "My terms are final. I will not negotiate any of them. So, as the humans say, 'Take it or leave it.'"

I looked around the group, making sure the others were okay with the terms of the deal. I wasn't going to force them into anything. Each of them nodded back to me. They wanted me to accept. I squeezed Alex's hand, wondering if this was going to be goodbye for a while. Hades would most likely separate us as soon as I agreed to the deal.

"I love you," Alex whispered.

"I love you, too." My voice shook. I wasn't ready to leave him yet. He nodded toward Hades, waiting for me to give our answer. I reached out my hand, thinking we'd shake on the deal, but Hades laughed.

"I don't shake hands. Your word will bind this deal."

No loopholes there. He was going to make me say it. I trembled as I breathed in, and on the exhale I said, "Deal."

Hades' grin stretched across his face. "Then I shall send you all to your new stations. Remember, we serve the dead with a smile." He laughed at his own bad joke, and since none of us were laughing, he waved his hand in the air and sent us all off on our own swirling clouds of smoke.

Alex's hand was ripped from mine. I hadn't been able to say goodbye or kiss him one last time. I was thankful that the last words I'd said to him were "I love you."

I couldn't see where I was going, and it made me wonder how I was supposed to take souls to their afterlives when the only way I'd traveled down here was by a swirling cloud of smoke. Had Hades set me up to fail again?

I wasn't surprised at all when I was set down in front of the palace. I knew I'd be assigned here. I wasn't the guard type. Ethan, Tony, Carson, and—would Hades let Chase in on this deal, or would he honor our decision to leave Chase behind? Seconds later, a cloud of smoke landed next to me.

"Surprise," Chase said as the smoke disappeared.

My heart sank. I'd been hoping Alex would be with me. As much as I knew Hades wouldn't keep us together, the naïve little girl in me was still praying it would happen.

"Happy to see me?" Chase moved toward me, but I started up the steps to the palace.

"Don't talk to me. We'll escort different souls. As far as I'm concerned, you don't exist." I stormed up the steps and to the front door. I opened it just far enough to slip inside and let it slam in Chase's face. *Thank you very much, Hades, you son of a bitch.*

The palace was dark. Everything was black and made of cold stone. I didn't know where to go, so I headed straight forward. Hades had said the judges were in the forecourt, whatever that was. At the end of the entryway stood two tall black vases filled with asphodels. I was so busy looking at them and thinking about how I was supposed to get to Matt that I didn't notice Chase walk up behind me.

"Pretty awesome. You know, if we play our cards right, I bet Hades will give us our own thrones like that."

I was about to tell Chase to shut up, when what he'd said fully registered. Thrones. I looked up and saw a narrow little hallway leading to a throne room.

Chase bowed and held out his hand to me. "Ladies first."

"Don't even think about touching me. In fact, don't talk to me either. I don't need much encouragement to send you flying on your ass with my poisoned blood."

"Feisty! I like it. This place is really improving your edge." He winked and had a stupid smirk plastered on his face.

God, I wanted to hit him! I turned on my heel and walked into the throne room. Two of the thrones, the biggest ones, were empty. I guessed they were reserved for Hades and Persephone. The other three thrones were occupied by three guys. Hooded guys. All I could see of them were their hands, draped over the edges of their armrests. Judging by the wrinkles, I figured it was a good thing their faces were covered in shadows.

"I'm Jodi Marshall. Hades sent me to escort the souls to their afterlives once they've been judged." I don't know why, but I bowed. Why piss off the guys who would ultimately decide your fate? I'd have to face my own judgment some day.

The judge in the middle nodded slightly, and I assumed that meant they accepted my position. I stepped off to the side, not knowing what I was supposed to do. I didn't see any souls waiting to be judged.

Chase stepped up and waved two fingers in the air. "Hey. Name's Chase Baxter. My deal's the same as hers. Just tell me who to bring where." He didn't bow.

"You would do well to show us the same respect Miss Marshall showed us," the judge in the middle said.

Chase mumbled something under his breath, but he bowed and met me at the side of the thrones.

"What the hell was that?" I asked him.

"I thought you weren't talking to me." He said it like he wasn't surprised at all that I was speaking to him.

"I'm not. Forget I said anything."

The doors of the palace creaked open, almost as if announcing the soul that was walking through them. Funny, but I didn't remember the doors making any noise at all for me or Chase. An older man walked in. I still couldn't get over the fact that souls looked exactly like the living. You couldn't tell they weren't whole beings with regular bodies. Hell, I'd even touched Matt. I knew there was a word for that. Tony had used it in a lecture once when he was explaining how souls looked in the underworld. *Corporeal*. It meant they could touch things and be touched in return. They weren't the same as when we raised them. Something happened down here to make them more lifelike. Ironic.

This guy had to be pushing seventy. He had a slight limp on his left side. Something told me he walked that way more out of habit than necessity. No way would his limp follow him into the afterlife. He just couldn't change the way he walked after limping for so long.

When I stopped to think about it, I realized my little lie to Hades about knowing what the souls were thinking and feeling wasn't really a lie after all. I could tell a lot about this guy just from being near him. It was like my necromancer blood was tuning in to the soul. Reading it.

The judges sat forward in their thrones, and the middle one spoke. "Justin Mercer, you are here before us to be judged for your sins. We shall review your life and decide how you will spend eternity. Await your judgment."

I made a mental note to figure out who was who as far as the judges were concerned. If I was going to be working with them, even without being fully in my body after I raised my human soul, it would be easier to know which judge I was addressing. We waited while they deliberated. All three lowered their heads as if watching mini television screens in their laps. I wondered if they were streaming this guy's life on their smartphones. Of course, I had a feeling all of the methods of communication and transportation down here were light years ahead of what we had up top.

After several moments of silence, they raised their heads and nodded to one another. The middle judge spoke again. "Justin Mercer, you will spend eternity in Tartarus paying for the wrongful doings in your lifetime."

"Sweet!" Chase said. "I got this one." He walked forward and grabbed the man by his arm. The guy was crying and begging for his soul, but the judges waved their hands. The palace doors opened, and Chase dragged the man out, looking way too happy to do it. It was almost too much to watch.

I was still trying to get my heartbeat back to normal when a couple walked into the palace. They were young. Only about eighteen, if I had to guess. She was blonde and tiny. He was blond, too, and average height. By the way they clung to each other, I knew they were definitely a couple, not brother and sister.

They looked at me strangely, and I felt my mouth curve into a smile. I must have been totally creeping them out smiling at them like that, but all I could think was that they were perfect. They were Matt's and my way out of here.

# Chapter 9

Finally, I managed to stop gawking and waved them toward me. They didn't look like the kind of people who'd end up in Tartarus—not that I thought Alex, Arianna, or the others deserved to be there, either.

The couple walked toward me, and the girl began to sob. "It's okay. The judges won't hurt you. They just want to evaluate your life and see which afterlife you belong in." I put my hand on her shoulder and directed the two of them to the open space in front of the three thrones.

Once again, the judge in the middle leaned forward. "Elizabeth Roseman and Brian Gehris, you are here before us to be judged for your sins. We shall review your lives and decide how you will spend eternity. Await your judgments."

Apparently, things were pretty scripted around here. Either that, or this guy had been giving the same speech for eternity, and he said the same thing every time without even thinking about it.

While the judges reviewed the lives of Liz—she looked more like a Liz than an Elizabeth to me—and Brian, I stared at them, trying to picture Matt and me in their bodies. I'd never visualized myself as a blonde before, and her hair was pin-straight. I was going to miss my waves. Brian was better than average in the looks department, but he had nothing on Matt. It was definitely going to be a step back for him, but I doubted he'd mind.

"It has been decided," the middle judge said. "You both will spend your afterlives in the Fields of Asphodel. While your lives were not full of sin, they were not full of great deeds, either. Your existence in the underworld will be much the same."

That was how they viewed it? I hardly called wandering around aimlessly neither good nor bad. It downright sucked. Still, I was glad I didn't have to take them to Tartarus.

"Follow me," I told them. As we left the palace, we passed Chase.

"Wow, he put up a fight." He laughed, as if there was something funny about dooming a soul to eternal punishment.

"Go crawl in a hole," I said, ushering the souls past him.

"You just can't stop talking to me, can you, Jodi?" I really did try to ignore him, but something about Chase demanded attention. He was like a little child. The more you ignored him, the more he kicked and screamed.

Liz and Brian were silent the entire way to the Fields. At first, I wondered how I'd even find my way there, considering I'd only traveled by black cloud since I got here, but my body moved on autopilot. Another one of Hades' tricks, I was sure. As we approached the gate, I saw Alex's dirty-blond hair. My heart sped up at the sight of him. Now I knew where he was. I'd be able to see him before I raised my soul.

He was leaning over the gate and calling out Matt's name. Crap! I'd forgotten Matt had wandered off while I was striking yet another deal with Hades. I couldn't leave until I found him. I owed him that much. He wouldn't be here at all if it weren't for me.

"Alex." He jumped down from the gate and whirled around at the sound of my voice.

"Jodi!" He rushed to me, scooping me in his arms. I squeezed him tightly, not wanting to ever let go.

"I thought Hades had sent you to guard the gates of Tartarus. I figured he'd send most of the guys there." I leaned my head back to look at his beautiful face.

"I thought he was going to, too, but here I am." He smiled at me and lowered his lips to mine.

As much as I didn't want the kiss to end, I had a feeling Hades would show up and personally put an end to our reunion if we didn't knock it off soon. "Alex." His name was barely a whisper on my lips, proof that I didn't really want to get his attention. I really wanted him to wrap me in his arms and…well, that would have to wait until we were out of the underworld.

He sighed, resting his forehead against mine. "Sometimes you make me forget we're in Hell."

Liz gasped at the word, obviously unfamiliar with the levels of the underworld.

I turned to her. "It's okay. You aren't going anyplace bad." Well, not entirely bad at least. It definitely wasn't good either. I wondered if Liz and Brian would even remember each other after they'd spent some time in the Fields of Asphodel.

Alex opened the gate and stepped aside for them to enter. They peered in, looking very unsure.

"It's fields of flowers. They're called asphodels. There's nothing in there that will hurt you. I promise. It's safe." I left out the part about losing all sense of who you were.

As they entered the field, I whispered to Alex, "I heard you calling Matt. No luck finding him yet?"

"No. My guess is he's doing his pattern again. He'll find the gate eventually, but…" He looked at Liz and Brian. "I'm guessing you want to use their bodies."

"Yeah. They're kind of perfect."

"They're a couple, you know." Of course he'd notice that.

"I know, but that doesn't really matter. They won't be themselves. They'll be Matt and me."

"Right." Was he really still jealous of Matt? "And did you notice the engagement ring on the girl's hand?"

Engagement ring? No, I hadn't.

"You're not really going to pretend to be his fiancée, are you?"

That would be way more than Alex could handle. "No." I doubted Liz would be buried with the ring anyway. At least she wouldn't have it on in the morgue when I took over her body.

It wasn't the best time to bring up Matt again, but we were kind of crunched for minutes here. "We have to find Matt. Like, right now."

Alex sighed. "Seriously, I want major brownie points for this. I'm talking watching the movies I want to watch, eating the food I want to eat…" His mouth curved in a devilish grin. I knew where he was going with this.

"Yeah, yeah, but you know, you lose points when you try to tell me you deserve…certain things." I couldn't bring myself to say the word "sex."

He held his hands up in defense. "I wasn't going to say that. I was simply going to say all the alone time with you I want." He raised an eyebrow. "But it's interesting to see where your mind is."

"Ha ha." I laced my fingers through his, and we both became completely serious again. This was goodbye, and we both knew it. Even if it was only for now, neither of us wanted to be apart.

"Hey," Alex called out to Liz and Brian, waving them back to the gate. They looked nervous as they approached us. Did they really think we were the bad guys? "Can you two look for a guy walking in a weird spiral kind of pattern? He's tall with dark hair, and his name is Matt, but he might not respond to it. We need to talk to him. Think you can find him and bring him here?"

Liz stared at Alex like he'd just described a puppy getting hit by a car. She was horrified. "Wh-why wouldn't he respond to his own name? And why is he wandering around?" Her eyes met mine, and she reached for my hands.

Alex put his arm up to block her. "Sorry, but once you're inside, I can't let you out. Not even your hands."

Tears fell from her eyes. I wished there was something I could do for her.

"You'll be okay. Matt's been through a lot. He didn't die under normal circumstances."

"We died in a car crash," Brian said. "Trauma to our heads, I think. Will we forget who we are, too?"

Car crash. I hoped their bodies weren't too badly banged up. I didn't want to put Matt and me in busted-up and broken shells. Putting our souls into the bodies would heal them to a certain extent, but not completely.

"You'll be okay." God, couldn't I think of anything better to say? "Will you find Matt for us? Please?"

Liz nodded. Brian took her hand, and they disappeared into the asphodels.

I stared in the direction they'd gone. "What if they can't find their way back? I'm afraid if I use my powers to call out to Matt's soul, Hades will sense me doing it and stop me." And that would be the end of our deal.

Alex didn't answer. He just put his hand on my shoulder.

"Hey, who's guarding this place with you?"

"Arianna."

I looked around. "Where is she?"

"Hades said he needed to see her. Something about Abby."

Hades wasn't the type to reunite families, so what was the deal? "What's wrong with Abby, and why would Hades need help from Arianna?"

"Abby did something wrong. Didn't follow orders specifically. Hades is punishing her extra."

No, he was making Arianna punish Abby. "That's torture for Arianna! Abby's her daughter. No matter how bad Abby is, Arianna still loves her."

Alex wrapped me in a hug. "I know. Hopefully, she'll be back soon." He stroked my hair, trying to keep me calm, but I was like a bomb ready to explode. We had to find Matt so I could get out of here and figure out a way to put an end to all of this.

The faint scent of smoke made me pull away from Alex. A swirling cloud of black was coming our way. I prayed it was Arianna being transported here by Hades, but my history of stellar bad luck told me differently.

Hades dropped down next to us. "Well, what do we have here?"

"I was escorting two souls to the Fields," I said, trying to stand my ground.

"Ah." He stroked his chin. For a brief moment, I was mesmerized by him. The guy was seriously hot. Not that it overrode the fact that he was a complete jackass. "I take it the souls are inside the gate now?"

"Yes." I hoped they wouldn't return with Matt while Hades was still here.

"Then you have somewhere else to be, Jodi Marshall." Hades' glare zeroed in on me. "Don't make me have Arianna torture another person she loves today. You're like another daughter to her, you know."

I glanced at Alex quickly, communicating a silent *goodbye for now*, but said aloud, "I'm going." Without even looking at Hades, I turned and walked away.

Chase was coming out of the palace with a young girl in tow. "Hey, Jodi. What do you think? Can I make this good girl go bad on the way to the Elysian Fields?" He laughed.

"Don't you ever get tired of hearing yourself talk?" I glared at him before reaching for the girl's hand. "I'll take you there. Trust me, you don't want to be anywhere near this guy." The girl was more than happy to go with me and get away from Chase.

"Be sure to tell her all about our history together on the way. Start with how you couldn't keep your hands off me!" Chase yelled after us.

I stopped. I knew I should ignore him, but I couldn't. "Your mom would be so proud." My voice was laced with sarcasm. His mom was his weakness.

His jaw clenched, and for once, he didn't have a snappy comeback. Satisfied, I smiled at the girl and walked her to the Elysian Fields.

The gate to Heaven was beyond words. It glowed a brilliant shade of yellow, with a hint of pure white mixed in. The warmth that came from beyond the gate was intense, but in a completely peaceful way. Happiness. That's what awaited this girl. She was one of the lucky ones.

I was so in awe of the Elysian Fields that I didn't even notice Carol and Jared standing next to us.

"Hey, Jodi." Jared smiled at me. "Thanks for working this out for us. It sure beats those asphodels and, of course, Tartarus."

I nodded. Couldn't argue with that.

Carol gently put her arm around the girl and walked her to the gate, which opened immediately for her. "Go ahead in." The girl smiled as she disappeared inside and the gate closed behind her. Yup, she was lucky.

I motioned for Jared and Carol to come closer so I could whisper. "I found the two souls I'll be using. They're in the Fields of Asphodel looking for Matt right now. I'm going to sneak over there before I head back to the palace. If they've found Matt and brought him to Alex, then I'm going to try to raise our souls."

"So, this is goodbye?" Jared reached his hand out to me.

"You want to shake? Really?"

"I didn't think I should hug you. I mean, you're Alex's girl, but you used to be with Matt, and even though he and I aren't cousins by blood, I appreciate you looking out for him."

Jared and Matt had been close. I'd always envied the Serpentarius Ophi and how they seemed to have such control over their powers. They were around humans a lot more than the rest of us. "See you soon, Jared." I gave him a quick hug.

"Just so you know, I'm telling Alex you hugged me."

I smiled. "Got it."

Carol hugged me, too, and I started back toward Alex and, hopefully, Matt. I still didn't really know how to raise my human soul. I figured it would be pretty much like raising any soul, except I'd be feeling broken in two after I did it. That was the part I was worried about.

As I got closer, I saw that Arianna was back. I couldn't help it. I ran to her and threw my arms around her. "Are you okay?" I asked, my head buried in her hair.

"I'm okay." Her voice was still shaky. She was trying to put on a strong face, but she was shattered inside. She pulled away from me. "Someone's here to see you."

I looked up to see Liz and Brian, and my shoulders sank. They must not have found Matt.

Liz fidgeted with her hands. "We wanted to say thank you for being so nice to us."

Brian nodded. "And we wanted to let you know we found Matt. Well, actually he found us. He was on his way back here, and he bumped into us. He's walking kind of funny, but he should be here any minute."

They'd found Matt! This was it. We could leave. I could save Matt. I could save Alex and Arianna and everyone.

Tears spilled from my eyes. I waved to Liz and Brian as they walked off into the Fields.

"Jodi?" Alex gently took my arm.

"I'm going to miss you." I could barely say the words. Alex and I had been through so much in the past few months. It seemed wrong to leave him behind.

He pulled me to him and kissed me. To hell with Hades. I had to say goodbye to Alex. When he pulled away, Alex turned to Matt, who was now at the gate. "Take care of her, or I'll send you to Tartarus myself."

Matt stared back at him, not comprehending a thing.

"So," I said, "I guess now I rip my soul apart."

# Chapter 10

My hands shook as I willed my blood to mix in my veins. This was going to be painful. Maybe so painful I wouldn't be able to go through with it. No, I wouldn't think like that. I'd find the strength to do this. No matter what.

Arianna touched my arm. "You must raise Matt's soul first, Jodi. Once you raise your human soul, you won't have the power to raise Matt."

She was right. How stupid of me. My fear was taking over and clouding my judgment.

"And another thing." Arianna looked around, making sure there was no sign of Hades. He could show up at any moment, and that would be the end of our plan. We'd be right back in Tartarus. No more time off for good behavior. We'd be done.

"Hurry, Arianna. We don't have much time."

"I know, but you have to locate the bodies of the souls you are reaching out to first. Find them with your blood."

"That's, like, the opposite of what I'm used to doing."

"I know. It won't be easy, but you need to figure it out fast."

Alex took my hands in his. "You can do this. Take some of my power if you need to."

I'd never taken power from anyone but Chase. "It's too risky. I may hurt you or leave you completely defenseless. I have to do this on my own."

"Too bad Chase isn't around. You could drain his power." Alex's face hardened. Chase had that effect on him.

"I don't need Chase for anything. Trust me." I took a deep breath and closed my eyes. I willed my blood to mix again, and I searched for Liz and Brian's bodies. Knowing their names and how they'd died helped. My blood had a purpose, targets to seek out. Images flashed through my mind so fast I couldn't make out a single one. But then I saw the hospital morgue. The bodies.

"I got it." I opened my eyes. I didn't need to see the bodies anymore. My blood knew where they were. That was enough. "Where's Matt?"

Alex reached for the gate, but Arianna stopped him. "If Matt steps across that gateway, Hades will be alerted. He'll think Matt is trying to break out of the Fields. Jodi has to raise him from where he is."

That was too close. We'd almost ruined everything. I walked to the gate and stared at Matt. He was looking at me with a vague sense of recognition. "I'll see you soon," I said, and I willed my blood to raise Matt's soul. To put him inside Brian's body. I had to work quickly and hope Hades was too busy to notice a soul leaving. With any luck, Matt's soul would blend in with the ones the Ophi still left on Earth were raising. It should've been more difficult, but some part of Matt must have understood I was helping him, because his soul didn't fight me. He floated away, and as soon as he was in Brian's body, I turned to Alex and Arianna. "My turn."

Alex pulled me to him and pressed his lips against mine. Before he let go, he whispered, "Don't forget about me when you're human. Please."

My body shook with a combination of my blood wanting to finish what it had started and with the heartache of leaving Alex. "Never. I love you." I was already pushing my Gorgon blood and soul away to free my human soul.

The last thing I saw was Alex mouthing the words "I love you" in return. His actual words were drowned out by the screaming in my head. My blood was raising my human soul. I felt like I was being ripped in half—because I was. My former strength and power were replaced with pain and weakness. My human soul floated from the underworld and through the ground. I smelled the dirt and worms as I searched for my new body. It felt like someone was pulling me through concrete. The pain was worse than what I'd gone through in Tartarus. When Hades made us relive the raisings of our victims, it wasn't as torturous as the real thing. Not by a long shot.

Even the air felt like it was crushing me from every angle. My soul twisted and writhed in torment. Just when I thought I couldn't handle it anymore, my soul found Liz's body. I was slammed into it with such force I felt like I'd shatter. Only I wasn't whole. Not yet. I bounced around inside Liz's body, instinctively looking for a way out. This wasn't home. This wasn't me.

I felt her skull sealing back up and her skin pulling itself together where she'd been cut in the car accident. The body burned and itched; it wasn't as painful as hellfire, but a close second. Finally, the body sealed around me, locking me inside. I was a prisoner in someone else's corpse. To say it was disorienting was an understatement. I couldn't see a thing. I thought I was blind for a second before I realized I was under a sheet. No, not a sheet. I was in a body bag. I had to get out. Matt was trapped on the gurney next to me, and he had no idea what was happening to him. He must have been terrified.

I groped for the zipper on the body bag, but muffled voices sounded in my head, making me raise my hands to cover my ears. It was like a buzzing that wouldn't stop. I kicked at the body bag and screamed to block out the noise in my mind. I was losing it. Raising my human soul had driven me mad.

No. Tony had said I'd have to tune out one of my bodies—or one half of my soul. Was I hearing what was happening in the underworld? I settled down, being absolutely still, and listened.

"She really did it." Alex's voice was a faint echo.

"We'll have to keep an eye on her. She's moving on autopilot now. I'm not sure anything is really registering." Arianna's words made me panic. If I was acting weird in the underworld, Hades would notice.

"She reminds me of the souls in the Fields of Asphodel, dazed."

"She'll learn to tune out one soul for a while to give herself some peace. It will make her body robotic, just going through the motions rather than thinking, but we'll get her through it."

Alex closed his eyes and swallowed hard. "How will she get back if she doesn't have any powers in human form?"

"She can still summon her human soul from down here. Her Gorgon soul is strong enough."

"Does she know that? Does she know she'll have to keep checking in with us?" Alex was panicking. He had no idea I was listening in and seeing everything they were saying.

"She'll be okay. Let's give her time to get settled in her new body, and then we'll try calling her here."

"If Hades suspects what Jodi's done, he'll bring her back himself."

I was sure he'd find the most painful way possible, too. My head pounded as Alex and Arianna's faces invaded my vision. I was seeing double—the body bag and the underworld at the same time.

"She's opening her eyes," Alex said.

Arianna grabbed Alex's hand as he reached for me. "Don't touch her. Just let her be for now. She must be going through a lot."

Arianna was right. I had to focus on my human soul and getting out of this bag. I tried to block out the underworld completely by throwing myself into finding a way to bust out of this bag. Where was that zipper? I reached up by my head, but the bag was fully zipped—of course. Damn it! I jabbed my pointer finger at the end of the zipper, hoping to make it poke through. Trying to undo a zipper from the inside wasn't going to be easy by any means. It took a few tries, but I finally forced my finger through, making a small opening at the top of the bag. Now I had to work the zipper down the rest of my body. I hooked my finger over the zipper and tugged. It was awkward, and the zipper snagged on my hair, so I had to tug at Liz's blonde strands to get free. Little by little, I pried more of my body through.

When I got the bag open to just below my knees, I bent my leg and used my foot to unzip the bag the rest of the way. Using my elbows, I propped myself up and looked around to make sure no one was in the morgue. I felt like I was in a horror movie, because, just like those dead guys that rose from the slabs and walked out of the hospital, I was a zombie. We had to be inside one of those walk-in refrigerators because the room was freezing cold and the walls were silver, like they were made of steel or some other metal to keep the room cold enough to preserve the dead bodies.

I sat up and stretched my limbs, trying to get used to Liz's body. It was completely foreign to me. Luckily, since I'd raised myself, I didn't need to wait for anyone's permission to speak or do anything else. My blood was controlling me, allowing me to be more than just a normal zombie. Matt would be a different story, though.

There was no sign of movement in the body bag next to me. Where was Matt? I slid off the metal table and unzipped Matt's bag. "Come on, Matt. Open your eyes." I couldn't risk someone walking in here and finding us. It was bad enough we were going to leave the hospital with two missing corpses on their hands. Thankfully, we'd be going far away from here so the police wouldn't be able to track us down.

Why wasn't Matt moving? I looked down at Liz's body. That was it! My human half was useless in this situation. I needed my Ophi powers to command him. I closed my eyes and tuned in to my body in the underworld. I was in the palace again. Chase was going on and on about another soul he'd taken to Tartarus. I ignored him and focused on sending a message to Matt's soul. "Be free. Live out your life in Brian's body." As soon as the message was sent, I shifted my focus again.

I heard him stir and opened my eyes. "Matt." I reached for him, but he pulled away. "It's okay. You're all right. Talk to me, Matt. Say something."

"Stay back." His voice was strained, and he swallowed hard. "Who are you? How do you know me?"

Of course he didn't recognize me. I was in Liz's body. How could I be so stupid? "Matt, it's me, Jodi."

He shook his head. "No. You don't look anything like Jodi."

"Please, just let me help you out of there. I promise I'll explain everything." I reached for him again, but he sat up on his own and looked around.

"Did you put me here? Is this a—"

"Morgue, yes. And I did put you here, but it's not what you think." He'd never guess this on his own, and unfortunately the truth was probably much worse than whatever he was thinking.

"Is this some sort of prank? Did you knock me out and..." His eyes widened as he ran his hands along the bag. "You put me in a body bag?"

"No. Not really. I mean, yes, technically I put you in here, but—" This was coming out all wrong. How the hell did I tell my ex-boyfriend—no wait, we'd never officially broken up—that I had brought him back to life?

He used the sides of the metal slab to stand up, and he stared at me, looking like he was seeing a ghost, or worse, a monster. "Where's Jodi? What did you do to her? We were together in her backyard, and then I don't remember anything. You knocked me out, didn't you?"

"No." What I'd done to him that day in my backyard was much worse. I'd stopped his heart forever. I shivered, partly at the memory and partly at how cold it was in the morgue. I guess I should at least be thankful that he didn't remember Hades raising him in the graveyard at the school. "Please, Matt. I *am* Jodi. I know I look different, but it's me. It's really me."

He turned and headed for the door, his movements jerky in the unfamiliar body. "Jodi!" he yelled.

"Matt!" I grabbed his arm and raised a finger to my lips to quiet him before someone came to see what was going on in the morgue. "It's me. I'm in someone else's body, but it's me."

"Are you crazy? Did someone do something to you, too? Is that what you're trying to tell me? It wasn't you who hurt me and Jodi? Someone else did it, and they hurt you, too?"

I shook my head, not knowing how to make him believe me. I should've known this would happen. But he was Matt. He knew me that night in the cemetery at school when Hades brought him back. He'd even recognized me in the Fields of Asphodel when every other part of his memory had faded away. He didn't know himself, but he still knew me. I'd just assumed he'd know me now.

"Ask me anything. I'll do anything to prove to you that I'm Jodi."

"Listen, I'm sorry if you're hurt, but you have to understand you're not Jodi. Jodi is my girlfriend. She has brown, wavy hair and the most amazing green eyes. She looks nothing like you." His voice was soft and sympathetic.

This wasn't working. He thought I was some poor girl who'd wound up at the end of a prank gone wrong.

"Matt, my name is Jodi Marshall. My birthday is December eighth. My best friend is Melodie. She's your best friend, too. She introduced us. You and I have been dating—or at least we were until—"

"Until that guy came along. Alec or something." His face looked strained as he struggled with the memory.

"Alex. His name is Alex."

"I hate that guy. He tried to hurt Jodi."

Damn it. He still didn't believe I was me. Not even after I'd spouted all that off. "How would I know all this if I wasn't Jodi?"

"Are you friends with Alex? Did he put you up to this?" Matt's head turned from side to side as he scanned the morgue. "Where is he? Does he have Jodi?"

"No!" I was more frustrated with myself than Matt. None of this was his fault. I looked around helplessly for an answer. My eyes fell on the steel walls. Matt would be able to see his reflection in them if I could just get him to focus on that instead of trying to find me—or what I usually looked like at least. "Come look at this."

He put his hands up in defense. "Listen, I get that you're upset, but—"

"Look at your reflection." I tried to keep the annoyance out of my voice, but he wasn't listening to me.

"My reflection?" He stared down at his hospital gown. "Where are my clothes?"

"Look at your hand, Matt. You have a birthmark on the side of your left palm, right? Or you did, but it's not there now."

Matt stared in horror at his hand. "What's going on?"

"Look." I pulled him closer to the steel wall and under the lights. He held his eyes on me for a moment before looking into it. The second he saw his reflection, he gasped. "That's not me."

# Chapter 11

I didn't know where to start, but at least he'd be more open to hearing the crazy things that had happened now that he saw he wasn't in his own body.

"Am I dreaming?" Matt shook his head, still staring at his reflection—well, at Brian's reflection. "That's the only explanation. That's not me. Not my face."

"Okay, Matt, please listen to me. I *am* Jodi. I look different, just like you. And, no, you're not dreaming. This is all real. It's going to sound unbelievable, but I need you to trust me."

He raised his eyes to me. "Jodi? It's really you?"

I nodded, tears forming in my eyes.

He rushed over to me, pressing his lips against mine. I froze, not knowing what to do. He thought we were still together. Matt didn't know anything about me and Alex. To him, I was still his girlfriend. I was human now, which meant that he and I *could* be together. That fact wasn't lost on me, but neither was the fact that I loved Alex. Still, my unresolved feelings for Matt were lingering, keeping me from pulling out of the kiss.

My lips gently parted, and without really meaning to, I was kissing him back. This was how our first kiss should've been. I wouldn't stop his heart this time. Being with him felt right. In this moment, being with Matt was what made sense.

But Alex. I slowly pulled away from Matt, leaning my head against his chest. Tears dripped onto his hospital gown. My tears. For once, I didn't have to worry about what that would mean. I wasn't a danger to him.

"Don't cry. I'm here. I don't know what happened to us, but it'll be okay. I promise." Great. Now he was the one reassuring me. This wasn't at all what was supposed to happen.

"You don't understand." I stood up straight, trying to find the courage to break his heart. We couldn't be together. No matter how right that kiss had felt, it couldn't happen again. I wouldn't do that to Alex. I wouldn't cheat on him. Crap! Technically, I already had, but I was putting an end to it now. I wasn't the kind of girl to kiss another guy behind her boyfriend's back, but this was such a gray area. I was technically Matt's girlfriend, so I'd technically cheated on him with Alex. Only Matt had died, and that sort of ended our relationship, whether he was aware of it or not. Now, I was Alex's girlfriend, and here I was kissing Matt. Ugh! I hated technicalities. There wasn't room for them when it came to human emotions.

"Jodi, what is it? Do you know what happened to us?" He was looking at me like he just wanted to make things better—for me. All he cared about was me. God, this was going to be so hard.

"We're in other people's bodies. I promise I'll explain everything, but right now we need to get out of here without anyone seeing us."

"How? We're in hospital gowns, and we don't have money to take a cab anywhere."

He was right. I looked around, spotting the files at the ends of our gurneys. I pulled out Liz's. "Elizabeth Roseman. It says she didn't have any living relatives."

Matt pulled Brian's file. "Brian Gehris. That's whose body I'm in?"
"Yes."

Matt shook his head, trying to wrap his mind around everything I was telling him. "Personal belongings. He must have had a wallet on him when he died, right? The file says he was killed in a car accident."

I looked around again, wondering if they'd have personal belongings stored in here to return to the families. Not likely. This place was empty, sterile. "There's nothing here."

"Okay, then how about…" Matt walked to the closet in the corner and pulled out some hospital scrubs and white sneakers.

"Perfect!" I motioned for Matt to turn around while I got dressed. Just like always, he was a perfect gentleman. My sneakers were big, but they'd do. Once we were both outfitted like hospital staff, we checked the hall and prepared to make our exit. We had to get out of there before someone came for the bodies. They wouldn't leave them here for long, or they'd decay. That also meant we had to get out of this town quickly so no one recognized Liz and Brian suddenly walking around after being pronounced dead. I could see the back exit, and judging by the darkness on the other side of the window, it was night. That would help. We kept our heads down and walked out of the morgue as if we worked there. We even took Liz and Brian's files and pretended to study them to avoid talking to anyone we passed on the way out.

Outside, we ditched the files in the dumpster and walked down the road and across the street to a cemetery, of all places. At least I felt at home in one of those.

"I can't believe we pulled that off," Matt said.

I swallowed the lump in my throat and took Matt's hands in mine. Yeah, Alex wouldn't like this either. Still, I owed it to Matt to be gentle. He'd been nothing but good to me. "Matt, there's something you don't know about me. I'm not who you think I am."

He raised his hand to my head. "Did you hurt yourself? Were we knocked out? You're not making sense. I know you. I knew you the day I met you. When Melodie introduced us, I could tell you were an amazing person. You're sweet and caring. Not to mention you're smoking hot. I have to admit I don't like this blonde look on you, though. It's all wrong."

I couldn't have this conversation right now. "We need to get out of here." I didn't want to stick around the cemetery. It was too close to the hospital, and someone might see us.

"Where do you want to go?"

"We should find some other clothes so we don't stick out in a crowd."

"Where are we?" Matt looked around. "This doesn't look like the cemetery at home."

"I don't really know. We'll have to figure that out." I scouted out the road. "For now, let's just get out of here. We can talk on the way."

He took my hand, lacing his fingers through mine as we walked. "I think someone did some sort of spell on us. You know, like witches or something. I never thought they were real, but how else do you explain this?"

A nervous laugh escaped my lips. "How about a group of necromancers called the Ophi raised our souls and put us in the bodies of two recently killed teenagers?"

He cocked his head at me. "Is this some prank? Are you in on it? Should I be looking for Melodie lurking in the shadows?"

"No." I squeezed his hand. "Do you trust me? Really trust me?"

The smile left his face. "Jodi, look. There's something I want to say. I know it's early, we've only been dating for a little while, but I meant what I said about when we first met. I felt like I knew you. The whole time we were friends, before we started dating, I kept wishing you'd look at me the way I looked at you."

Oh, God, where was he going with this? Please, don't let him say the L-word. I couldn't handle it right now.

"I don't want to scare you away, but I can't hold this in any longer. Jodi—"

"Matt, don't."

"I love you."

My insides felt like they'd turned to stone. My heart wasn't able to pump blood to the rest of my body. I felt too heavy to hold myself up. Thankfully, we were at the gate at the other end of the cemetery, so I used it for support as we kept moving.

"It's okay if you don't love me back. I know it's soon." He brushed my hair off my shoulder. "But I do love you, Jodi. So, if you want to know if I trust you, the answer is yes. With all my heart."

I lost it. I cried, big heaping sobs. This would've been easier if Matt remembered me killing him. If he remembered being a zombie and killing that bunny. If he remembered that I'd been the one responsible for his death, not once but twice. Instead, he loved me.

"Please, don't cry. I didn't mean to upset you." He tugged my hand, making me stop, and raised my chin. Leaning forward, he pressed his lips to mine.

Damn it! Why wasn't I stopping him?

"You died," I blurted out.

Matt pulled away, looking shocked. "I don't know what's going on, why we were in that morgue or these bodies, but we aren't dead." He reached for my hand, taking it in both of his.

"Not anymore, but we were." I started walking again, preparing to let it all out. Everything from start to finish. "You remember being at my house and kissing me, right?"

"Yeah." He dragged the word out, not sure where I was going with this. I wasn't so sure either. How did I explain the next part?

"All right, well, something happened when we kissed." The way he was staring at me was tearing me up inside. Here I was telling him unbelievable things, and he was just looking at me like he wanted to kiss me again. "You died that day, Matt. It was my fault. My blood isn't like yours. It's poisonous. I didn't know it when we got together. Things started happening to people and animals around me. I was killing people with my tears and my blood, and I brought a deer, a squirrel, and a rat back to life with it, too."

"Oh, Jodi, what happened to you?" He thought I'd lost my mind.

"I was born this way, but my powers didn't kick in until just recently. I'm not human, Matt. I'm a necromancer."

"A necromancer? Isn't that someone who can raise the dead?" He was honestly trying to follow along with me, which just proved what a great guy he was. He should've been cursing and telling me I was crazy. But Matt was amazing. I'd forgotten how much I cared about him.

"Yes. I was born under the thirteenth sign of the zodiac, Ophiuchus. People like me have Gorgon blood in our veins. It's poisonous to humans."

"Whoa, this is sounding a lot like a lecture Mr. Quimby gave in lit class. Did he put you up to this?"

I sighed. "It's not a joke, Matt. I'm being completely serious."

Just like that he nodded, taking my word for it and waiting for me to continue.

"I'm a descendent of Medusa. When you kissed me, my blood poisoned you and stopped your heart." The warmth running down my face was the only indication that I was crying. "I didn't mean to kiss you. When I found out what I was—what I am—I was going to end it, stop seeing you. I didn't want to hurt you. I cared about you so much. But before I could explain, you kissed me, and I couldn't even think because I'd wanted to kiss you for weeks. I think I might have been falling in love with you, and I got so wrapped up in the moment that—"

He pulled me to him and kissed me again. My God, why wouldn't he stop doing that? I pulled back, and he smiled. Not at all the reaction I was expecting. "If I wasn't trapped in someone else's body, I'd tell you you're crazy."

"Sometimes, I think I am."

He brushed the tears from my cheek. It wasn't fair. I could touch him now without hurting him. Now that I could be with him, I wasn't available.

"What changed? Why can I kiss you now? And how am I alive and in this body?"

I started walking again. I had to keep us moving, no matter how much Matt wanted to stop and talk about all this. "I raised you...and myself. This isn't really me, not all of me anyway. I sort of pissed off Hades, and he took me and the other Ophi to the underworld. I raised the human half of my soul. It sort of died a couple months back when I drank Medusa's blood."

"You drank blood?" His voice cracked. Finally, I'd freaked him out.

"It sounds worse than it was. I had to do it. I would've died if I didn't. Alex would've died."

"Alex?" He stiffened. "You mean that guy—"

"I-I'm with him."

Matt's eyes widened, and his jaw clenched. "That's not funny, Jodi. I'm sorry if I freaked you out when I said 'I love you,' but don't you think you're going a little too far? I mean, that's the guy who stalked you, who assaulted me."

"I know, but there's an explanation for all that."

Matt's face twisted in disgust. I reached for him, but he pulled away.

"Alex was only trying to help me. I just didn't know it. He's like me. He saved my mom. I killed her, Matt. It was an accident. We were cooking, and I cut my hand. I tried to stay away, to tell her the truth about me, but she grabbed my hand and then... If Alex hadn't been there, she'd be dead. He saved her, and then I left. I went with him to a school to study with other Ophi. He's really sweet."

"How soon?"

"How soon what?"

"How soon after I died did you take off with him?"

I closed my eyes, feeling the threat of tears again. "Matt."

"I have to know. I'm trying to be really patient and understanding right now, but I need to know this."

"I don't want you to hate me. I was crushed when you died."

"How soon?"

Payback really was a bitch. This was proof. I was paying for everything I'd done wrong. This was supposed to be my way of making up for all the things I'd done to Matt. I'd saved him from the underworld, yet here he was with me and in more pain than he'd been in Hades' hands.

I bit my lower lip and inhaled deeply. "I left the night of your funeral."

A strange half-cough, half-laugh escaped Matt's lips. "The night of my funeral? Wow."

"My mom died. I couldn't stick around and chance killing her again. What if Alex wasn't there when it happened again? I couldn't risk it."

"And when did you and Alex…" He couldn't even say the words.

"It sort of happened gradually. I didn't plan on it. You have to understand it nearly killed me to lose you." I didn't want to tell him about me bringing him back wrong, about how I watched him rip apart a bunny with his teeth. He didn't need to know that.

Refusing to look at me, Matt stared off at the open road as we kept in the cover of the trees. "Does he treat you well?"

"Do you really want to talk about him?" I didn't want to rub his face in the fact that I'd moved on. He didn't deserve that.

"No. How long has it been since I died, and why am I in the wrong body now?"

"A few months. I couldn't bring you back. Not at first, anyway. When Hades took me and the others to the underworld, I found you. You were wandering around in this place called the Fields of Asphodel. I didn't think you belonged there. You're too good to be trapped in an afterlife where you felt nothing at all. And when you recognized me, I knew I had to free you, raise your soul. I found a young couple who'd just died, and I raised us both."

He turned to me, meeting my eyes for the first time in minutes. "You wanted to be with me again? Is that why you did this?"

I could've lied, made him believe I did this all for us, but when I returned my soul, it would crush his heart all over again.

"I have to free my friends. They're trapped and being tortured. My body is still being tortured, too. My soul can't stay split like this."

"So, we can't be together, even though you're human right now."

"I won't be human for long." He was silent for a while, and I didn't know what to say to make this easier on him.

"Do you need help finding a way to free your friends?"

I nodded. "But I understand if you don't want to help me."

He took my hand and squeezed it. "I'll help you. I can't change the way I feel about you, though."

Did he hate me now? Was that what he was trying to tell me?

"I won't try to pressure you into changing your mind about me, but I won't hide my feelings either. I'm still in love with you."

Pain tore through my insides. It was going to be torture for both of us to be this close and unable to act on all these unresolved feelings. My body felt like it was being hit by a thousand hammers at once.

"Jodi?" Matt squinted at me and grabbed me by my shoulders as my eyes rolled back into my head.

It wasn't heartache I was feeling. My body was being tortured in Tartarus, and the pain was forcing me to tune into the Ophi half of my soul.

# Chapter 12

I cried out in pain, and Matt carefully lowered me to the grass so I wouldn't hurt myself. I saw glimpses of Victoria looming over me, smiling as she continued to deliver my torture. "Service with a smile," she'd called it. She was talking to me, but I couldn't hear her over my own screams. I felt the hellfire burning me from the inside out. This wasn't the normal torture. I wasn't reliving a death I'd caused. Victoria was burning me the same way Hades had after I'd raised the entire cemetery in my sleep.

"You ready to torture your father's soul yet?" Victoria asked, easing up only enough for me to answer.

My dad? "No!" What had I missed? Hades was torturing me by trying to make me torture my own father?

"Then I guess I get the pleasure of torturing you both." Victoria smiled, and I turned to see my seventeen-year-old father on the ground next to me in Tartarus. His eyes said he was more concerned for me than himself.

"Jodi!" My name echoed in my ears. Matt's hand was on my face. "Look at me. Focus on me." His voice was firm, demanding my attention.

I choked back the fire in my throat. My eyes watered, and I clenched my teeth against the searing pain shooting through me. Dad's cries tore through me worse than the hellfire.

"Jodi!" Matt was screaming now. "Damn it, listen to me!" Matt had never yelled at me. Never cursed at me.

I opened my eyes, seeing double. Victoria's image hovered over Matt's with a faint ghostly glow.

"Good," Matt said. "Tune it out. It's just me, okay. You're not there. You're here with me." He took my face in his hands. *Please, don't kiss me.* Alex—he was near me, near my body in Tartarus. Matt leaned toward me as I shoved the image of the underworld out of my mind. I turned my head away from Matt, and he paused inches from my face.

"I'm okay now." But my dad wasn't. I never thought I'd see him again, but of course Hades would make me watch Dad suffer.

Matt hung his head in relief. "I was trying to shock you out of it. I wasn't really going to kiss you again. I know you're with... I guess it worked."

"I'm going to have to learn to keep those thoughts out. Hopefully, my Ophi half is doing a better job tuning out what's going on here."

"It's almost like you're two people now."

"I know. Even with all the crazy things I've been going through, this tops them all."

"You okay to get up?"

I nodded. "I think so."

He gave me his hand and pulled me up, going slowly to make sure I was really all right. "What do we do now?"

"I have to get back to the school. Medusa's spirit is trapped in a statue we have there. Normally, I can call her and she'll appear in my mind, but I don't have any of my Ophi powers now. I'm hoping, if I connect to the statue, I'll be able to talk to her."

Matt rubbed the back of his neck. "Medusa's spirit? Really?"

"I know how it sounds, but it's true. Listen, you don't have to come along. You can start over. Go somewhere no one knows Brian."

"I don't have anyone anymore." He looked down at his feet. "Except you."

"Do you want to come with me?"

"Do you mind?"

"No. Actually, I was kind of hoping you'd come along. We didn't really get to say goodbye to each other. I've been carrying the memory of you and the last time we were together for months now. I'd like a better memory for when I—"

"Go back to being Ophi and can't be around me anymore?" His big brown eyes spoke volumes.

"You know, all Ophi have green eyes. It's really nice to see your brown eyes again, even if these aren't really yours."

He smiled. "I always loved your eyes."

Things were getting weird again. These feelings just wouldn't go away, especially when we stared into each other's eyes like this.

"We should go. We can't exactly stay in this town. Someone will recognize Liz and Brian." We started walking again. Our only chance of not drawing attention to ourselves was to find one of those donation bins and get some normal clothes.

We came to a fork in the road. "Which way?" Matt asked.

Neither of us had a clue where we were. "Let's go right," I said. "It's the right side of Medusa's body—and mine—that has the power to restore life. Seems like a good way to go."

"Whatever you say." Matt smiled at me, a smile that said he'd follow me anywhere. This was not going to be easy. Matt was a gentleman, and I knew he wouldn't try anything as long as I was adamant about Alex. But what if my human soul couldn't hold on to my Ophi feelings for Alex?

We walked along the road in silence. No cars drove by, and the streetlights were few and far between. I tripped over a dead animal, and Matt grabbed my arm to keep me from faceplanting in the dirt on the shoulder of the road.

"You know, a few months ago, I would've been afraid I'd raise the poor thing."

"I still can't believe you can do that."

"It takes some getting used to."

We came to a traffic light, and we both smiled. This was a good sign. It meant we were getting closer to civilization. Maybe we'd find somewhere to get clean clothes. At this point, I wasn't opposed to stealing from a clothing store. I'd find a way to pay for it later.

"Right again?" Matt asked at the intersection.

I nodded. It was only our second right so we wouldn't be heading in a circle or square that would lead back to the hospital or cemetery.

We walked about another half mile before we started to see lights. Neon lights.

"Stores!" I never thought I'd be so happy to see a store, especially a drugstore.

"Look." Matt sounded equally as happy. He pointed to the sign across the street from the drugstore. It was a secondhand shop, and outside was a donation bin.

"Yes!" I whirled around and hugged Matt. He lifted me off the ground and squeezed me. Our faces were inches apart, and we stared at each other. My smile slowly faded, and I lowered my eyes. "Sorry."

Matt didn't say a word as he lowered me to the ground. "Ladies first." He motioned for me to lead the way.

Alex, Alex, Alex, Alex. Alex was counting on me. He was probably worried sick about me. I couldn't do anything to jeopardize what I had with him. Matt was only temporary. I wouldn't be human forever. I tried so hard to convince myself of all these things. To be rational. Only… the human heart isn't rational. A huge part of me wanted to finish what Matt and I had started.

The metal container creaked as Matt held open the lid. "So, do I dive in and start digging for something appropriate?"

"How about you reach in? I don't want to have to pry you out of there if you get stuck."

He laughed. "Okay." He reached his arms in and pulled out a yellow tube top. I shook my head, and he tried again. This time he got a pair of neon-green pants.

"Oh, they're so you," I said.

"Remember you have to be seen with me."

"Touché."

Matt reached in again. "Oh, I've got the perfect outfit for you. So perfect that I'll agree to wear the green pants if you put this on." This was going to be bad. Matt held up the most hideous floral and paisley-print dress that only a senile old great-great-grandma would wear. "What do you think?"

I shook my head. "I don't think it goes with my eyes. Darn." I faked an upset tone.

"All right, your turn. I can't reach anything else."

"My arms are shorter than yours. How do you expect me to reach in there?"

"I'll hold you up. I bet you'd fit in there just fine."

"You won't let me fall in?" I knew he wouldn't. I trusted Matt with my life. The only reason I'd asked was because…well, I was flirting. I cursed myself for it.

"I'd never let anything happen to you." He was dead serious.

I nodded, and he waved me closer. As I put my hands on the metal container, Matt placed his hands on my waist. He counted to three and lifted me up. Leaning forward, I reached both my arms into the container. I was dangling upside-down, held up by Matt's arms. I tried to push the warm feel of his touch from my mind as I sifted through the clothes. Most were nowhere near my size or Matt's. I was about to give up hope when I found what felt like a t-shirt and a pair of jeans near the bottom of the bin. They felt big, so I guessed they were men's. I also grabbed another smaller pair of jeans and a lightweight zip-up hoodie.

"Okay. Pull me out of here."

Matt carefully brought me back out of the container. His body pressed up against mine. He cleared his throat and backed away, running his fingers through his hair and avoiding my eyes. Yup. We both felt the pull between us.

I forced myself to look at the clothes in my hands under the light of the thrift store sign. "Hopefully these will work." I handed Matt the jeans and shirt.

"We should find a bathroom." He pointed to the gas station two stores down. "That'll work."

We walked in silence again. I wished Matt and I could go back to the way we used to be, when we were just friends. I missed him, and this tension between us was unbearable. We decided it wasn't safe for both of us to go inside the gas station to get the bathroom keys, so Matt went alone, while I stayed outside and worried that someone would recognize him.

A few minutes later, he came back holding two keys. "No problem. The kid working the register didn't even look up from his phone when he gave me the keys." Speaking of not looking up, Matt was having trouble looking at me now. Just great. This was going to be extremely awkward.

I took the key and opened the bathroom door, going straight for the sink. Seeing Liz's face stare back at me in the mirror was the weirdest feeling. I shook it off and turned on the cold water. I needed something to shock myself out of whatever it was I was going through. I splashed water on my face, but it didn't help at all.

I stared at the tag on the jeans. Squeezing myself into them wasn't going to be easy. I held my breath and tugged them on. It felt like someone was strangling my waist, but I managed to button them. They actually reminded me of the jeans Melodie had made me buy. The ones I'd worn on my date with Matt. Being human again was making me tap into all those memories I'd tried to put in the back of my mind when I became the leader of the Ophi. I wondered if my Ophi memories would fade while I was here. I couldn't imagine Alex becoming nothing but a memory.

A knock on the door made me jump. I took one last look at Liz's reflection—now my reflection—and stepped outside.

Matt held his hands out at his sides. "Well, what do you think?" He had on a deep orange shirt. I used to love him in that color. Something about his dark hair and eyes against the rich orange was really...sexy. But Matt wasn't a brunette anymore. He was a blond. The color didn't have the same effect on his features.

"Looks a little snug." I stuck to safe comments, ones that didn't comment on how hot I'd thought he was—the real Matt, at least.

"Yours, too. Though I remember the jeans you wore on our date to that nightclub, Serpentarius, were killer on you. This girl doesn't...well, she's not you."

Yeah, I knew what he meant. Not that I was complaining about Liz. She was pretty fit, but too teeny tiny—though not as tiny as these size-zero jeans. I wasn't exactly big, but I had a few inches on her—not to mention a few curves.

I fidgeted, feeling uncomfortable, which was ridiculous considering I wasn't even in my own body. "Um, I guess we should figure out where we are."

"Already found out. When I was in the convenience store, I checked out the paper. We're in some town called Springfield."

"That doesn't exactly narrow it down. There are a ton of Springfields across the country."

"Not a problem. Did you really think I'd leave it at that? I checked out a few brochures they had for activities in the area. I'm pretty sure I know where we are." Of course he did, because Matt was perfect. He thought of everything.

"How far from home?"

"I'm guessing about four hours by bus."

"Bus?"

"Yup. Next one leaves at six. We've got two hours."

Alone with Matt for two hours waiting for a bus. I would've killed for this opportunity a few months ago. Now, it terrified me. Even when I wasn't a threat to him, I was still afraid to be around him. "We don't have any money."

Matt looked away as if ashamed. "I sort of stole some money from the register."

"What? How?" Matt wasn't the type to steal. I couldn't imagine how he'd pulled this off.

"I told the kid the coffee maker was empty, so when he went to refill it…" He shrugged.

I couldn't complain. We needed money, and Matt had done what he had to in order to get us out of this town. He was protecting me, even if it meant doing something completely out of character.

"We should go to the bus station and try to get some sleep." Matt cocked his head at me. "What is it? Why do you look like you lost your puppy?"

How did I explain this to him? *Well, Matt, after splitting my soul, I feel like a complete psycho with a split personality. I still love Alex, but looking at you, I just want to throw myself in your arms and kiss you.*

"Just tired, I guess." Yeah, that was a better answer.

"The cashier said the bus station was two blocks down on the left."

A car pulled into the parking lot, so we decided to leave the bathroom keys in the door locks instead of risking going back inside the store again. The fewer people who saw us, the better. While we walked, I kept my hands shoved in my pockets. I wasn't afraid of Matt trying to hold my hand. I was afraid of *me* wanting to hold *his*. I loved Alex, and if I was fully in the underworld with him, it would be *his* arms I'd want around me. *His* hand I'd be holding. But this part of me—my completely human soul—had never been with Alex. Matt and I had a history together, one based on me being normal, not Ophi.

We stepped into the bus station and found the bus we needed. Matt pointed the way, gently placing his hand on the small of my back. He used to do that all the time when we walked down the halls at school, but now…

He looked down at his hand. "Sorry. Old habits and all that."

I shook my head. "It's okay." No, it wasn't.

I looked at the empty wooden bench. It wasn't exactly sanitary.

"Here." Matt sat down and motioned for me to join him. "You can put your head in my lap so your hair doesn't stick to whatever this substance is coating the bench. My guess is year-old chewing gum and…well, I don't want to know what else."

Put my head in his lap and sleep? That was way too intimate.

"Jodi." He frowned at me. "You know you can trust me. I'm not going to do anything to you while you sleep."

He wasn't the one I was worried about. "I know that." It was four in the morning, and I was exhausted, so I curled up on the bench next to him and rested my head on the edge of his lap, not daring to touch any more of him than necessary.

I closed my eyes and wondered what Alex was doing.

# Chapter 13

Heat prickled against my skin as I led the soul past Tony and Ethan and into the depths of Tartarus. He cowered behind me, not wanting to follow but unable to stop his legs from moving. I knew the feeling. Hades had done the same thing to me on several occasions.

"Please, don't make me go. I'm sorry. For everything. Please." He grabbed my hand, squeezing it with every sobbing heave of his body.

"I'm sorry, but there's nothing I can do. Once the judges make their decision, I have to follow their judgment. They said to bring you here. I'm powerless to change your fate." Even as the words left my mouth, they felt foreign. I was going through the motions down here. The only reason I was aware of what my body and Ophi soul were doing in the underworld was because my human soul was asleep. When I tuned out one soul, the other took over.

The man, Henry Something-or-Other, continued to wail. Knowing what awaited him in Tartarus, I couldn't help feeling sorry for the guy, even if he had done terrible things in his life. I wasn't really one to judge.

"Oh, good. Another one." Abby smirked. "Who knew there were so many damned sinners in the world?"

"You're one to talk. Your punishment didn't end too long ago."

Her eyes burned into mine. "And it will be time for yours again soon."

I turned away, not wanting to see Henry's horror or the look of pleasure on Abby's face, and headed back to the palace. As I passed the Fields of Asphodel, I felt a pull in that direction.

"Jodi."

Alex. I fought the urge to run into his arms. I had to be careful in case Hades was watching us. We never really knew where he was. Ever since we'd made the deal with him, we'd seen him less and less. It was strange, but the second I tuned in to my Ophi soul, I had access to all my memories in the underworld. I just had to be careful not to access them all at once. Between the torture and bringing souls to their own personal forms of Hell, it got overwhelming really quickly.

I walked slowly to Alex, looking around for signs of Hades. "Hey."

"You came." He looked deep into my eyes. "It's you. How? Did you release your soul already?"

"No. My human soul is sleeping, and that brought my focus back here. It's happened before, though. When we were in Tartarus. The pain yanked my focus back to my body." Just in time to see my dad. That image was hard to get past.

"The double vision thing is tough, huh? Tony said it would be, but I've been hoping he was wrong." He reached for my hand, lacing my fingers through his. God, I missed him.

"Is it okay to be holding hands like this? I mean, will Hades—"

"He's been leaving the underworld a lot. No clue where he's going, but we end up unsupervised. He thinks we're all still under his control, but when he's gone we can do whatever we want. Our powers are too strong for him to keep a hold on."

"He doesn't have a clue, does he?"

"Not at all. Something's going on. He's too busy to notice us."

"That can't be good. What could he be looking for?" The thought hit me like a speeding Mack truck. "Do you think he knows what I've done?" I clutched Alex's hand, squeezing it so hard he looked down at it.

"Easy, Jodi. I don't think he suspects anything, but you *have* been different since you left."

"Different how?"

"Every time you go by the Fields, I call out to you, but this is the first time you've responded."

I'd been ignoring him. "I'm so sorry."

He shook his head, dismissing it. "You're not all here. I get it." He got quiet for a moment, which could only mean he was thinking of how to ask about Matt.

"Things aren't going so well for the human me, either. Matt had a tough time adjusting at first, but after I showed him his reflection—Brian's reflection—he was pretty much up for believing anything I said. I left out some things, though. I didn't want to overload him."

Alex's head jerked up. "What kind of things?"

"The whole 'I brought him back wrong' thing. You know, the bunny-eating incident."

"Anything else?"

"He knows about us. I told him."

He nodded and started breathing normally again. "Good. If he does anything, tries anything—"

"Matt's not like that. He knows how I feel about you." I didn't want to tell him about the kiss—*kisses*. Or that Matt had said he still loved me. It wasn't the right time to tell him. I didn't know how much time I had left before I woke up and my focus shifted back to my human soul.

"I don't want to, but I should go. I only have a couple hours to rest before the bus comes to take Matt and me back to the school."

"He agreed to go with you?"

"Yeah. He needs to get used to his new body and decide how he's going to start his life over."

"Wait, you're not ever going to release his soul? I thought this was just a temporary thing, to give him a break from his afterlife."

"No. He deserves to live, Alex. I can't let him die again."

"Jodi, he's a zombie. Maybe you gave him permission to act like himself, but he's still not alive. He's been dead too long."

I hadn't thought about that, but Matt seemed so different. He wasn't like the other souls I'd brought back. He seemed so alive.

"I don't know. I'll figure it out. There's still time for me to decide what to do about him."

"Please think about this…"

Alex's image faded as Matt gently shook my shoulder. "The bus is here."

I sat up, rubbing my eyes. Alex was gone. I was with my human soul again. With Matt. I hadn't gotten the chance to say goodbye or tell Alex I loved him.

"You okay?" Matt rubbed my arm, concern all over his face.

"Bad dream." This going back and forth between souls was too much for me to handle. Matt wouldn't be able to understand.

"I know what you mean. My dream was really strange."

We got on the bus and found seats in the back, away from everyone else. Not many people were on the bus this early in the morning.

"What was it about?" I kept my voice barely above a whisper in case Matt's dream had been of the underworld, too.

"You. Me. That Alex guy and some other people I don't know. We were in a cemetery, and this guy was telling you to choose your dad and me. He must have meant over Alex. At first, I thought the dream was just my mind trying to process you being with Alex now, but then something weird happened. The guy said you weren't allowed to have any kids. Strange, right?"

Not strange. Matt's dream was exactly what had happened in the cemetery the night Hades brought him back to life.

"Then you and I talked, but you were crying, so I wiped a tear from your cheek. I don't remember anything else, so that must be when I woke up."

No, that was when he'd died…again. My mouth couldn't form words. I couldn't tell him the truth, could I? How would he react to knowing I'd killed him again? That he'd once been in Heaven, and because of me Hades had sentenced him to eternity in the Fields of Asphodel, where he barely knew his own name?

"Matt, how much about me do you really want to know?" Letting him decide for himself was the only fair thing to do.

"What do you mean? You told me about what you can do." He looked around to make sure no one was eavesdropping, even though we hadn't said anything too bizarre. Yet.

"I've done a lot of bad things, not all on purpose." I played with the hem of my shirt. "There's more to tell you about us. You and me."

He straightened up in the seat and stared at me. "Go on."

"Your dream, it wasn't a dream. It was a memory. That really did happen." He shook his head, but I continued. "Matt, when you kissed me in my backyard and you died, I brought you back to life. Only, I did it wrong and Alex had to…" I couldn't say it. He'd hate Alex even more.

"What did he do to me?" His fists were clenched at his sides.

"He had to release your soul, only he wasn't powerful enough to do it yet so he poisoned you with his blood. You died again."

"He killed me?" His voice was way too loud, and a few people turned around to look at us.

We both slumped down in the seats, hiding from view.

"He had to. You weren't you anymore. It was your body, but your soul didn't fully return. You were a zombie. I watched you rip apart a bunny."

His hands flew to his face, covering his eyes. "Please, tell me you're making this up. I've handled a lot since we came back. I've believed a bunch of crazy stuff, but this is too much."

"I'm sorry. Do you want me to stop?"

He lowered his hands. "No. Keep going. How did I end up in the cemetery with you?"

"It was months later. Hades had this plan to get me to wipe out the Ophi line, but I refused. He raised you—only this time, you weren't a zombie. You were you. Human. Alive. When you touched my tear you died again." I looked away, unable to face him after such a huge confession.

He didn't say anything for a long time. We rode along, watching the scenery go by. Part of me felt like an idiot for unloading all that on him. Maybe ignorance really was bliss. But didn't he have a right to know what had happened to him, no matter how bad it was?

The bus pulled up to a stop, and a bunch of people got out. Matt and I had at least another two stops before we'd be close enough to walk to the school. I wondered how long he'd keep up the silent treatment. Once the bus was back on the road, I turned to look at Matt.

"Do you hate me?"

He sighed and shifted in the seat so he was facing me. "I could never hate you."

"Then why the silent treatment? I figured you'd yell or ask more questions, but you didn't do or say anything."

He brushed a strand of blonde hair out of my face. "Have I mentioned how much I miss your hair?"

Me too. In the right lighting, my crazy waves almost looked Medusa-like. In a non-creepy-snake kind of way. Without my powers or my hair, I wasn't feeling connected to Medusa at all, and she was the one I had to talk to if I was going to save the Ophi.

"Did I lose you?"

"Sorry, just thinking."

"I figured that." He fidgeted with his hands, like he didn't know what to do with them. "Look, there's something I need to ask. I'm not trying to be the guy who steals someone else's girlfriend—"

"I know you're not like that." Was I saying this to convince him not to go there? Or did I really know this was true?

"I just need to know. If I hadn't touched your tears, if I hadn't died again that night in the cemetery, what would you have chosen?"

He meant *who* would I have chosen. Instinctively, I reached for his hand, but I stopped before our fingers grazed each other. I tucked my hands under my legs to keep from touching Matt. "You have to understand that there is no way for us to be together. My powers have killed you more than once. I won't put you in danger again."

"You aren't a danger to me now. Can't we stay like this?"

Stay like this? Forever? "I don't know if that's even possible. My soul is split. I didn't want to mention this, but my dream last night wasn't a dream, either. While I was sleeping, my focus slipped back to the underworld where my body and Ophi soul were delivering someone to Tartarus. I saw Alex. He said I've been kind of out of it, not responding to him when he calls to me."

I couldn't help noticing the way Matt's eyes lit up at that.

"Maybe you're becoming fully human again. Maybe your Ophi soul is fading away. Can it do that?"

"Honestly, I don't know, but I don't think so. I'm stronger as an Ophi. I have a lot of power. Here," I released my hands from under my legs and motioned to the bus, "I'm defenseless."

"And you don't want to give up the power you had."

I thought about how some Ophi had turned evil as a result of having too much power or even just craving too much power. It had happened to Victoria, Troy, Abby, and Chase, just to name a few. I didn't want it to happen to me, too.

"I don't, but to be honest, the power scares me a little, too."

"Is this life really so bad? Being human? Being with me?"

This time he took my hands in his. My heart ached, knowing what he was really asking. He wanted me to take Hades up on his offer that night in the cemetery. He wanted me to choose him.

"Hades could make it so we could be together. You'd be human. I bet he'd love that idea."

Maybe he would, but I'd have to give up Alex. I'd have to let Hades keep the souls of my friends forever. "Matt, you don't understand what that would mean. I'd be sacrificing every Ophi for my own happiness."

"So, you admit you'd be happy with me?" Hope filled his eyes.

"I was happy with you before all this happened, but a lot has changed. I love Alex."

"You said you thought you were falling in love with me. I already love you, Jodi. We'd be perfect together. I think you know that."

Maybe I did. Suddenly, this all felt like a huge test. A one-question multiple-choice test worth all the points in the world.

Who would I rather be?

A. Ophi and be with Alex

or

B. Human and be with Matt.

# Chapter 14

Matt stared at me while I struggled to make sense of what was happening. I was literally two different people right now, and they both wanted different things. I couldn't please both. Ultimately, I'd have to make a choice, one that would hurt more than just one half of my soul.

"Am I wrong?" Matt said, breaking me from my internal debate.

I slowly pulled my hands from his. "It's just not that simple. Believe me, I wish I could separate both halves of me and choose you *and* Alex. But this is about more than which guy I want to be with."

Matt nodded. "You're right. I'm sorry. I said I wouldn't push you, and here I am putting pressure on you. I shouldn't have said any of that."

"Do you ever wish you'd chosen Melodie instead?" The question came out of nowhere, but Melodie had been in love with Matt. I'd found that out right before I'd killed him.

"Melodie? She's one of my best friends. I don't think of her like that."

"I was one of your best friends, too."

He smiled and waved off my comment. "Nah, I was only pretending to be your friend because I wanted to date you."

"That's not you. You're too good a guy to do something so deceitful."

"Ouch, the nice guy speech. That hurts."

"I love that you're the nice guy. It's actually what attracted me to you in the first place."

"Really?" He wagged his eyebrows at me. "It wasn't my tall, dark, and handsome physique?"

I laughed.

"What? It's not *that* funny." He looked mildly hurt.

"No, it's not that. It's…well, do I need to show you a mirror? You're not tall or dark anymore, and as for handsome, Brian had nothing on you." Crap! I'd just flirted again.

"Good to know." He sat back in the seat, looking pleased with himself.

Just great. How was I going to survive this trip if I couldn't stop flirting with him? It wasn't fair to either one of us—or to Alex, for that matter.

After the next stop, Matt dozed off for a bit. I felt guilty for being happy about that, but I needed a break from everything. Mostly from the guilt of killing the guy who loved me and then bringing him back to life only to break his heart.

The brakes squeaked as we approached our stop. I nudged Matt. "We're here."

He looked around, kind of dazed before standing up and motioning for me to go first. "After you."

"Thanks." I tried my best not to come in too much contact with Matt as I squeezed between him and the seat on my way to the aisle. I walked to the front of the bus, being careful not to look closely at anyone. Not that anyone would recognize me, but I wouldn't exactly be able to keep the horrified look off my face if I did see anyone from my old life.

"Mel?" Matt said behind me.

No! No, no, no. I whipped my head up in time to see Matt gawking at Melodie boarding the bus. Where was her new car? Why on earth was she taking the bus?

I turned to Matt and grabbed his hand. "We better hurry or we'll be late." I pulled him past Melodie as if we'd never seen her before.

"Wait up." Matt was tugging my arm, but I kept going. After the bus doors closed, I let go of him. "What the hell, Jodi?"

"Don't call me that. It's too risky."

"Why? We don't look like ourselves."

"It doesn't matter. A guy and a girl with the same names as two kids who used to live here? People will assume we're together because we're traveling together. There are too many connections to our old lives. Melodie is another one. You can't talk to people we knew. You might slip up and say something that will let them know who you really are."

Matt smiled. "No one is going to believe this. We could flat-out tell people the truth, and they'd laugh in our faces."

"Let's not test that theory, okay?" Why wasn't he getting how serious this was?

"So you're not the least bit curious about what your mom's up to? How she's doing?"

Mom. Of course I'd give anything to see her again. But I couldn't. Could I?

Matt took me by the shoulders and peered into my eyes. "Come on. What's the harm in checking in on our old lives? Making sure the people we left behind are okay?"

"What if they're not?" My eyes burned with the threat of tears. "I couldn't handle it if my mom wasn't okay. I wouldn't be able to leave."

"I get it." He sighed and let go of me. "But I want to see my parents and my sister. If I'm really getting another shot at life, then I need to know they're all okay."

I started to protest, but he gently pressed a finger to my lips. "If they're not, then I'll find a way to make it okay." I could see the wheels turning in his mind. "I could even be, like, an exchange student or something. I could live in my own home again and be part of the family."

"Matt." He was getting his hopes up. Things never worked out that nicely.

"I know it's a long shot, but what if it could happen? If there's any chance, I want to try."

How could I deny him this after everything I'd done to him? "Okay, we'll go check on them, but I can't stay long. I have to get to the school. The others are counting on me."

He smiled so wide I could see all the money Brian's parents must have spent on dental work. "Let's call a cab."

"And what? Show up on their doorstep?" That would never work.

He thought for a moment. "I could show up at Amber's art studio. She goes every day after school."

"We don't even know what day it is. Time moves differently in the underworld. We don't know how much time has passed." It was April when Hades took me and the other Ophi, but the air was warm now. I was guessing it was late May or early June. Maybe even later, judging by how hot I was in this hoodie.

"We have to start somewhere." Matt walked to the traffic light and headed toward the grocery store. "Maybe they have a phone we can use." Of course, we didn't have any money left to call a cab or pay for one.

"Who are you going to call?"

"Amber's cell."

"What? Are you crazy? You can't even think about telling her who you really are."

"I won't. I'll tell her I'm new at school and one of her friends gave me her number."

"And what are you going to do when your own sister thinks you're hitting on her?"

Matt's face twisted in disgust. "Oh, gross."

"Yeah, well, that's what she's going to think. Trust me."

He kicked a rock on the ground, looking defeated. "So then, what do we do?"

"Come on." I tugged his arm, pulling him inside the grocery store. I grabbed a newspaper from the stand by the door. "Yes!" A few people turned and stared at me. "Sorry." I turned away from them, focusing on Matt. "It's Friday. Serpentarius is open to humans." I could go talk to Mason, and Matt could look for Amber or some other kids from school who might be able to tell him about his family.

"To humans?"

"It's an Ophi safe house, kind of like the school I need to get back to. Only the owners open the club to humans every Friday night. They even have humans on staff, so there aren't any slip-ups."

"Slip-ups?"

I widened my eyes, waiting for him to get the meaning behind my words.

"Oh." His forehead creased with worry lines. "Do you think my cousin knows about the Ophi?"

Matt had no idea Jared was an Ophi. Just great, another thing I'd have to break to him. "Matt, your cousin isn't really your cousin by blood, right?"

"How did you know?"

"Because Jared is an Ophi. He's with the others in the underworld."

He looked like he'd been sucker-punched. "Wow."

"He was one of the few Ophi who worked when humans were allowed in the club. He never used his powers, and he was really careful. That's why he could be around you and your family without hurting any of you."

"This is so crazy. All my life I had no idea Ophi existed, and now I find out I know two of them, my cousin and my girlfriend." He lowered his eyes. "Though I guess he's not technically my cousin, and you're not my girlfriend anymore."

The pain on his face made me think I deserved the torture my Ophi soul was being put through in Tartarus. I didn't have the strength to address the issue of Matt and me, so I focused on Jared. "He's a great guy. The longer I stay here, the guiltier I feel."

"Jodi, look—"

"No." I returned the paper to the shelf and walked back outside, nearly getting run over by an old lady pushing a shopping cart. "I promised I'd help you get settled. Besides, if we go to Serpentarius, you could try to get info about your parents while I talk to Mason and figure out how to break the others out of the underworld. It's a win-win."

"Great, except it's morning. The club won't open for hours."

True. I could go back to the school in the meantime and talk to Medusa. Would I be able to touch the statue in my human form? Medusa might not recognize me in Liz's body. Panic rushed through me. I needed to talk to Mason before I tried to talk to Medusa. He might know something, like how I could connect to the statue without being fried in the process.

"Want to check out the school?" I didn't know where else to go, only that I wanted to avoid seeing my mom. It would be too hard to leave her again.

Matt looked away, and I knew exactly what he was thinking.

I tugged on his sleeve. "Let's go."

He tilted his head in surprise. "Really? Just like that? You're not going to warn me about how dangerous this could be for me? How it might screw me up forever if things aren't the way I want them to be?"

"If you say you can handle it, and it's something you need to do, then I trust you. But…" I waited for him to stop smiling and made sure he was listening. "We have to make a stop first."

"Where?"

"You'll see. The question is, how are we going to get there?"

"Steal a car?" Matt laughed, but when he saw I didn't, he stopped. "No way. Who are you, and what have you done with Jodi Marshall?"

"Shh!" I pushed him away from the door and the people walking out of the store. "No one can hear you call me that."

"Sorry." He looked down at me. I was pressed up against him in an alcove next to the cart return. I could feel his heart race as we huddled together. I cleared my throat and backed away.

"Okay. We just have to remember to be more careful. That's all." Yeah, more careful not to get that close again. I said Alex's name over and over in my mind.

"Right, but are you serious about the car thing?"

"What choice do we have?" I scanned the parking lot, looking for a clunker, something I wouldn't feel bad about taking. "There." I pointed to a beat-up sedan that looked older than me.

"Are you kidding? The person driving that thing obviously can't afford a new car. If he could, he wouldn't be caught dead in that." Matt looked over the cars. "That one." I heard the smile in his voice as I followed his gaze.

"No way. Matt, that's a BMW."

"Exactly. That guy's got money."

"Unless he blew it all on an expensive car during a midlife crisis."

He shrugged. "Might teach him a lesson to have it stolen."

It was my turn to stare at him in disbelief. "You've changed since…" I didn't want say "since coming back from the dead."

"Desperate times, I guess. So, what do you say?"

"Do you know how to hotwire a car?"

"If I said yes, would you judge me for it?"

Was there another side to Matt? A reason why he ended up in the Fields of Asphodel instead of the Elysian Fields, where all the good souls went?

"Let's get this over with." The memory of stealing Melodie's car was all too present in my head. This wasn't as bad. I didn't know this person, and I hoped Matt was right about this guy having a lot of money.

We crouched down between the rows of cars, staying out of view. Matt tried the door. Locked. Of course. No alarm, though. That was surprising.

"How are we going to get in?" He looked at me as if I had the answer.

I didn't have anything to pick the lock. Could you even pick a lock on a car? There was only one thing I could think of.

"Any chance there is an alarm on this but that we didn't trip it?"

"Sure. All we did was try the door. That's not enough to set off an alarm." He studied my face like he was trying to read my thoughts. "But why would you want to set off the alarm?"

"If we trip the alarm, one of the store employees will announce that the car's alarm is going off. Then the owner will come out to reset it. When he unlocks the doors, we'll jump in."

"Please, tell me you're kidding."

"Not even a little bit."

Matt threw his head back and stared at the clouds. "I really am starting to think we're completely different people."

"Does that mean you don't want to do this?"

"No." He looked at me again. "It means I do."

Matt motioned for me to go around to the other side of the car. We couldn't be sure the owner wouldn't come inspect the car when the alarm sounded. If he did, we'd have to move fast.

Matt started tugging on the door handles and bumping the car with his body. The alarm blared in my ears. I peered through the window, watching the grocery store doors for someone coming out with keys in their hands to disable the alarm. It felt like an eternity before the doors opened. A man in his late forties with a really bad dye job—I must have been right about the midlife crisis—came out. He stood on his toes, trying to see the car over the others in the lot.

"Get ready," Matt said in a loud whisper.

The man was about four cars away when he unlocked the doors and shut off the alarm.

"Now!" I pulled open the door and threw myself into the passenger seat. Matt was inside and fumbling under the steering wheel quicker than I could put on my seatbelt.

"Hey!" the guy yelled as he saw me through the windshield.

"Matt, hurry up! He sees us." The guy had keys. No way would we be able to keep him out of the car.

He was only one car away now. I undid my seatbelt, getting ready to run. I couldn't get arrested. It would ruin everything.

"Matt!"

# Chapter 15

The engine roared to life at the same time the locks clicked open. Matt sat up and put the car in reverse as the guy opened the driver's side door.

"Go!" I yelled.

Matt didn't bother trying to close the door. He backed out of the spot, dragging the guy with us. He held on like he was waterskiing through the parking lot. Matt slammed on the brakes, sending the guy flying forward and the door slamming shut.

"Nice. Now drive!"

We sped out of there, fumbling for our seatbelts. My breath caught in my throat as I looked in the side mirror. The guy was on his feet with his cell phone pressed to his ear.

"He's calling the cops. We can't keep this car. He saw us. He can ID us."

"Jodi, calm down." Matt reached for my hand. His touch sent shivers through my arm. Not exactly calming.

"Let's get away from here and then dump the car. We'll hide out for the rest of the day and walk to Serpentarius tonight."

"No way." Matt's hands were back on the steering wheel, and his eyes focused on the road. "I'm not giving up on seeing my family."

"I have an idea. Go to the cemetery." It was where I'd been planning to take him to begin with.

"Why? You can't raise souls. You're human now."

"I know. There's something I want you to see."

"What could possibly—" He turned to look at me, only glancing at the road long enough to keep us from colliding with a tree or telephone pole. "You want me to see my grave, don't you?"

"Yes."

He shook his head. "Why? That's twisted, Jodi."

"No, it's not. If you're going to move on with your life, you have to say goodbye to who you used to be."

"Is this your plan to convince me not to see my family?"

"No. This is one step in getting you to be okay so I can return to the other Ophi." There, I'd said it. He knew my plan. He knew what I wanted for him. He knew I didn't see a future for us.

"So, you're sure that you're going to go back to what you were, a necromancer? You don't even want to consider staying with me?"

I'd considered it, all right. Too much. I shouldn't have been having any of these feelings for him. I should've been focusing on Alex and the others. This had to end. The split personality thing was killing me.

"Matt, I have to go back."

"You know, you're trying to convince me to move on, let go of the past, but you won't do the same."

I swallowed hard, getting up the courage to say what I had to say next. "You are my past. Alex is my present and my future."

He looked hurt for a moment. "You're wrong. Look around. *I* am your present, and I could be your future, if you'd let me."

He wasn't letting go. I decided not to say anything else. He wasn't going to listen, and I didn't want to argue. He pulled into the cemetery and parked near the entrance. We left the car, and I led him to the place where he was buried.

He slowed as we approached the headstone. This wasn't going to be easy on him, but it was something he had to do.

"Do you know what the worst part about dying at seventeen is?"

Instead of answering, I waited for him to continue.

"It's not missing out on graduation or going to college. It's missing out on being in love." I stared at him, wondering why he thought that. It wasn't the typical guy answer. Most guys would've said the worst part was dying a virgin. *Was* Matt a virgin?

"I never got to experience the kind of love my mom said only teens can have. The kind that consumes you. Makes you do stupid crap, and you don't even care because someone else thinks you're the greatest thing on earth."

He wanted that with me. The thought tore me up. He'd died kissing me, falling in love with me. And I'd just told him I was leaving him.

"You know, we technically never broke up."

"I know. I just kind of figured the relationship is assumed over when—"

"One person dies?"

I was thinking when one person kills the other, but his way was nicer. I turned away. This was getting way too emotional for me to handle.

Matt stepped closer to me and lifted my chin.

"Matt, don't." My voice shook, and his touch brought goosebumps to my skin.

"I know I said I wouldn't do this, but I'm desperate." He looked me in the eyes. "Pick me." His words were like a knife to my heart.

I opened my mouth, not knowing what to say, but his lips came crashing down on mine. His arms wrapped around me, lifting me off the ground. I froze for a moment, but as Matt continued to kiss me, I felt myself giving in. My eyes closed, and I kissed him back. We may have been in two completely foreign bodies, but together we were still Matt and Jodi. We fit. We made sense. We had great chemistry.

We stayed like that for several minutes, only pausing long enough to take a breath every once in a while. Then, I heard sirens approaching. I pulled away and saw the glow of red and blue lights coming toward the cemetery. They'd spotted the stolen car.

"We need to get out of here." I pulled Matt with me out the back exit and through the houses. I could easily get to my house from here. I'd done this exact route the night of Matt's funeral. But I didn't want to go home. I wasn't ready to. Still, I found myself ducking into my backyard, behind the shed. The exact spot where Matt had attacked the bunny.

We sat with our backs against the shed, catching our breath.

"I'd be lying if I said that wasn't fun." Matt smiled at me. I knew he meant the part about us kissing more than the part where we ran from the cops. I was completely leading him on by making out with him on top of his grave like that. God, what was happening to me?

"Look, about what happened…I'm confused. I don't know how to handle this double life I'm living right now."

"You still have feelings for me." He said it so matter-of-factly.

"Yes, I do. I won't deny that, but I love Alex. I can't deny that, either. I need time to make sense of what's going on with me." I leaned my head back on the shed. "I need you to stop kissing me. I can't control myself around you."

"Yes, you can. There have been plenty of times that you stopped me from kissing you—before all this and now."

That was true. Before I ran away with Alex, Matt and I had missed out on plenty of opportunities to kiss each other, and mostly because of me. And there was the incident outside the grocery store. I'd resisted the urge to kiss him then.

"You gave in to that kiss in the cemetery because you wanted to kiss me. I know you won't kiss me without wanting to, and I'm not about to stop you if it's what you want."

Man, that was confusing. "You think *I* brought that on in the cemetery? That was all *you*."

"You didn't stop me. You kissed me back."

"I know, but you started it. You have to stop that. If I kiss you first, then have at it. Go nuts. I give you permission. But if I don't, please…"

I hated putting these rules on our relationship. It wasn't fair to him. It wasn't fair to Alex. Hell, it wasn't even fair to me. I was losing it.

"Is this a game to you?" He looked beyond hurt.

"No. I know I'm screwing up royally. I suck at being two people. You don't deserve this."

"Want to make it up to me?"

Now if it were Alex who'd asked that, I'd assume he wanted to make out again. But Matt wasn't Alex. He had more self-control, most of the time anyway.

"What can I do?"

"Make me a sandwich. This Brian guy has the same appetite I had."

I laughed, relieved he'd said something to break the tension.

"Your mom should be at work, right? I didn't see her car in the driveway."

"Yeah. We can go in the back way. There's a hidden key in the lantern."

Matt stood up and gave me his hand. Always the gentleman. He followed me to the back door, and I reached inside the lantern for the spare key. Even though I knew Mom wasn't home, my hands shook as I turned the key in the lock. I was going inside my house for the first time since I'd killed my mom and Alex had brought her back to life. How different would my home look? Would my room still be the same? Would there be any evidence at all that I'd lived here?

Matt put his hand on my shoulder, as if he knew exactly what I was thinking. "I'm right here with you."

I nodded and turned the doorknob. The kitchen looked the same. The table was set with four green placemats. The counter still had a bowl of fresh fruit. That was a good sign. Mom had moved on, continued to live without me.

I walked to the refrigerator and pulled it open. I gasped when I saw several packages of chicken, more green peppers than I could count, and two bags of onions.

"What's wrong? You look like you saw a ghost."

Yeah, the ghost of our last meal together—or at least the meal we'd been preparing when I'd cut myself and bled on Mom, stopping her heart.

"She keeps making the meal we were cooking the night…" I couldn't say it.

"Maybe it's not as bad as you're thinking. There's some steak in there, too. Maybe the chicken and stuff is just her way of keeping you around, you know? Remembering the good times."

"Except it wasn't a good time." My throat burned as I sucked back the tears, refusing to let them out. "She died, and I left."

"Does she know she died?"

"I don't know. Alex brought her back, and we left before she came to."

"So, maybe she's making the meal over and over, hoping you'll come back."

Ugh, this was torture. Worse than I'd thought.

"You could tell her the truth. I believed you. She's your mom. I'm sure she'll believe you, too. You could get a second chance. We both could."

I closed the refrigerator door and walked over to the table, slumping into one of the wooden chairs. "Please, don't use this to try to make me choose you."

"You know that's not what I'm doing."

I did know that. It wasn't Matt's style. He genuinely wanted me to be happy, to have another chance with my mom, to be human again.

I had to know how far this went. How much my mom was holding on to the memory of me. I stood up, letting the chair squeak across the floor.

"Where are you going?" Matt's eyes darted back and forth between mine.

"My room."

"Are you sure that's a good idea?"

I didn't care at that point. I had to know. I took the stairs two at a time, with Matt right behind me. My bedroom door was shut. I hesitated. Thankfully, Matt didn't push or try to convince me not to do this. He waited patiently, letting me make up my own mind.

I counted to twenty and opened the door. Immediately, I felt the slight breeze coming from the open window. I'd always kept it open, even in the dead of winter. Mom was continuing to do the same. My bed was made, and my desk still had my schoolbooks strewn across it. She hadn't touched them.

I walked to the closet, noticing the faint stain on the off-white carpet from when I'd bled on it while trying to catch the rat I'd brought back to life. As I remembered Mom and me working together, huddled on my bed, trying to catch the thing, I broke down. I fell to the floor, sinking into my misery.

Matt rushed to me and rocked me back and forth in his arms. He smoothed my hair and whispered, "It's okay. Get it out."

I had a lot to get out. I cried huge tears, ones that sucked the air out of my lungs and made me choke. I felt my nose run, but I didn't care. The pain inside me was too much. I had to get it out, like Matt said.

We sat like that for hours, until I'd cried every last tear inside me. Then, we stared out the window, not saying a word. I didn't move at all. I let my body go numb, tuning out feeling to every part of my body. Matt stayed silent, letting me handle this my own way.

Finally, I heard the sound of tires pulling up the driveway. Mom! The little girl inside me wanted to go running down the stairs and throw myself into her arms, but I knew that wouldn't be a good idea. I would never be able to leave her again. Still, could I leave things the way they were? She obviously wasn't getting over losing me.

"Jodi, come on. We'll slip out the window." Matt was on his feet, holding his hand out to me.

"No." I made a split-second decision.

"What do you mean?" He narrowed his eyes at me, trying to figure out what was going through my mind now.

"I'm tired of being two different people. I can't do this to her. She deserves to know the truth."

"Are you sure?" He looked worried for me.

I nodded, even though my bottom lip quivered.

The front door shut, and Mom's footsteps sounded on the stairs. She was coming.

"Last chance to change your mind." This was proof Matt was an amazing guy. If all he was worried about was getting me back, he would've encouraged me to tell my mom the truth. But he cared more about me doing what I thought was best, whether that meant I stayed with him or not.

"I have to do this." I braced myself as Mom reached the top of the stairs. She immediately noticed my open door and turned toward Matt and me.

Her eyes widened. "Who are you? How did you get in my house?"

"Mom, it's okay. It's me, Jodi."

# Chapter 16

She looked horrified. "I'm calling the police." She turned and raced down the stairs.

Matt met my eyes, waiting to see what I was going to do. I rushed from the room and to the kitchen, where I knew Mom would be on the phone.

"Mom, please!" I reached for the phone, wrestling it from her hands.

"911. What is your emergency?" I heard the operator's voice on the other line.

"Sorry, hit the wrong button," I said and quickly ended the call.

"Who are you people?" Mom's face was red with anger and hurt. "How dare you come in here and talk about Jodi?"

"Mom." My voice shook as I fought the urge to cry. "Please, listen to me. Do you remember what happened the night I left?"

"Get out. I don't know who you are, but I want you gone. Now!" She pointed to the door as if I didn't already know where it was.

"Please, hear me out, and then if you still want me to leave I will. We both will."

"Please, Ms. Marshall." Matt motioned to the kitchen table. "Sit down and talk to us. Five minutes. That's all we're asking for."

Even though Matt was talking, Mom kept her eyes on me.

"I can make us some tea. You always drink tea when you get home from work."

She tilted her head to the side and stared into my eyes like she was trying to see my soul.

"I know I don't look like myself, Mom, but you'd know me anywhere. You have to. You're my mom."

"What happened to you?" She said the words slowly, like they were hard to get out.

"Everything I told you about Alex and me being different was true." I walked around her, placing her cell on the counter and going for the teapot on the stove. I filled it with water and placed it on the burner, turning it on high.

Matt walked Mom to the table and sat down. She waited for me to sit and then finally gave in.

"Alex? That boy who came here after you cut yourself?"

"Yes. He's like me. We're different. Not entirely human. Well, I *am* human now, but that's a long story."

She shook her head. All this information must have been giving her one hell of a headache.

"Okay, how do I start?" Poisoned blood, zombie deer, evil Ophi trying to kill me, Hades taking me to the underworld? Leading with any of those would've sent her over the edge. "Dad," I blurted out. "I met Dad."

"Melodie told me that. She said she saw you. You stole her car and left her at the park." She shook her head, obviously not believing that either.

I still felt awful about what I'd done to Mel. "Yes, I did." I lowered my head. "But, I had to. Mom…" I reached for her hands, but she pulled back. She still wasn't convinced I was her daughter. I put my hands in my lap. "My blood is different than yours, and it's because of Dad. He didn't walk out on you like you thought he did. He had to leave to protect both of us. He's not human."

Mom made a sound like a gurgled laugh. "That I could almost believe."

"He died about a month after I was born."

Her eyes shot up to meet mine. "You said you met him."

"I did. Alex took me to a place. It operates as a school for people like me. They—*we*—call ourselves Ophi. We're all born under the thirteenth sign of the zodiac, Ophiuchus. We're necromancers. I met Dad because we raised his soul." I left off the part about Victoria raising Dad to torture me.

"Okay, that's enough. I've listened. I don't believe you. This is some school prank, and I don't want to be part of it." She stood up and shook her head. "You know, for a moment, I thought maybe you two knew something about Jodi—what happened to her. But you're just messing with me, and that's really cruel."

"Mom, we're not. Please. I'm telling you the truth. I'm Jodi. This is Matt. You remember Matt. I had to raise our souls, so we're in different bodies, but we're still us." She stared at me with a look of horror, but not because she believed me. Because she couldn't believe I'd create such a crazy story. "I died, Mom. I killed myself. The human part of me, at least. Matt died, too. You know that. You were here. Only you didn't know it was because of me. My blood killed him. Just like it killed you."

She shook her head. "I'm not dead."

"Not anymore. Alex brought you back. It's part of what we can do. Alex saved your life, and then I left before I could hurt you again."

The teapot whistled on the stove, piercing the air like an alarm.

"I'll get it." Matt got up and walked to the stove while Mom and I continued to stare at each other.

"Please. If you love me, you should be able to see it's me. Even in this body. Look at me. Really look."

She walked around the table and stood in front of me. Normally we were the same height, but Liz's small frame was inches shorter than Mom.

"I haven't looked down at you in years."

"Get past the outside. That's not me. I'm in here." I put my hand to my heart. "Mom." My eyes watered, blurring my vision.

She moved closer, looking deep in my eyes. "Jodi?"

"Yes, it's me."

Her arms were around me a second later. I wasn't sure if she truly believed it was me or if she was just desperate to believe it was true. Either way, it felt amazing to be in her arms.

Matt walked past us, smiling at me. He placed three cups of tea on the table and sat down, waiting for us.

I tried to pull away, but Mom kept her grasp on my arms. "It's really you." It wasn't a question this time.

Matt motioned to Mom's chair. "This is a lot to take in. Maybe you should sit down and have some tea, Ms. Marshall."

I walked Mom back to her seat. She didn't take her eyes off me. "Tell me more, but go slowly."

I nodded and took a deep breath. Where had I left off? "Like I said, Alex took me to meet other people like me. That's where I met Dad. He's buried in the cemetery at the school."

"Is he—was he like you?"

"Yes. He was an Ophi, too. That's why he had to leave. We don't come into our powers until we're around sixteen or seventeen. It's different for some people. But once our powers come out, we're dangerous to humans…and animals." I remembered the deer. I could start there.

"The rabid deer," Mom said, beating me to it. "That was the one you hit with your car, wasn't it?"

"Yes. I bled on it, and it came back to life. Only I didn't know how to use my powers yet at that point, and what I raised was a mindless zombie deer."

"The nurse at school?"

I nodded. "I killed her with my tears when she checked me out after the car accident." I didn't want to run through the entire list, so I jumped ahead to the most important one. "You died when you touched the cut on my hand. You wanted to prove your blood was the same as mine, but it wasn't anymore. Alex saved you."

"And then you were gone." She sipped her tea, obviously needing time to process all this.

I drank my tea in two big gulps.

"You still haven't learned to enjoy your tea, have you?" Mom's mouth curved into a small smile. She'd always told me I drank tea all wrong.

"It tastes better hot," we said at the same time.

A tear fell from her eyes. If she hadn't been convinced I was her daughter before, she was now.

"Why didn't you tell me sooner? I thought you ran off with that boy. I thought you were so distraught over Matt's death that you couldn't deal with things around here anymore."

All of that was true. "I couldn't tell you sooner because I didn't have a handle on my powers yet. The only reason I'm here now is because I'm human. Alex and the others are trapped in the underworld with Hades."

Mom opened her mouth to talk, but I held up one finger to stop her.

"Yes, *that* Hades. He doesn't like the Ophi because we take his souls from the afterlife. He wanted to take all our souls and end the Ophi line with me. My body is still there."

"In Hell?"

"The underworld is actually broken up into three different places. Tartarus, which is Hell. The Elysian Fields, which is Heaven. And the Fields of Asphodel, which is where most people end up and roam around, not happy or sad."

"Where is your body?" Of course she'd ask that.

"It goes back and forth between working for Hades at the palace, escorting souls to their afterlives, and…"

"Oh, God." Mom raised her hand to her mouth.

"I'm okay, Mom. I raised my human soul. Well, really it was the human *part* of my soul. I can tune out the underworld and what's going on there."

"You aren't dangerous to me now? Does that mean you can stay?"

I wanted to. "No. I have to save the others like me, and I can't leave my Ophi half down there, either. It's being tortured. Sooner or later, the pain will be too much for me to tune out anymore." I wasn't sure if that was entirely true, but I was willing to bet Hades would make it true once he found out what I'd done.

"How are you going to save yourself and the others?"

"I have to go back to the school. Medusa's spirit is there. She's sort of my ancestor."

"Your what?" Mom's eyes practically bugged out of her head.

"I know. Crazy, right? But she's really nice. All those myths about her being mean, they aren't true. She was cursed. Before that, she was beautiful. And she cares about the Ophi. We're all her children in a way, because her blood is what gave us our powers."

Mom didn't look like she was breathing. "So, she's wandering around at that school?"

"No. Her spirit is trapped in a statue there, but I can connect to the statue and communicate with her. At least, I could when I had my Ophi powers. I'm not sure what it will do to me now."

Mom reached across the table. "Don't do anything that might hurt you. I lost you once. I can't do it again."

"Neither can I." Matt reached for my other hand. Neither of them was going to make this easy on me.

"I'm going to talk to some Ophi who are still here first and make sure I'll be okay." If Mason even knew what the statue would do to a human.

Mom squeezed my hand. "How long can you stay?"

"Matt wants to see his family, make sure they're okay."

Matt let go of my hand and finished his tea. "We should go soon."

"You aren't going to explain all this to them, are you?" Mom looked at Matt this time.

He shrugged. "Maybe. I mean, you believed Jodi. Why wouldn't my parents believe me?"

Mom sighed. "Your parents buried you, Matt. I'm not sure they'd be able to handle this."

"And I'm not sure I want that many people knowing the truth about me. It's too risky." I hated doing this to him. I mean, I'd told my mom everything, but I was telling him he couldn't be honest with his parents.

Mom finally let go of me. "You could stay here if you want."

"What?" Matt and I asked in unison.

"This place is too big for one person, and I'm guessing Jodi won't be staying here long. You're going back to your Ophi people as soon as you figure out how to save them, right?" She was doing her best to understand, and I loved her for it.

I nodded, looking down at my empty cup. It hurt too much to look at either of them, knowing I was hurting them both.

"All right, then. Having Matt around will remind me of you. It would make things a little easier, so really it would be helping both of us."

Matt looked at me, trying to see what I thought of the idea.

I shrugged. "I think you should do it. You could stay in town and keep an eye on your family."

"I could tell everyone that you're my nephew," Mom said. "We could even invite your parents over for dinner every now and then so you could spend time with them."

Matt had always been sensitive in a tough guy way. I'd never seen him tear up. Not once, but his tough exterior couldn't handle this. "I don't know what to say."

"Say you'll stay." I reached over, placing my hand on top of his. "I'd feel better knowing Mom's not alone, that you're not alone. I love you both." I did. On some level, I loved Matt.

He squeezed my hand. "Okay. I'll stay."

I knew he'd been waiting for me to say I loved him, and this wasn't exactly what he'd had in mind, but he was going to take it anyway.

Matt couldn't take his own life back, so I was giving him mine.

# Chapter 17

We sat in silence for a moment, unsure of what to do next. I knew Matt was going to get my room. The house only had two bedrooms. Of course, he didn't have any stuff to move in or anything, and I wasn't about to ask Mom for money. She'd always struggled to make ends meet.

"We'll have to find a job for you," I said to Matt. Since he had no ID, birth certificate, or anything, we'd have to hope for finding someone who'd pay him off the books, which wouldn't be easy. "And you can't call yourself Matt, either."

"Should I use this guy's name?" He held his hands up, looking at Brian's body.

Liz and Brian had lived four hours away, and it wasn't like Matt would be using Brian's last name. It could work.

"It's up to you. You could even name yourself if you want."

"Hmm." He drummed his fingers on the table as he thought.

Mom gave me a weak smile. She was handling all of this really well. Offering to give Matt a home, even temporarily, was more than I could've hoped for. Leaving wasn't going to be easy, but knowing Mom and Matt had each other made things almost bearable.

"Tyler." Matt nodded. "It's my middle name. Using it will make me feel more like me."

"I like it."

"Me too," Mom said, wrinkling her brow as she made a mental note of the name. Slip-ups couldn't happen.

I glanced at the clock on the wall. We'd been here all afternoon. "We should get going. Serpentarius is opening soon, and I want to get there before the crowd."

"Wait." Mom reached for my arm. "You both must be starving. Let me make you some dinner before you go hunting down information."

Matt was already drooling.

"Mom, we can grab something at the club. Really. Don't worry about it." I didn't want to impose on her any more than we already had.

"Nonsense. Come on, we can cook together just like old times." She was already heading to the refrigerator and taking out carrots. She hesitated and looked at me around the door. "You did say you're human now, right? You can't, you know…"

Yeah, I knew. "Totally human. In this body anyway."

"Good. Then slice up the carrots and get them cooking while I fix us some steaks and mashed potatoes."

I walked over to her and lowered my voice. "Where did you get the money for all this?"

She lowered her eyes as she put the steaks on the counter. "I don't have anyone to support anymore. It's just me. I was going to invite the neighbors over, just for some company, but this is much better."

She was going to invite the Sandersons to dinner? Things really *were* bad. I got started on the carrots, and Matt helped Mom with the grill. In no time, the house smelled delicious. I hadn't realized how hungry I was. I hadn't eaten at all in the underworld, and since coming back, I'd been too busy to think about food. Other than the tea, Liz's stomach was completely empty.

We ate dinner almost like a normal family. Mom kept smiling at me, but every once in a while she'd glance at the clock, and then her smile would fade. She knew we had time constraints. I tried to eat quickly without seeming like I was rushing to get out of there, but really, I was. I needed to talk to Mason. I had to let him know I was here and that I needed some information in order to save the others. He must be missing Carol like crazy.

I cleared our plates and loaded them into the dishwasher. Mom leaned against the counter with a dishtowel in her hand. Our eyes met, and she started crying.

"Mom, don't do that." My voice was shaking already. I'd be sobbing with her in a matter of seconds.

"I'm sorry. It's just that I didn't think I'd ever see you again, and even though you don't look like yourself anymore, I can still see you inside. I don't know how I didn't see it right away. I'm sorry it took me so long to believe you."

*Long*? She'd handled it really well. "You've been amazing." I hugged her and rubbed her back. "If you don't mind, can Matt and I stay here until I—?"

"For as long as you need. The longer the better, as far as I'm concerned. You can bunk with me."

I couldn't help laughing. There was the mom I was used to. The one who made sure I kept my distance from boys. "I'm with Alex, Mom, not Matt, but I'd love to bunk with you. It'll be like a sleepover."

"Good, because you're still my daughter, which means I make the rules here." Mom turned to Matt, who was putting the steak sauce back in the fridge. "That goes for you, too. I get that you're almost eighteen, but this is my house, so you're going to have to follow my rules."

"Yes, ma'am." Matt nodded. "I'm just happy you're letting me stay. I plan to get a job and help out around here. I won't be a problem at all."

"Well, I guess we should go." I wanted to run upstairs to my room and put on clothes that were actually mine, but Liz's body would drown in them. I did grab the little money I had stashed in my desk drawer. We wouldn't get into Serpentarius without paying the cover charge.

Mom pulled me in for another hug, squeezing me like she was afraid that, once I walked out that door, I'd never come back. This couldn't have been easy for her. I was asking her to accept so much without any proof at all.

"I love you, Mom," I whispered before I pulled away. "We'll be back later tonight."

She blinked back tears. "Not too late."

It was great to see glimpses of how things used to be.

Matt and I said goodbye. Mom insisted we take her car. Matt drove since I'm not very good with a stick. I couldn't help thinking about the last time Matt and I had gone to Serpentarius. I'd thought Alex was some psycho stalker. I'd thought Matt was the one for me. Now, my mind was a jumbled mess.

"Everything okay?" Matt snuck a glance at me. "I'm not used to you being so quiet."

"Still processing, I guess. I'm not sure I'm going to get used to wearing someone else's face."

"I know what you mean." Matt checked out his reflection in the rearview mirror. "He's not better-looking than me, is he?"

"No." I answered way too quickly. It was stupid slip-ups like that—comments that made it all too obvious my feelings for him were still there—that made being around him so difficult. Maybe bringing him along for all this had been a mistake. I should've raised his soul, explained what had happened to him, and moved on. Only, I couldn't. He deserved better than being dumped in a strange body and left to fend for himself.

"Any more flashes of what's going on with your body in the underworld?" He smirked as he said it. "That's never going to stop being weird for me. Talking about the underworld."

"Luckily, no. And after the last one, I'm not sure I could handle another. At least, not any time soon. I'll have to check in on the others eventually, though. Especially once I figure out what I'm going to do, how I'm going to get them out of there."

Matt was silent for the rest of the drive. I couldn't help wondering if he was waiting for me to change my mind about all of this. I couldn't help wondering if *I* actually would change my mind about all of this.

We parked, and Matt came around to open my door. He couldn't stop being a gentleman. "Thanks." I stepped out and stared at Serpentarius. All the answers I needed might be inside those walls. Nervous energy surged through me, feeling vaguely like the power I used to have in my blood. I missed that feeling.

"Hey, it's Jack, right?" Matt said as we approached the door. I recognized the guy from around town. He worked at the gas station on most days.

I tugged on Matt's arm and gave him a look that said, "What are you doing?" No one would recognize Matt in this body.

Jack narrowed his eyes at Matt and me. "Do I know you?"

"Um, yeah," I said, trying to play it cool. "We were here about a month ago. You gave us directions to—" Crap! Where was I going with this? I sucked at lying. "Um, what was that place called again?" I looked to Matt for help.

"The museum. The one with all the interactive science stuff."

"I did?" Jack's brow wrinkled as he struggled to remember something that had never happened.

"Yeah. We found it. Had a great time, too. And since you were so helpful and friendly—I mean you told us your name and everything— we decided to come back here. This place is awesome." Did that sound believable?

"Right. Glad I could help." Jack took our cover charges and waved us inside. "Have a nice night."

"Thanks." I gave him a small wave and ducked inside.

Matt put his hand on the small of my back and led me over to the bar. It wasn't crowded yet, so we ordered two bottles of water—using the last of my money—and sat down in the corner. "Sorry. That was stupid of me."

"It's okay." I took a sip of water to avoid lecturing him. After all, I'd just spilled everything to my mom.

"Maybe this was a mistake. Me coming along. Me being around people from my old life." At least he recognized that it was his old life. It couldn't be *his* life anymore.

"No. It's fine. You'll get the hang of it." I looked around, wanting to go straight to Mason, but I was worried about leaving Matt. What if he saw Amber or someone from school?

"Go." It was like he was reading my mind. "I'll be fine. I'll sit here and drink my water. No one will recognize me, so we don't have to worry about that. And I promise I won't talk to anyone I used to know."

I trusted him. Really I did, but there was so much at stake here. I couldn't help thinking I should bring him with me to see Mason.

"Jo—I mean, wait, what am I supposed to call you? We only came up with a name for me."

"Jodi is fine. In this body, nobody is going to question the name."

He nodded and took a big gulp from his water bottle. He'd almost downed the entire thing already. "Seriously, I'm good. You can trust me."

"I know I can."

"Then what is it?"

"Nothing." I stood up. "I'm going."

"Good luck." He sounded sincere and sad at the same time. He cared about me, so he wanted me to get the answers I needed. But that would also mean I'd be leaving soon, and he didn't want me to go.

I gave him a weak smile before heading toward the office in the back.

"Hang on," came a voice behind the bar. "Where do you think you're going?"

"Oh, um…" I didn't even think that getting to Mason's office would be a problem. Now I was wishing this place was more crowded. No one would notice me if the bar was full of people waving bills in the bartender's face. "I'm a friend of Mason's."

The guy eyed me suspiciously. "I've never seen you before, and Mason didn't say he was expecting anyone."

"Can you tell him Jodi is here to see him? Trust me, he'll let me back there."

The guy sighed and tossed a dishtowel onto the bar. "Wait here."

"Thanks."

I watched him go, hoping Mason wouldn't ask the guy to describe me in order to make sure it was really me. If he did, I'd never get into his office. It seemed to take forever, so I glanced back at Matt. A guy was walking over to him. *Oh, please be a worker just busing the tables.* Matt's water bottle was empty, and he'd finished mine, too. I tried not to panic. It was probably nothing. I was just on edge and reading too much into everything.

Matt's eyes rose, and he looked up at the guy approaching. I debated going over there, but it was too risky. The bartender had told me to stay put, and if I acted suspicious, the guy walking over to Matt might think we were up to something. I had to wait this out. See what happened.

I couldn't hear anything, but I saw the look of recognition on the guy's face, and I swore I read the word "Brian" on his lips. Oh, God! Someone recognized Brian!

Screw staying put. I rushed over to Matt, weaving through people coming into the club and heading for the bar. Of course it would start to fill up in here now.

"Hey." I grabbed Matt's arm. "I love this song. Let's dance."

Matt jumped up from his seat and followed me, but the guy came, too.

"Hang on!" He called after us. "I know you, too. You're Liz."

I stumbled as we reached the dance floor. This wasn't good.

Matt flashed me a look, not knowing what to do. I wasn't sure either. I took a deep breath and turned around.

"Sorry, you must have us confused for someone else." I took Matt's hands and started to dance, hoping the guy would take the hint and walk away.

He didn't. He stood his ground, staring at us.

"Seriously, buddy, sorry if you lost your friends, but it's kind of dark in here. These lights play tricks with your eyes. Maybe try checking the bathroom."

He shook his head. "Trust me, they wouldn't be in there. Corpses don't need to use the bathroom. Of course, they don't dance, either."

I stopped dancing.

"One of you want to tell me what the hell is going on?"

# Chapter 18

We had two options. Bolt out of here, looking totally guilty and drawing suspicion, which meant I wouldn't get to talk to Mason, or make this guy into the bad guy by accusing him of trying to freak us out. I was going with option two.

I twisted my face into a horrified expression. "Do you think this is funny? How dare you come up to us and say these things? We're just trying to have a good time here."

Matt suddenly found the ability to speak again. "Yeah, go away, before I get your ass tossed out of here."

The guy glared at us with such contempt. "I don't know how you did it. Did you stage the accident? Was it because your parents objected to you guys getting married?" He wasn't letting this go.

"I don't know who you think we are, but I'm Jodi and he's Tyler. I'm telling you, you've got the wrong people. I'm sorry if you're confused."

"I'm not confused. We were in the same business classes at Eastern University. I heard all about your accident before I got home for summer break. You guys died in a car crash."

Crap. He'd gone to school with Brian and Liz, and just our luck, he lived nearby. "Obviously, you lost two people you knew, but we aren't them." Since going on the offensive wasn't working, I figured appealing to his emotions might.

He stared at us for several seconds, not saying a word.

"Look, we need to go. We have an appointment with the owner." I took Matt's hand and pulled him toward the back office, leaving the guy gaping after us.

"Wow, I didn't see that one coming," Matt said. "Does this mean I can't stay here, in this town?"

"I don't know yet. Let's not jump to any conclusions. You could always dye your hair or something. We'll figure it out."

The bar was crazy now, littered with people shouting drink orders over the music. The bartender must not have been able to find me in the crowd after I ran off to help Matt. Maybe that was a good thing. Sneaking back to the office was probably the better way to go. I waited until the bartender had his back to us, and then we ducked down the hallway that led to Mason's office. I silently thanked Alex for telling me where it was. I'd never actually been in it before.

The door was shut and locked, so I had to knock.

"What?" Mason called from the other side, and by the sound of it, he wasn't happy about the interruption.

"It's Jodi, Mason."

A chair screeched across the floor and hard footsteps followed. The door swung open and Mason glared at me. "This isn't funny, little girl."

"Wait." I held my hands out so he couldn't slam the door in my face. "Mason, it's really me. I raised my human soul, and I needed a new body."

He looked past me at Matt. "Alex?"

Matt lowered his head.

"No. This is my friend Matt. I raised him, too. Look, it's a long story. Can we please come inside and sit down? I need to talk to you about something. About Carol." I hoped the mention of his wife would get him to let us in.

He stepped aside without saying a word. I walked past him, taking a seat in front of his desk, and Matt followed, standing next to me.

Mason walked around the desk and sat in his chair. He folded his hands, resting them on the accounting records sprawled out in front of him. He'd kept right on working while his family suffered in Tartarus. I wasn't sure how he'd managed it. "Tell me. How bad is it?"

"What have you heard?" I needed to know what he knew before I got into the gory details.

He let out an extra-long and loud breath that smelled strongly of coffee. "You raised a bunch of souls from the depths of Tartarus, and Hades came to claim what you had promised him according to the deal you'd made."

He blamed me for all of this. No wonder he wasn't happy to see me.

I swallowed hard. "You have to understand that I was set up. Chase was sent to the school by Hades to try to get me to end the Ophi race. Ethan, your own twin brother, helped him do it. They were trying to save Chase's mom."

"Charlotte." The name was barely a whisper on Mason's lips.

"Yes. I was set up. Hades made that deal with me, the one where I thought I was saving the Ophi, knowing he was going to send Chase after me. Knowing Chase was going to overpower me."

"You take no responsibility?" Mason raised an accusing eyebrow at me.

"Of course I take responsibility. I'm the Ophi leader. I should've figured it out sooner."

He leaned back in his chair. "I suppose I didn't help any, agreeing to let Ethan take my place. I should've at least told Carol what was going on."

Yes, he should have, but I wasn't about to agree to that. I couldn't risk making him angry when I needed his help.

"Look, we all made mistakes, and now the others are trapped in the underworld. My body's still there with the Ophi half of my soul."

"You split your soul." He nodded. "I didn't think that was even possible."

Not what I wanted to hear. He was supposed to know *more* than me, not less.

"Tony and Arianna talked me through it. Believe me, it wasn't easy. I have to tune out one part of my soul, and still I see glimpses of the underworld when I fall asleep or when—" Was he ready to hear about how we were being tortured?

"When what?" He leaned forward, almost halfway across his desk. "Is Hades…is he torturing you all?"

I nodded.

"My God. I thought he took your souls to strip your powers, but this is worse."

"Wait, he can do that? Take our powers?"

"If he takes your souls."

"But we're all alive down there."

He sat back again. "I'd assumed you were dead."

He thought Carol was dead. That was why he'd moved on. Because he'd thought there was no hope.

"No. We're all alive. I worked out a deal with Hades to get him to let us work for him in the underworld in exchange for being punished less."

"Another deal?" He shook his head. "Jodi, when will you learn? Hades doesn't make deals that don't benefit him."

"We're giving him more time with Persephone. He loves her."

Mason laughed, not a joyful laugh. More like a "God, Jodi's an idiot" laugh. "Persephone hates Hades. He's not using the time to be with her. She's not even *in* the underworld right now. This is her allotted time with Demeter. You've been played."

"What do you mean? What do you think he's doing?"

"I don't know, but you can be sure it's not good for the Ophi. You may have cut down on the torture, but you've put the rest of us, those of us still here," he tapped his finger on his desk, "in great danger."

No. Could I really have walked right into another one of Hades' traps? My throat closed, and I couldn't speak. I'd come here for help, but all I'd gotten was more bad news. I was in over my head.

"You think Hades is coming after the Ophi here?" Matt asked.

Mason looked at him, studying him hard. "Who are you, anyway?"

"He's human. I knew him before all this happened."

Mason scoffed. "Tell me you're kidding. Tell me you didn't bring a human along for the ride."

"Look." I stood up. "I came here because I promised the Ophi in the underworld that I'd find a way to free them. I promised Carol. So, you can either decide to keep bashing me for the crappy job I've done leading the Ophi, or you can help me save them. Make up your mind fast because you're wasting my time, and you're putting Carol through more torture in the process."

Matt stared at me. "I've never seen you like this. When did you get so strong?"

*Strong?* I was terrified.

"She has to be stronger," Mason said. "But at least this is a start." He looked down at his desk. "I need some time to look into this."

"I want to talk to Medusa, but I don't know if I can connect with the statue at the school while I'm human. While I look like this. She won't recognize me."

"She might kill you is what you mean." Well, if he wanted to be blunt about it, yes.

"Whoa, you could die?" Matt reached for my arm. "I don't like this."

Mason's eyes traveled back and forth between Matt and me. "Well, this is interesting. Does Alex know about this?"

"Yes, he does. Alex knows Matt." I left it at that. Mason didn't need to know the details of my screwed-up love life.

"Like I said, I'll need some time to look into this. Contact a few people and see if this sort of thing has ever been done before."

"How much time?" I couldn't sit around doing nothing while the others suffered, and who knew how badly I was suffering, too? I couldn't hold off the double vision forever. I might be in agonizing pain when it hit me again.

Mason put his hands on his hips and bit his lip. "A few days at least."

"We don't have that long. I can give you twenty-four hours, tops."

"Jodi—"

"It's for Carol, Mason. Carol." I had to make him understand. "You don't know what Hades is doing to us. She can't hold on much longer. Can you really make her wait another few days?"

His eyes closed as he took in a deep breath. "Twenty-four hours. I'll have your answer."

"Thank you." I turned and started for the door.

"Jodi," Mason called after me.

I looked back at him, noticing the worry lines creasing his forehead. "Be careful. The longer you're human, the more you'll distance yourself from being Ophi and from the people who care about you." He glanced at Matt, and I knew exactly what he meant.

I nodded and left the office before he could judge me any more.

Matt rolled his eyes. "He's a fun guy."

"He's under a lot of pressure. We all are."

"What now? We have twenty-four hours to wait." He looked toward the dance floor and playfully nudged my elbow.

"I can't. With everything going on, I can't dance my cares away. I'm sorry."

"I understand." He couldn't keep the hurt tone from his voice.

Suddenly the lights dimmed, and I felt weak in the knees. My breathing was labored. "Matt."

He grabbed me as I stumbled forward. Scooping me into his arms, he carried me to the ladies' room, locked the door behind us, and placed me on the counter by the sink.

"What is it? What's happening?"

"Tartarus," I said, before slumping forward on him.

Pain surged through every part of my body. I heard Victoria's laugh, but the searing heat that was attacking me kept me from seeing anything.

"Time is up!" Hades yelled.

My body slumped to the ground, motionless. Relief washed over me. At least I'd only checked in for the end of the torture session. A dark figured loomed over me as my vision returned. Hades. He stared into my eyes.

"Interesting." He turned to Victoria and the others who administered our punishment. "Increase their punishment by two hours each day."

What? We had a deal. "Why?" I managed to choke out.

"Come, come, Jodi Marshall. What kind of fool do you take me for?" Hades laced his fingers in front of him.

"I don't know what you're talking about."

He leaned down toward me, and the heat coming from his body made me flinch. "You're a smart girl. I'm sure you'll figure it out." He disappeared in a swirling cloud of black smoke.

We all got to our feet and walked out of Tartarus. Alex stayed close to me, looking at me like he hadn't seen me in days, which, considering how time moved down here, was probably true.

"Jodi?"

"It's me."

"When did you get back?"

"It happened during the torture. I was pulled out of Serpentarius. I was just talking to Mason, trying to get answers about the statue and connecting to Medusa."

"Are you okay?"

"Yeah. Mason's going to work on finding out if I can see Medusa without dying."

"That wasn't what I meant."

I knew that. He was worried about me, not how I was doing with the plan. "I'm fine, but what was with Hades just now? Did I miss something?"

Alex lowered his head. "He knows. He knows you've split your soul, and he's increasing the torture until you come back. We'll all die, Jodi. He's looked into your eyes a few times, and he saw you weren't fully here. I'm the only one who knows. He came to me. He's only letting me talk to you now so I can tell you this. So I can convince you to return." He stopped walking and kissed my lips. The emotion behind the kiss was overpowering. It ripped my soul apart...again. "Don't come back. Stay where you are. Be happy. Live the life you could've had if you hadn't come into your powers."

What? He couldn't mean that. "Alex, you don't know what you're saying."

"Yes, I do. I love you, Jodi. If this will save you," he spread his arms out wide, "from all of this, then I want you to do it."

# Chapter 19

Stay human? How could I? I'd be stuck like this forever, or at least until Hades killed my body and my Ophi soul with it. Then maybe I really would be free. But I'd be sacrificing all the Ophi to do it. Sacrificing Alex.

"Alex, I'm not leaving you here. I can't." My insides crumbled, and my legs weakened under my weight. I wasn't sure I was strong enough to do this. To fight *or* to flee.

He pulled me to him, wrapping his arms around me. "It's okay."

"No, it's not. I feel so weak. It's like I'm not really me without my powers, but at the same time, I feel normal." I lowered my eyes. "I saw my mom. I told her everything—about you, the school, my dad, Hades. She understood. I couldn't believe it, but she listened, and she accepted this is who I am. She's letting Matt and me stay with her while I'm there. After I go, Matt will continue to live there for a while so he can be near his family. They're going to tell everyone he's my mom's nephew."

Alex's body stiffened. "Your mom took him in? Just like that?"

"That's my mom."

"I thought she was overprotective when it came to you and guys."

"She is. I'm sleeping in her room, and Matt gets mine."

He smiled, obviously pleased with that arrangement. "She doesn't trust Matt to stay on the couch all night, huh?"

"Don't look so happy. She definitely wouldn't trust you."

"What's that supposed to mean?" He looked hurt.

"That I love you. If she saw us together, she'd know we wouldn't stay apart for the whole night."

His frown righted itself, and he leaned down to meet my lips. His hands cupped my face, pulling me closer to him. I clutched the sides of his shirt in my fists and pressed my chest against his.

"Now that's torture," Abby said, walking out of Tartarus. "If I have to watch any more of this, my eyes will burn for sure."

I shot her a look. "What are you doing out here? I thought Hades kept you guys locked up tight."

"What, Queen of the Ophi Jodi thinks she's the only one to get time off?"

I really didn't miss her. I'd tried to sympathize with why she was such a bitch. I mean, if my mom and sister shipped me off and didn't return my calls or letters, I'd be majorly pissed at the world too, but Abby didn't let you feel sorry for her. She cut you down and made you suffer with her.

"What do you want, Abby?" Alex glared at her like she was the most vile creature in the underworld.

She walked closer. Too close to Alex for my liking. "Hmm, what do I want?" She eyed him up and down.

"Back off, Abby." I stepped around Alex, blocking her from him. Before I could say or do anything else, I felt myself slipping away. I turned my head toward Alex and collapsed in his arms.

The last thing I heard before I was back in Liz's body was Abby saying, "Don't worry, Jodi. I'll take good care of our boy."

Damn it! Why now? I wasn't ready to leave, and Abby's little comment meant she knew what was going on with me, too. Did the whole freakin' underworld know what I was up to?

"Jodi?" Matt's eyes darted back and forth between mine.

"Yeah. It's over." I tilted my head back, silently pleading with the tears that wanted to come rushing out. These quick visits with Alex weren't enough.

"You were in something like a trance. I was talking to you, but you didn't respond. You stared back at me, and you didn't move at all. Does that happen to your body in the underworld, too? When you're here, I mean."

"No. I'm stronger in my body. I kind of move on autopilot, but apparently, it's not very convincing because Hades knows what I've done."

"What do you mean he knows? How?"

"Alex said he looked into my eyes a few times. Saw my soul was split or something." I hopped down from the counter.

"He can tell that just by looking at you?"

"He's the god of the underworld. Souls are kind of his thing." I checked out my reflection in the mirror for a whole two seconds before I turned away. I couldn't even bear to look at it. I wanted the next twenty-four hours to go away. I wanted to find out how to connect with Medusa and save Alex. The question was, how long would I feel this way? The longer I was in Liz's body, tuned in to my human soul, the more I became human. I really was going psycho.

"What are you going to do? Or should I ask what Hades is going to do?" Matt looked genuinely scared for me.

"Hades is torturing us overtime until I return. He told Alex to tell me that. He's using Alex to try to make me go back there."

Matt grabbed my arm. "Then you can't go."

"You're kidding, right? Did you hear what I said? He's torturing my body, and worse, he's torturing the others. If I don't get back there soon, he'll kill us all."

"But you won't really die. Just the Ophi half of you will."

"Matt, technically, we're both dead. These bodies are rentals."

He let go of me and stared at himself in the mirror. "Then why'd you bring me back?"

"What do you mean? I wanted to give you a second chance. Make up for all you've been through because of me."

"But you said it's only temporary."

"*You* don't have to be. You can stay here for as long as you want."

"This body…" Matt held a hand up, examining it like it was something completely foreign. "Will it decay on me?"

"No. It won't change at all."

"Ever?" His eyes widened.

I shook my head, seeing where he was going with this.

"So, while everyone else around me is growing old and dying, I'll be in this never-aging eighteen-year-old body?"

I hadn't thought about that. I was just so concerned with bringing him back, giving him more time. I looked away, ashamed of myself for not thinking ahead.

"I can't stay here. You know that, right?"

I did now. "Matt, I'm so sorry. I thought I was doing the right thing for you. I'm still pretty new at all this necromancer stuff. I didn't think this through."

He sighed. "Let's go home. I need something to eat, and then I'm calling it a night. We'll figure things out in the morning after we've both had time to sleep on this." I reached for him, but he shook his head. "Please, Jodi, let's just go. I really don't want to talk about it anymore tonight."

What could I do? I followed him out of the bathroom. The line outside was about a mile long, and a bunch of drunk girls started cursing at us and making rude comments about why Matt and I had locked ourselves in there. On the outside, I ignored them, but inside I couldn't help thinking how ironic it was that girls were thinking Matt and I had been hooking up in the girls' bathroom, just like some random girl had thought about Alex and me in this very same bathroom months before.

Yeah, my life was a little confusing.

The drive home was completely silent. Matt didn't say a word, and I was too upset to even put on the radio. I cracked my window, letting the coolness in the night air sting my damp cheeks. Up until then, I hadn't even noticed I was crying. Human emotions were killer.

Mom opened the front door as we pulled up in the driveway. For the first time since I'd known him, Matt didn't open my car door for me. He went straight to the house and to the kitchen.

I threw my arms around Mom and rested my head on her shoulder.

"Oh, baby." She kissed my hair. "I take it you didn't find out what you needed to?"

I pulled away, and she motioned to the couch. I sat down while she went to the kitchen, returning with two steaming cups of tea and handing one to me. "Here you go. Matt said he's having a quick snack and heading to bed." More like he was avoiding me.

"Mom, can I ask you something?"

"Sure, sweetie. What is it?"

"Is it better this way? Getting to spend a little more time with me, even if you know I can't stay?"

She held her teacup in her lap and sighed. "I know it's going to hurt like hell when you leave, but I wouldn't trade these few days for anything. I get to see my baby girl again." Her eyes filled with tears. "When you left, I had no idea if you were okay. All I wanted was to see you again. And then you sent me that email saying you were safe, but when I tried to reply, the email account had been closed. I was devastated. When Melodie told me she saw you, I kind of fell apart."

Hearing her recount all the awful things I'd done made me lose it all over again.

She reached for my hand and squeezed it. "But now you're here. I can see you're okay. You're stronger than I ever imagined you'd be."

Funny, because I didn't feel strong at all.

"Even if this is the last time I get to be with you, I'm grateful for it."

I put my cup on the coffee table and curled up in a ball with my head on her lap. She moved her tea to the table as well and stroked my hair.

"Maybe now that you know about me, we could see each other sometimes. We'd have to be really careful, but we could do it."

"Sweetie, I would love that. I'll even promise not to touch you if I have to."

"Then it's settled. Even after I go back to my Ophi body and soul, we'll still get together. We could do holidays."

"I do make a mean turkey." Mom laughed.

"Yes, you do. And I promise to stay away from any knives. I'll strictly be the stirrer or flipper or whatever else you can do to food while it cooks."

"Taste tester?" Mom asked.

"No. Too risky. My saliva is poisonous too. I'll have to be in charge of loading the dishwasher, too. Oh, and taking out the garbage after I use the napkins."

"Now, *that* I'm not going to argue with." Even though I was facing the coffee table, I could hear the smile in Mom's voice. She was doing her best to make me feel better. To prove we could still be a family even though I was an Ophi.

"You're the best. You know that?" I tilted my head to see her face.

"Yeah, well, it's a tough job and the pay sucks, but I love you, so what can I say?" She smiled, and it felt so much like old times.

We hung out and talked about everything—Alex, the school, Alex, the underworld, Alex—until midnight. By then, we were both exhausted, and we dragged ourselves upstairs to bed. Mom took the side of the bed closest to the door. Even after all that talk about Alex, she was still worried about me and Matt. He'd gone to bed hours ago. It was strange to think about him sleeping in my bed. No guy had ever been in my bed before, and a week ago, I would've thought the only guy to occupy my bed would be Alex. But somehow, I was being magically transported back through time, to months ago when it was Matt who appeared in all my dreams.

I still wasn't sure what to do about Matt, and because he wasn't speaking to me right now, I had no idea if he even wanted to stay here anymore. If he asked me to release his soul and let him return to his afterlife, it might destroy me. I'd already sent him there twice, and each time it got worse. First he was in Heaven. Then he was in the Fields of Asphodel, totally oblivious to every emotion. If I sent him back to Hades a third time, would he end up in Tartarus?

That thought haunted me as my eyes finally closed, and it stuck with me all night—mostly because I was back in the underworld delivering another soul. My body suddenly stopped moving on autopilot as my focus came crashing back to my Ophi soul. I staggered for a moment before I felt the searing heat of the Phlegethon, the river of fire that surrounded Tartarus. Somehow, Hades had made it so we could pass through it. Of course that was only when we were delivering souls. If we tried to escape during torture time, we'd be burned alive.

My eyes came into focus as I got my bearings.

"Are you okay? You look like you freaked out for a second." I knew that voice. But, no. That was impossible. It couldn't be. I must not have adjusted from the switch, from returning to my Ophi soul.

I turned to face the soul I was escorting.

Amber! Matt's sister. Immediately I knew what was going on. Hades had sent Alex to try to reason with me earlier. He'd even increased the torture for me and the group. When both of those didn't get immediate results, he'd decided to play really dirty. He'd gone after Matt's sister.

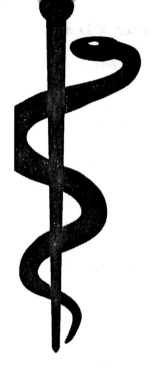

# Chapter 20

I couldn't breathe as I stared at Amber's innocent face. First Matt, and now Amber. Hades was avoiding me, not confronting me about what I'd done. He was making me suffer, forcing me to return to save the people I cared about.

Amber cocked her head to the side and stared into my eyes. "Jodi? Can you hear me now? You were so spacey before. I tried to talk to you, but you didn't answer me. Where are you taking me? Is Matt here? Will I see him? Are you dead, too?"

Each one of her questions was like a stab in the heart. She had no idea what was going on. She thought she was going to see her brother again. That I was taking her to him.

I opened my mouth, but my throat closed up, only allowing a squeak to escape. This couldn't be happening. I willed my blood to mix, to give me strength. I had to put an end to this now. Matt couldn't lose Amber—and to Tartarus, of all places. Amber was a sweetheart. No way did she deserve this. The only reason she was here was because of me. My skin rippled as my power surged through my veins.

Amber stepped back, her eyes widening at the sight of my flesh moving as if snakes were crawling under it. "What's happening to you?"

I found my strength and screamed at the top of my lungs, "Hades!" I yelled his name over and over, refusing to stop until he came. Until he undid what he'd done. Until he brought Amber back to life, and not as a zombie.

A swirl of black smoke approached from above. I stopped yelling and focused all my energy, my anger, into making my blood boil. If he didn't listen, I'd start raising every soul in this place until he stopped me. That meant I was most likely going to die in a matter of minutes, but I didn't care.

Hades appeared out of the smoke and smiled at me. Smiled. Of all things. He was enjoying my misery. "Nice to see you again, Jodi Marshall. You've been away for so long."

How long had it been? I felt like the last slip into my Ophi soul hadn't been long ago at all.

"Enough with the small talk. We both know what I've been doing, and I just discovered what you've been doing." I motioned to Amber. "I'm not taking her to Tartarus." I kept my voice firm, steady, masking my fear with the power in my blood.

"Oh, no?" He smiled again, looking amused.

"No. You're going to bring her back to life. She didn't deserve to die. You only took her to punish me. You knew it would destroy Matt, and that I'd come back here to stop you."

Hades shrugged, playing innocent. "How do you know it wasn't simply her time to die?"

"Don't play games with me. We both know you're trying whatever you can to get me back here, *fully* back. You're desperate. You thought having Alex talk to me would be enough."

Hades laughed. "It would've been if you weren't so focused on your human side. Have you noticed your emotions have changed? Old feelings returning to you?"

Crap! He could read me like a freakin' book.

"Matt seems to be very important to you again. I thought maybe taking his sister would get your attention, and here you are."

"I didn't know you took her. This just happens when I fall asleep. My mind strays back to my Ophi soul."

Hades clasped his hands in front of him. "No. That's not quite how it works. You come back here for a reason. Your Ophi soul calls you because it feels there's something you need to see."

Was that true? Was I trying to warn myself? "You're saying I brought my focus back here because I wanted to save Amber?"

"Exactly."

"Fine. Then that's what I'm going to do. Now bring her back, and not as a zombie. I want her back the way she was."

He smirked. "It's so cute how you think you can make demands of me." His eyes narrowed. "No, wait. It's just annoying." He stepped forward so his face was only inches from mine. The heat radiating off him burned my skin. I tried to back away, but my feet were planted firmly on the ground. He was holding me there. "Return your human soul to your body or Amber spends eternity in Tartarus. There will be no deal this time. If you don't do as I say, she will burn, over and over and over again." He stood up tall again, and the searing pain stopped. "Your decision, of course." He brushed his sleeve as if he didn't have a care in the world.

What was I supposed to do? If I saved Amber, I'd be sacrificing the Ophi. Alex's face popped into my head. Arianna, Leticia, Tony, Jared, Carol, McKenzie, Lexi—even Ethan. I couldn't let them all be trapped here until Hades decided to kill them. I'd given up on Chase. He belonged with Hades. But the others… And trying to raise all the souls in the underworld wasn't going to work. Hades would kill me before I succeeded.

I turned to Amber. "I'm so sorry. You don't deserve this, and if I could save you, I would."

"You *can* save her." Hades moved closer to Amber. "She has the power to save your soul. She's just choosing not to. She wants you to suffer."

"That's not true!" I focused on Amber, pleading with her with my eyes. "Listen to me. He wants you to hate me, to think this is my fault, but *he* did this. If I save you, I'd be killing eight other people. I can't do that. It's awful, but losing one soul is better than losing eight."

"Come now. Don't lie to the poor girl. The people you are choosing to save aren't really people at all. They're monsters."

"No, they're not." I faced him head-on. "I'm not. You can call us monsters, but what we do is nothing compared to what you do. You're torturing Amber to get what you want." I turned back to her. "That's the truth, Amber. *He's* doing this to you."

Her eyes filled with tears as she stared at the gate to Tartarus. "Is it going to hurt?"

Hades smiled. "More than you could imagine."

Amber began to sob. "But why? I'm not a bad person."

I gently touched her arm. "No, you're not." I glared at Hades. "He is." I hugged Amber and whispered in her ear, "I'll try everything I can to get you out of here. I promise. Try to hold on. Try to shut off your mind until I can figure this out."

"Matt...he isn't in there too, is he?"

"No." I didn't have the heart to tell her he was alive again. That would only make things worse.

"Good." Her body shook as she took a deep breath and tried to regain her composure.

"I'm so sorry." I didn't know what else to say.

"So, I guess you'll be escorting her inside?" Hades asked.

I didn't respond, not wanting to give him the satisfaction of admitting defeat.

Amber looked at me and reached for my hand. My eyes shut, futilely trying to hold back the tears.

"I don't blame you, Jodi."

Well, that did it. It was like a dam breaking. I stepped forward, leading Amber to the afterlife she didn't deserve as Hades' laughter bellowed behind us. Part of me wished I'd return to my human soul so I didn't have to endure this. It was almost as much torture for me as it was for her, especially since I knew how painful the punishments were in this place.

Tony stepped toward me from the gates of Tartarus and wrapped me in a hug. Somehow he seemed to know that, no matter how strong I was supposed to be, I needed support. I smiled up at him as I pulled back and wiped my tears. He knew me well enough to know I didn't want to discuss what had just happened, so he motioned for Ethan to step aside and let Amber and me pass.

I held her hand as I escorted her to Bristol, one of the Ophi from the school who had chosen to follow Victoria and Troy's evil plan and landed herself in here.

I swallowed the lump in my throat as I approached her. "I want you to know that Hades is torturing this girl—Amber—because he is trying to hurt me. She didn't do anything wrong. She's innocent."

Bristol stared at me completely unfeeling for a moment, but then her eyes flickered to Amber, who was trying to keep a brave face but was failing miserably.

"Bristol, please, I'm begging you to go easy on her. She doesn't deserve this."

"Oh, and *I* deserved this?" She held her arms out wide, gesturing to her own imprisonment. An imprisonment I'd doomed her to.

"You came after me. You chose to follow Victoria. What was I supposed to do? She was going to kill me, and you volunteered to help."

She lowered her head. "I thought Victoria was right. I thought we had to wage a war against Hades to avoid something like this." She raised her eyes to mine. "Not all of us could be the Chosen One and instinctively know the right thing to do. I chose wrong."

"Is that really how you feel?"

She glanced at Victoria about twenty feet away, torturing a soul and smiling wickedly. "I hate her. She's pure evil." Her gaze returned to me. "I'm sorry for trying to hurt you."

I nodded. "I'll make a deal with you." Apparently, all I did anymore was make deals. "If you take care of Amber as best as you can without letting Hades get too suspicious, I'll find a way to take you with me when I free my friends."

She raised her brows. "You'd do that? Even after I—"

I held up my hand to stop her. "Consider it done. Just promise me you'll take care of Amber for me."

"I promise." She fidgeted with her hands. "Should we shake on it or something?"

"No, that would look too suspicious. We can't let anyone know we're working together. It would be bad for both of us."

"Got it. I'll pretend I still hate you."

"Good."

"But, Jodi?"

"Yeah?"

"I don't, and I really appreciate what you said. Even if you fail, and we don't get out of here, the fact that you're willing to forgive me and save me from this…well, it means a lot."

I nodded, not wanting to smile since Bristol and I weren't supposed to be friendly to each other. I turned to Amber and squeezed her hand. "You'll be okay. Stick by Bristol."

She managed to raise one corner of her mouth a fraction of an inch. I hugged her one last time and left Tartarus. I should've headed back to the palace and waited for my next soul, but instead I went straight for the Fields of Asphodel.

Alex and Arianna were at the gate. My mouth curved into a smile the second their faces came into focus. I rushed for them, and they wrapped me into a group hug.

"God, I missed you guys."

Arianna kissed the side of my head. "Sweetheart, you have no idea."

I stepped out of their arms and took them in from head to toe. They both looked worn out, and Arianna had several bruises and burn marks on her arms.

"Ari, what happened?" I gently took her hand to get a closer look.

"Don't you worry about that. I can handle myself just fine. You have enough going on, so don't give it another thought."

I looked to Alex for an explanation. He sighed. "Hades has been going harder on some of us lately."

"Because of me." I let go of Arianna's hand and inhaled as deeply as I could to stop myself from screaming my head off. If I alerted Hades to my whereabouts, he'd be here and forcing me back to the palace. He wouldn't approve of my visits with Alex or any of the others.

Arianna gave Alex a reprimanding look. "Don't you go listening to him. I mean it, Jodi. He had no right to tell you that. We're fine."

She was wrong about so many things. They weren't fine, and Alex had to tell me that because I needed to know.

"Hades was really angry when he found out his plan to have me bring you back didn't work."

"I know." I closed my eyes, trying to erase the image of Amber looking helpless and scared from my brain. "He killed Matt's sister and had me escort her to Tartarus. That's why I'm here. My Ophi soul called me back to save Amber."

"Did you?" Alex asked.

"No, but I made a deal with Bristol."

"Bristol?" Alex shook his head. "I don't know if you can trust her. She—"

"I think she really feels like she made a mistake helping Victoria and Troy. She wants to get out of here just as much as we do, and she apologized for trying to hurt me."

"You believe her?" Alex wasn't buying it.

"I have to. She's agreed to take care of Amber until I can find a way to get her out of here."

"Jodi, if Hades took her, then all you can hope for is to raise her soul. She'd be—"

"Maybe not. If I can figure out how to stop Hades from messing with us for good, then maybe I can convince him to bring Amber back—human."

Alex put his hands on his hips. "That's asking for a lot."

"I know." I was resting all our hope on Medusa knowing the answer, knowing how to defeat Hades. If she didn't…

Alex moved toward me and took both my hands. "There's something else you need to know."

Not more bad news. I couldn't handle anything else.

"Hades is still trying to use me to get to you, so take this however you want, but I have to tell you."

This was going to be awful. No, devastating.

"Tell me."

"He told me where he's been going."

"Is he hunting down other Ophi?" That was what I'd assumed.

"He's hunting you. He wants to kill you in human form. It's his back-up plan since his other scare tactics to bring you back here aren't working. The only problem is, he doesn't know what body you've chosen to occupy." He closed his eyes for a moment and swallowed before continuing. "But, Jodi, he said that, if he doesn't find you in the next two days, he's going to take your mom."

# Chapter 21

Mom. My legs shook, and my eyes rolled back into my head. I felt Alex's arms around me as I slipped away. When my eyes opened again, I was in Mom's bed. I stared at her sleeping peacefully beside me. Tears dotted my pillowcase. This wasn't fair. I wasn't supposed to be able to hurt her now that I was in human form, but she still wasn't safe around me. I had to talk to Medusa and find a way out of this mess in two days, or Mom was going to die because of me.

Even though it was only just past three, I stayed awake, watching Mom sleep and wondering if Mason had found out anything yet. We were going to see him at six. That gave me the day to spend with Mom. Of course, I knew Matt was going to want to get in touch with his family or, at the very least, peek in at them to make sure they were okay. Only they weren't. Amber was dead. They were probably complete wrecks and making funeral arrangements. How was I going to explain that to Matt?

I wasn't going to have to worry about him loving me anymore. That was for sure. Once he found out I was the reason his sister was dead, he'd hate me forever. I wondered how Hades had done it. Did he take her in her sleep? That would mean her family didn't even know she was dead yet. Or had he tortured her and made her death painful? A car accident, maybe? I had to know.

I slipped out of bed, careful not to wake Mom, and I sat down at the desk in the corner. Mom's laptop was open, and luckily it was still on. I brought it out of sleep mode and immediately searched the Internet for Amber's name. Chills ran across my arms as I clicked "search." A few seconds later—our connection was slow—a list of results came up on the screen. The very first one was what I was looking for but hoping I wouldn't find.

"Sixteen-year-old Amber Davenport dies of a brain aneurysm."

Silent sobs burst out of me. I turned to Mom, wondering if Hades would take her the same way. I couldn't let that happen. I'd go to Mason this evening, and from there I was going to the school to visit with Medusa. And if all else failed, I'd give Hades what he wanted. I'd throw in my white flag to save my mom. I knew how hypocritical that was. I'd told Amber I couldn't save her at the expense of eight others, and here I was, ready to save my mom over them. But she was my mom.

I cried until Mom woke up at seven. She rubbed her eyes and sat up when she saw I wasn't in bed but at her desk.

"Honey, what is it?" She threw the blankets off her and rushed over to me, wrapping her arms around my shaking, tear-soaked body.

"Mom, there's something I didn't tell you yesterday. When I raised my human soul, my Ophi half remained in the underworld."

"You did tell me that." She patted my head, probably thinking I was hysterical, which I was.

"There's more, though. I can see glimpses of what's happening in the underworld. Hades is trying everything he can think of to make me go back there. He knows what I've done."

"How?" She pulled away and looked back and forth between my eyes.

"I'm like a robot down there, going through the motions. He could tell something was wrong, and then when I focused on my Ophi soul and was actually feeling everything that was happening, he noticed. He threatened me by punishing the other Ophi. He even had Alex tell me he knew what I'd done, thinking Alex would be enough to make me return. But when that didn't work, he…" The tears came again. I turned to the screen, which still had the article about Amber's death open on it.

Mom's eyes widened, and her hand covered her mouth. She shook her head. "I should've heard about this. I could've prepared you, but I don't watch the news anymore. I don't talk to many…" Her voice trailed off, which was good because I couldn't listen to this. Not on top of what had happened to Amber. Mom had completely shut down because I left. She didn't go out, except for work. I'd turned her into a walking zombie, only worse because she was alive.

"Did you see her?"

I nodded. "Hades made me take Amber to Tartarus. That's Hell—literally. I got one of the Ophi who tried to kill me…" Her eyes were bulging out of their sockets at this point. "Long story. Anyway, I got her to agree to go easy on Amber if I freed her along with my friends. I'm going to get Amber out of there. I won't let her die."

"Can you do that? I mean, she's already dead."

"I'm a necromancer, so I can bring her back. Or at least my Ophi half can. But I don't want her to be like *this*." I held my arms out. "I want her to be human again. Alive. I'm going to make Hades do it. He's the only one who can."

"What makes you think he'll do it?"

"I have to talk to Medusa. Hopefully she'll know how to stop Hades for good." Mom started to protest, but I shook my head. "I know it's a long shot, but what else can I do?"

She hugged me, and I felt her body shake as she began to cry. She was worried about me. Worried I wouldn't survive this fight. I was, too.

Mom and I finally managed to compose ourselves enough to shower, get dressed, and head downstairs for breakfast. As we neared the kitchen, the smell of pancakes filled the air. Mom and I looked at each other and smiled.

Matt was at the stove, placing the pancakes on plates. "Hope you're hungry. I made way too many."

Mom and I took our plates, still smiling. Mom even kissed Matt's cheek. Great, now she chose to like him, after I'd killed him and we'd stopped seeing each other. "This is such a nice surprise. Thank you."

"You're welcome, Ms. Marshall." Matt leaned his cheek toward me, waiting for me to kiss it, too. I laughed and shoved a pancake in my mouth, pointing to it and shrugging. Better luck next time, Matt.

Breakfast was so nice, I almost forgot about Amber and having to tell Matt that his sister was dead because of me. Now I wished I *had* kissed his cheek before I lost him forever. Mom kept glancing at me while I ate. She was waiting for me to break the news.

"So," Matt said after polishing off his large stack of pancakes. "I was thinking I'd try to meet up with Amber. She always hangs out at this art gallery on Saturdays. They feature local talent, and she's dying to get her stuff in there."

Mom reached for my hand as I struggled to breathe.

"What?" Matt looked back and forth between us. "Did I miss something?"

"Matt." That was all I had. His name. I couldn't think of what else to say. *I brought your sister's soul to Tartarus last night* was just too awful.

"Jodi was able to see herself in the underworld last night," Mom said, trying her best to help.

Matt's eyes flew to me. "Is Hades messing with you still? Did he hurt you?"

Of course he was worried about me. That was Matt. He had no idea he should be worrying about himself and his family.

"I don't know how to tell you this." My voice shook.

"You're leaving, aren't you?" He slumped back in the chair.

"No." Man, I wished I could mix my blood and get up some courage right now. "I saw Amber."

Matt's brow furrowed. "No, you must have been dreaming. You couldn't have seen Amber. She's not..." The horror must have been all over my face because Matt stood up, knocking his chair over, and stormed upstairs.

Mom reached for my hand, but I pulled away.

"I have to go talk to him. He needs to hear this from me."

She nodded.

I raced up the stairs, taking them two at a time. The light was on in my room, and I knew exactly where I'd find Matt. At my laptop.

He already had the article up on the screen. Why didn't the connection work that quickly for me?

"Matt, I'm so sorry. I know that sounds like the stupidest thing to say right now, but I'm going to fix this. I'll bring her back. I have one of the Ophi taking care of her while I'm here, and as soon as I figure out how to stop Hades for good, I'm going to bring Amber back here, to you." The words spilled from my lips. I wanted to get them out as quickly as possible to ease Matt's pain.

"Is she...like I was...in that place wandering around without a clue who she is?"

That would've been heaven compared to Tartarus. When I didn't answer, he turned to look at me.

"Jodi, where is she?"

"Tartarus." The second I said it, I burst into tears and reached for him, but Matt stood up and punched my desk.

I pulled away in horror as he cried out. He'd definitely broken his hand. Mom rushed into the room. She took one look at Matt cradling his hand and said, "I'll get my keys. You need a doctor."

"I'll take him." Being around Mom was risky. If Hades wanted to find me, he'd definitely come here. He was giving me two days—and I hoped he meant two days in *this* time and not in the underworld where time moved more quickly—before he took Mom. As long as I wasn't here when he showed up—which I was sure he would today, hoping he'd find me—she'd be okay for a little while longer.

"I'll go with you. You're both upset, and neither one of you should be driving."

"Mom, Hades is looking for me. Alex told me last night. He's going to come here, and if he finds me, he'll hurt you to get me to do whatever he wants me to. I can't put you through that. I've hurt enough people already."

Mom grabbed me by the shoulders. "None of this is your fault. Do you hear me? None of it."

If only that were true. Maybe I hadn't asked for any of this, but it still had happened because of me. "I need to take Matt, and I need to distance myself from you. I love you, Mom, and I already lost you once. If Hades takes you..." I shook my head. "I'll never forgive myself. Please, let me do this."

Mom hugged me tight. "Okay, you can go. Take my car. But don't stay away. I just got you back, and I'm not ready to say goodbye yet."

"I'll make sure we get some more time together. Somehow."

Mom released me. "Keys are in my purse."

"I love you." I kissed her cheek before taking Matt's good hand and leading him downstairs.

"I understand if you hate me."

"I don't hate you. Your mom was right. This isn't your fault."

Why did everyone have to be so understanding? It made me hate myself more. I grabbed Mom's keys, and we headed out. The hospital wasn't far, so we got to the emergency room in record time, mostly because I wanted to get away from Mom as quickly as possible, but also because Matt coached me on when to shift.

The receptionist barely looked at us even though we were standing directly in front of her. "Fill these out and take a seat."

I took the clipboard and scanned the papers. Damn it! Matt didn't have insurance. He didn't even have an address anymore, unless we counted Mom's, but I didn't want any bills showing up there. She didn't need to be burdened with Matt's medical expenses.

Matt stared at me and sighed. He tugged me away from the receptionist, not that she'd given us a second thought. She was already deep into her crossword puzzle again. I didn't think anyone still did those.

"We should go. I can't pay for this."

"We're not leaving. You're hurt. I'm sure you broke something. You're going to need a cast."

He pointed his good hand at the papers. "So what, we lie our way though all this? They need to see my insurance card."

True. Unless he didn't have insurance. No, they overcharged people who didn't have insurance.

I held up a finger to Matt and walked back to the receptionist. "Excuse me, ma'am."

"Fill these out and take a seat." She held out another clipboard without looking up.

"No. I already have one."

"Then take a seat."

"There's a problem." Finally, she looked up at me. I hoped this worked. "You see, we're from out of town. We got here this morning on the bus, but when we went to use the restrooms at the bus station all our bags were stolen."

"You left your bags unattended in the bus station." She said it like we were the two stupidest people on the planet.

"Dumb. I know. But you see, Tyler," I motioned to Matt, "got so upset that we'd been robbed that he kind of punched a wooden bench."

The lady shook her head and rolled her eyes. "I'd give you a lecture, but I think the broken hand kind of sums it up."

Matt nodded, playing along.

"All right. Fill out your address and all the information you can. If you don't remember all your insurance information, fill in what you know and leave the rest blank. We'll mail you the bill—I'm assuming you don't have cash on you."

Matt and I shook our heads.

"Of course not." She rolled her eyes again. "We'll mail you the bill, and you can fax us your new insurance card when you get it. We'll bill your insurance at that time, and you can settle your co-pay."

"Thank you." I gave her a huge smile and led Matt to some empty chairs. I started filling in bogus information. "Hmm, Tyler Gross." I giggled. There were very few times I was able to laugh anymore. I was going to enjoy this.

He groaned. "Come on. Really?"

"It's funny." I continued. "Address. 666 Hades Junction."

Even Matt laughed at that one.

After I finished filling out the paperwork and turned it back in to the receptionist, who rolled her eyes at me for the third time, we waited while everyone else was called in before Matt. Finally, a woman came into the waiting room.

"Tyler Gross."

We both turned at the sound of Matt's fake name. Only neither one of us laughed this time. The nurse who'd called Tyler's name…was Matt's mom.

# Chapter 22

I nudged Matt, widening my eyes and nodding in his mother's direction. "What is she doing here? Amber just…shouldn't she be at home?"

"You didn't read the entire article about Amber, did you?"

No, I hadn't. After I found out it was an aneurysm, I didn't want to know anything else. I shook my head.

"Amber died a month ago."

A month ago? "No, that can't be. Hades took her to get back at me."

"I don't think so, Jodi. Amber used to get these really bad headaches all the time. I can't help thinking she was meant to die when she did."

"That would mean Hades had me *move* her."

Matt balled his good hand into a fist. "He took her out of Heaven and put her in Hell to get back at you."

"Those aren't the terms he uses, but yes. That's exactly what he did."

Matt looked like he was about to hit something and break his other hand.

"I'm so sorry." He couldn't deny it was my fault now. Maybe I hadn't been the reason Amber died, but I was the reason she was in Tartarus. "Why wasn't she buried next to you, though? We should've seen her grave."

He shook his head. "Amber always said she'd rather be cremated than buried. She was claustrophobic. She insisted she would be even in death." That was Amber. Very quirky. "I don't know if I can do this." He glanced at his mom. "She never worked in the ER. She was always stationed in the maternity ward."

"You wanted to see her, remember? This is good. You'll be able to check on her without randomly showing up on her doorstep."

"Tyler Gross?" she called again, looking around the waiting room.

"Here." I stood up and grabbed Matt's arm, pulling him up. "He's a little out of it from the pain."

Mrs. Davenport nodded. "Right this way, please."

We followed her through the set of double doors and into an examination room.

"Okay, why don't you hop up on the examination table, and I'll take a look at that hand."

I sat in the chair in the corner and gave Matt a small encouraging smile. He breathed out loudly, trying to get control of his emotions. I knew how he felt. I had been terrified to see my mom. He'd thought it would be so easy, checking up on our families. Now, he was seeing that there was nothing easy about it.

Mrs. Davenport flipped through Matt's paperwork. "It says here that you did this punching a wooden bench after your bags were stolen from the bus station."

"She wrote that on the form?" Man, that receptionist just couldn't stop taking digs at us. If it wasn't a flat-out lie, I'd be insulted.

"Afraid so. Clarice has a strange sense of humor. Most people don't get her." Mrs. Davenport smiled at us, and I couldn't help remembering the way she'd always invited me to dinner and told me I should stop by more often. She was such a caring person.

She gently turned Matt's hand, looking at it from all angles. "Well, I'm going to wager you broke at least one bone in there, but we'll need an x-ray to see the extent of the damage."

"Will he be in a cast?" If Matt had to come back to get the cast removed, it would really screw up our "mail us the bill, and we'll get our insurance to take care of it later" plan. He'd have to find a different hospital to pull the same scam on, and he'd have to do it without me.

"Most likely. I'm pretty certain he has some broken bones."

Matt mouthed a "sorry" to me, making me want to melt into the chair. If Hades hadn't tried to get back at me through Amber, this wouldn't have happened. I should be the one apologizing. Again.

"You can stay here while we go get this x-rayed and speak with the doctor and the radiology technician."

I nodded.

Matt followed his mom out of the room. He still hadn't said a word to her. I hoped he'd get over it enough to at least say something. He'd regret it if he blew this opportunity to talk to his mom again. Of course, there was the danger of him getting too comfortable and spilling everything to her in front of the doctor and the countless other people who were examining him.

I tapped my foot for what seemed like an eternity before they both returned, this time with the doctor, a middle-aged man with a mustache who didn't say a word as he walked over to the sink and wrote on his clipboard. Mrs. Davenport put Matt's x-ray up on one of those light boxes.

"Yup. There and there. Can you see the fractures?"

"Guess I won't be punching anything for a while." Matt gave his mom a small smile. My heart sank when I saw the way he looked at her. God, I hoped she didn't notice. She'd think he was having some cougar fantasy or something.

"Should I go to the waiting room while he's getting the cast put on?"

"If you'd like. Completely up to you and Tyler." When she said his name, her eyes lit up for a split second. "I always liked the name Tyler. I wanted to name my son that, but my husband insisted on Matt." She lowered her eyes. "Tyler was his middle name." She was still grieving.

Matt opened his mouth, but I jumped up and said, "You know, I think I'll stay if that's okay with you, Tyler." He looked at me, coming out of his trance. "I figure you could use the emotional support."

"Yeah." He reached for my hand and squeezed it. Alex would've hated it, especially since Matt still had strong feelings for me. But Matt needed me right now, and I wasn't about to deny him something so small as holding my hand for support.

"You two make such a cute couple," Mrs. Davenport said, eying us.

Oh well, I went with it. "Thank you, Mrs. Davenport."

She wrinkled her brow. "How did you know my name?"

Damn it! "Oh, um, you told us when you called Tyler into the examination room."

"I did?" She shook her head. "I must be tired. I always introduce myself as Emily. Mrs. Davenport makes me sound old. But then again, I don't usually work in the ER. Someone called out sick, and I got stuck working a double. They pulled me from the maternity ward."

"Well, I'm glad you're here," Matt said, on the verge of sounding like a cougar hunter again.

"Yeah, you've been really nice." I jumped right in, trying to make this better. "Some people, like the receptionist, weren't exactly nice about how this happened."

Mrs. Davenport looked over her shoulder at the doctor, who was washing his hands at the sink, and then she leaned closer to us and whispered, "Don't let Clarice get to you. A few months back, she slipped off the toilet in the ladies' room after insisting that she only uses the bathroom after the janitors wash the seats." She giggled. "Apparently, the seat was so slippery clean, she shot right off it."

We all laughed, breaking the tension that Matt had caused. I had to keep him under control. If he couldn't hold it together, how was I supposed to leave him here when I went to save the others from Hades?

"You all ready to get plastered?" Mrs. Davenport asked.

Matt and I looked at each other like we'd both lost our minds—or she had.

She laughed again. "I mean your cast. God, I haven't laughed like this in months. I've been going through a rough time, but you kids have really cheered me up."

Being around Matt was making her happy again. Maybe this visit would turn out all right after all.

"Come on. You can pick your color of cast wrap. We have red, blue, green, yellow… I'm guessing you don't want pink, but some guys do like purple."

Matt and I exchanged glances. He wasn't the purple type. My smile faded when I realized why Matt disliked purple so much. Amber's entire room was purple. Matt always said it looked like a grape exploded in there. He must have been thinking the same thing because he lowered his eyes.

Mrs. Davenport gazed out the window. "You know, my daughter loved purple. My son hated it. She always tried to get him to wear purple shirts. He never would. And now…" She turned back to us. "Well, I don't need to bore you with my drama."

"I'll take purple," Matt said.

It took all my strength not to cry. I clenched my teeth and fought the tears as Mrs. Davenport put a cast on Matt. She had no idea her son was sitting in front of her. My heart ached, and I wanted to tell her the truth. I wanted to let her know she hadn't lost both her children. I wanted to make up for taking Matt from her and for sending her daughter to Hell. But I couldn't. If we even tried to explain this, she'd think we were crazy, and she'd call security. That would be the end of Matt's time with her. We had to stick to the original plan. He was my mom's nephew. At least he'd be able to see his parents that way.

After the doctor finished wrapping Matt's hand in a purple cast and made a quick exit, Mrs. Davenport took a black permanent marker from the table behind her and handed it to me. "Want to do the honors?"

I looked at Matt and knew what he wanted. "Actually, I think you should sign it, Nurse Davenport."

"Oh, please, call me Emily, and I don't think Tyler wants me to sign it. He doesn't even know me."

If only she knew how wrong she was.

"I *would* like you to sign it," Matt said. "You've been really nice, almost motherly."

*Oh, God, Matt. Please, don't slip up. Don't say anything suspicious.*

"All in the job description, but if you insist." She took the marker and signed her name across the back of his hand. She held his hand while she did it, and Matt's bottom lip quivered a little. I held my breath until she let go of him. "There you go. Now, since you aren't from around here, I guess this is goodbye."

"You might see him again. His aunt lives here. He's going to be staying with her for a while." He couldn't stay forever because he wouldn't age, and people would definitely notice that, but at least he'd have some time before it got risky to be here.

"Oh, really? Who's your aunt? Maybe I know her."

"Laura Marshall," Matt said.

Mrs. Davenport's face lit up. "I know Laura well. Our kids used to…" Her smile melted away. "They used to date."

Neither Matt nor I knew what to say, so we stayed silent.

"I'm sure Laura is happy to have you. She's been through a lot since Jodi disappeared. Not that I need to tell you. You know all about that, I'm sure."

Matt nodded.

"I can imagine how she feels. I've lost both my children. But poor Laura, she never had any closure. She doesn't know if Jodi is alive or…" Her voice trailed off. Her eyes watered, but she forced a smile. "There I go again. Telling you two about my troubles."

"It's no problem, really," I said. "We appreciate how nice you've been."

"Well, it was really nice meeting both of you. You made me smile for the first time in a long time." She took one of my hands and Matt's good hand in hers. "Thank you for that."

I swallowed hard, afraid if I said anything I'd start bawling.

She let go and turned to Matt. "And, Tyler, I do hope I'll see you again. We should all get together for dinner sometime after you're settled."

"I'd really like that."

We said goodbye and left. Matt walked slower than a tortoise. He didn't want to leave his mom. I glanced at the clock in the waiting room. It was mid-afternoon already. We'd spent most of the day in the hospital.

"Hungry?" I asked.

The thought of food seemed to perk him up a little.

"Oh, wait. No money." I reached into my pockets, hoping to find a twenty stuffed in there, and to my surprise, I did. Attached to it was a pink Post-it note. *Buy yourselves some lunch.* Mom must have snuck it into my pocket when she'd hugged me. I held the bill up to Matt. "It's on my mom."

We drove to Alberto's. Matt's idea, of course. It was the place we went on our second-to-last date, back when I thought Alex was stalking me, and I referred to him as Green Eyes because I didn't know his name yet. I wasn't sure how Matt was feeling about me right now. He had to have a little resentment toward me. I'd killed him and sent Amber to

Hell. He was a great guy, as perfect as anyone could get, but that was too much to get past. Wasn't it?

"Bagel and vanilla milkshake?" he asked.

"You remember that's what I had when we came here?"

"Of course. I wasn't lying when I said I was in love with you."

Was. So, he wasn't anymore. That was good. I loved Alex. Things would be easier if Matt didn't have those feelings for me. But then why did I feel bad about it?

"You had a foot-long sub and ate all of it." I was suddenly feeling nostalgic.

"I'm surprised you remember."

"Why? I cared about you a lot. Wasn't it obvious?"

The waitress came to take our order. I recognized her from school. Wendy Something-or-Other.

"Hey, Wendy," Matt said with a big smile.

She cocked her head to the side.

"Um, your nametag." I pointed to the big block letters.

"Right!" She laughed. "You had me for a second."

I forced a laughed and nudged Matt under the table with my foot.

"Just a little game I play when I go out to eat. It's funny how many people think I'm psychic or something." He placed our orders, and once Wendy was out of earshot, he said, "Sorry. I promise I'll get used to this."

"It's okay." After all my screw-ups, Matt's were nothing major. "So, back to my question. Did I not make my feelings for you clear?"

"You did, but you were so distracted the day we came here. That guy—" He tapped his finger on his cast and avoided my eyes. "Alex was following you, and there was the whole thing with the school nurse."

There had been a lot going on. I'd come into my Ophi powers and was suddenly dangerous to every living thing around me.

"I was thinking." He raised his eyes to mine. "We're going to see that Mason guy again tonight, and I'm guessing you'll be going back to..." He swallowed hard and before he could continue, our food arrived.

"Anything else I can get for you?" Wendy asked.

"No, I think we're good," I said.

Matt took a sip of his milkshake before he continued. "I've only got a few hours to convince you that you're better off here with me. I want you to allow me to do that. To give me four hours to prove I'm the best guy for you. That this is the life you should choose." He reached his good hand across the table and laced his fingers through mine.

As much as I wanted to protest, to tell him I loved Alex, I couldn't. I squeezed his hand.

# Chapter 23

Thankfully, Alex had no clue what I was doing here. If he did, we'd be over before I got back to the underworld. *If* I went back. After everything that had happened, I was doubting my own existence. Maybe Hades was right. Maybe the Ophi didn't deserve to be alive. We caused pain for the souls we raised. We were better suited for the underworld. At least there, we couldn't hurt the living. I couldn't help wondering if I'd been going about this all wrong. What if I should've been getting Hades to agree to let us stay in the underworld and help him with the souls in exchange for no more punishments for ourselves? He just might make that deal because it would mean there'd be no more Ophi in the world, assuming he took the remaining few to the underworld with us.

It was too much to think about. I'd promised Matt four hours, and I was going to give him that much. We finished our food and drove to the park. Since it was Saturday, it was pretty crowded, but we found a place on the other side of the lake where it was quiet. Matt grabbed two towels from the pavilion and laid them on the grass. We lay on our backs, staring up at the clouds. The sky couldn't have been more beautiful.

Matt rolled onto his side, propping his head up in his good hand. "What's it like?"

I turned my head, wishing it was Matt's face I was seeing and not Brian's. "Are you asking what it's like to be an Ophi?"

"Yeah. I mean, why do you want to go back to that? You're human again. I'd think you'd jump at the chance to be back with your mom." He reached his hand with the cast toward my face, brushing my cheek lightly with his fingertips. "With me."

Right now, that *was* what I wanted. "It's complicated. I'm their leader. If I don't go back, I'm damning them all."

"Can't someone else lead them? I mean, someone must have been in charge before you got there—to that school."

Yeah, and she was a power-crazed bitch who liked torturing the souls in Tartarus. Who liked torturing me in particular.

"Let's just say that didn't work out so well." Of course, Tony or Arianna *could* lead the others. They both knew everything there was to know about being an Ophi. There was just one problem. Neither had my power. "I'm the only one, Matt. I'm stronger than the others. I'm tied more closely to Medusa."

"Can't you raise Medusa? Get her to lead the Ophi?"

If only I could. "Medusa's soul is trapped inside a statue. It took a bunch of Ophi to put her there, and most of them died in the process. No way could I raise her."

"Why'd they want to trap her, anyway? Isn't she like a mom to all of you?"

"That's actually the reason they did it. Hades was going to take her power and her soul. He would've tortured her. What the Ophi did saved her from that. It protected her from Hades. He can't touch her."

Matt shimmied toward me, coming onto my towel. I turned sideways so we were only inches apart. "Okay, forget being Ophi. I know at least part of you wants to stay here. Tell me why. What do you miss about being human?"

"This." I reached for his arm. "You."

He leaned forward like he was going to kiss me, but I kept going. "Mom, Melodie, my old life—I miss all of it."

He sighed, obviously hurt that I'd stopped him from kissing me.

"You could have all that again. You have it now. Well, not Melodie, but you could tell her the truth. She wouldn't go blabbing to anyone."

I shook my head. "No. We can't tell anyone else. It's too risky. Besides, Melodie is going off to college in a year, anyway."

"All right, then forget about Melodie. I'm never going to age. If you don't stay, I'll outlive everyone I know and love. Immortality isn't worth it if you're alone."

I was trying not to think about that part. Leaving Matt would mean sentencing him to a lonely existence. "I could always check in with you, and when you're ready to move on, I could release your soul."

"Back to that place? Those fields? I don't want to just wander for all eternity, either. This is my best option, Jodi, but if you aren't here with me, I don't want it. Watching everyone I love die while I stay like this would be a living Hell."

His words cut through me, making my throat sting with the unfairness of it all. "Do you wish I never brought you back?"

"No. I wish you'd love me like you love him."

Alex. Matt wanted me to look at him the way I looked at Alex. If I was still connected to my Ophi soul, my conflicted emotions would be sending my blood bubbling and mixing under my skin. I'd be raising every dead body in a ten-mile radius. But I wasn't Ophi. I was human.

I swallowed hard and leaned forward, pressing my lips to Matt's. He gently tipped me onto my back, holding himself above me with his elbows. His body pressed against mine, our limbs tangling. This felt right. Matt and I were supposed to be together…if I was human. Which I was now. He deepened the kiss, and I struggled to breathe, but I didn't care. I couldn't get enough of Matt.

I was getting dizzy from lack of oxygen. No, not lack of oxygen. I was losing my connection to my human soul. Drifting away.

Matt pulled back slightly. "Jodi?"

My eyes met his for a split second before they closed.

"No, don't go back to him. Stay with me." He pressed his lips to mine again, but I only felt them for a second before I was back in the underworld.

I shook my head, trying to focus on my surroundings. I was in the palace. The judges stood before me.

"Melodie Chambers, you will spend your afterlife in the Fields of Asphodel."

Melodie? I stared at the girl, taking in every feature. Brown hair, blue eyes, athletic build. My blood simmered. She turned toward me, seeing me for what must have been the first time.

"Jodi?"

My blood boiled now, making my skin ripple. She stared in horror.

"Escort her to the afterlife," the middle judge said.

I stepped toward Melodie, stopping two feet in front of her. "Mel."

"It *is* you." She stared at my arms, still rippling with the power of my blood. "What's happening to you?"

"It's a long story. Mel, I'm so sorry. For everything. For waving you down that day. For taking your car and leaving you stranded without a phone. For being the reason you're here."

"What do you mean, the reason I'm here? I died, didn't I? You couldn't have been responsible for that. If you're here, then that means you're dead, too."

"No. It's different for me. But forget about that. How did you die?"

"This truck came out of nowhere. I was at a traffic light, and it turned green. But when I drove through it, this truck barreled right into me."

Oh, God, Hades had made it painful. I was going to kill him. Could you kill the god of the underworld?

"I said, escort her to the afterlife," the middle judge said, his voice so loud it shook the palace walls.

I turned to him, allowing my blood to surge and bubble in my veins. "No. She shouldn't be here. If you're going to judge souls, then you should know how they arrived here. You don't have all the information. Hades isn't playing by the rules. He's taking people. People I care about, just to get back at me. You can't let him do that. You're here to fairly judge people."

I couldn't see their faces under their hoods, but since they weren't stopping me, I went on. "Did you know he took a soul out of the Elysian Fields and had me move her to Tartarus?"

The hooded judges turned their heads back and forth, checking with each other.

"What proof do you have of this?" the middle one asked.

"I took her there. She was my human boyfriend's sister. She died a month ago from a brain aneurysm. You determined she belonged in the Elysian Fields, but he overruled your judgment to punish me."

They murmured among themselves for a few minutes. Hades was in charge here, so maybe appealing to these three was pointless, but it seemed like I'd struck a nerve.

Finally, the middle judge spoke. "Hades is the ruler here. We are meant to pass judgment. That is all. If Hades desires to have a soul moved, he has that right. While we stand by our decision, we will not speak against our lord." He motioned to Melodie. "Now, please escort this soul to her afterlife."

"You don't even care that Melodie wasn't supposed to die? That Hades killed her?"

"We do not determine who dies or when they die. We only judge the life they lived and decide what afterlife would be most suitable."

This wasn't working. If I wanted Hades to bring Melodie back, I was going to have to talk to him directly and be prepared to offer something big in exchange.

I took Melodie by the arm and led her through the palace doors.

"Jodi, what's happening? Where are you taking me? What are the Fields of whatever they called it?" Her voice was riddled with panic.

"Don't worry. I'm going to get you out of here. You weren't supposed to die. Hades was looking for me, but he found you first. He's using you to get to me. I'll talk to him, make him fix this." I wasn't sure I could, but what else was I supposed to say to her?

"Is the place I'm going bad? Did I do something wrong to end up here?"

I stopped walking and hugged her tightly. "You didn't do anything wrong. You're a good person. I'm going to make this right." I still wasn't sure how, but I wasn't going to stop until she was out of this place. Maybe Amber's time really had come, but Melodie's hadn't. I'd find a way to fix this.

Her tears wet my shoulder, but I let her cry. She had every right to be upset, and I wasn't going to rush her off to the Fields of Asphodel where she'd forget who she was. When she finally pulled away and wiped her eyes, she gave me a questioning look.

"Why did you steal my car that day at the park? You were acting so strange. Not at all like yourself."

"I know. A lot's happened. I've changed. I'm not the same person anymore. I didn't mean to steal your car, but you wouldn't keep away from me, and I didn't want to hurt you."

"You don't think stealing my car and abandoning me in the park without a cell phone hurt me?"

"I know it did, and I'm so sorry. But believe me, Mel, I saved your life that day. I can't explain how, so I need you to just take my word for it. I love you. You're my best friend, and I did what I needed to do to protect you." I look down at my shoes. "I'd do it again if I had to."

"Was I supposed to die sooner or something? Did you take my car so I couldn't get into a car accident? Are you psychic?" She wasn't going to stop questioning me.

"Remember I said I found my dad?"

She nodded.

"Well, I found out he's not quite…" I took a deep breath, and on the exhale, I blurted out, "…human."

Her head jerked back like someone punched her in the jaw. "Is this a joke?"

"Look where we are. Do you really think I'd joke at a time like this?"

She sighed. "Okay, explain."

"My dad is something called an Ophi. It's a type of necromancer descended from Medusa and born under the thirteenth sign of the zodiac."

Her eyes widened. "Do you mean what Mr. Quimby was teaching us about?"

"Yes! Tony—I mean, Mr. Quimby is an Ophi, too. And so am I."

"Whoa." She raised her hands between us. "You're telling me you're a necromancer?"

I nodded. "Remember Mr. Quimby taught us about the blood on the left side of Medusa's body being poisonous? Well, my blood is poisonous to humans. That's why I left you in the park. I was afraid I'd hurt you." My body shook as I breathed. I had to tell Melodie the truth about Matt. I had to tell her I killed the guy she was in love with when he kissed me.

"This is crazy, you know that." She said it as a statement, not a question.

"There's more. When I found out what I am, I was planning to break up with Matt. I didn't want to risk hurting him. Only when we went outside—"

"The day he died?" Her face contorted, twisting in an expression of sheer horror. "*You*? You killed Matt?"

"Mel, I'm so sorry. He kissed me, and before I could stop him…it was too late. I tried to use the part of my powers that can raise the dead, but I didn't know what I was doing. Please, believe me. I never meant to hurt him." I reached for her, but she backed away.

"Don't touch me." She looked at my hands like they were radioactive waste.

"I can't hurt you here."

"Apparently, you can." She was right. I'd broken her heart…again. First, I'd stolen the guy she was in love with, and then I'd killed him.

"Mel—"

"Is he here? Will I see him?"

"No." The word was barely a whisper. "I raised his soul. He deserved another chance at life."

"How? If you couldn't do it before, how did you do it now?"

"I'm more powerful now. I can do a lot of things. I even raised half of my own soul. The human half."

Her eyes widened. "You're with him now, aren't you? The human you, I mean. My God! You killed him, and he still wants to be with you! Unbelievable!"

"It's not like that. I'm with Alex." Only I'd been making out with Matt when my consciousness was pulled back into my Ophi soul.

"Alex? Is he that guy you ran off with?"

"Yes. He's here. We're being punished by Hades."

"Good." That word, and her look of pure hatred, barreled into me. "Mel."

"I'm sorry, Jodi, but look what you've done. You killed Matt. You killed me."

"I didn't kill you. Hades did."

"To get back at you. That's what you told those freaky hooded guys. Same difference." She crossed her arms. "I can't believe I was ever friends with you."

Hades knew this would happen. He knew Melodie would hate me for everything I'd done. For what I'd become. Deep down, she must have always resented me, even when we were friends. She'd wanted Matt, but he turned her down because he was into me. Even though it wasn't my fault, she held it against me, and I couldn't really blame her.

I hadn't even noticed she had feelings for Matt until I was about to break up with him. What kind of friend was I?

"I don't know what to say to make you understand. I didn't ask for any of this to happen. I was happy with you and Matt and my mom. Things were just about perfect. This got sprung on me."

"Am I supposed to hug you and tell you it's okay?" She narrowed her eyes at me. "Because it's not okay. Even if you don't mean to kill someone, they're still dead. You can't undo it."

"Yes, I can. I'm a necromancer. I brought Matt back. He looks different now because he's in a different body. But he's okay. He saw his mom."

"His sister is dead. Do you know that? Does he?"

"Yes." I lowered my eyes.

"Are you responsible for her death, too?"

"No!" My God, she thought I was a monster.

"Sorry, but I can't believe that. Everyone around you is dead or some freaky undead creation of yours." Her face went stone cold. "You deserve whatever punishment Hades is giving you. You deserve to rot in Hell!"

# Chapter 24

My throat constricted, squeezing the air out of me. My best friend hated me. Thought I was some killer or psycho necromancer. Nothing I said was going to change her mind. Maybe she was right. Maybe I did deserve what I was getting.

"I'll take you to the Fields of Asphodel." I didn't look at her. I just started walking again, hoping she'd follow. If she didn't, Chase or even Hades might show up, and they'd make her pay for being disobedient. Even if she hated me, Melodie didn't deserve any of this. She wasn't supposed to die yet. This was my fault. I glanced behind me to make sure she was following. She kept her eyes glued to the ground, and I thought I saw a tear drip down her cheek. Was she crying because she knew she wasn't supposed to be here? Was she scared? Or did she feel bad about the way things between us were ending?

Alex's figure came into view, and his face lit up when he saw me. I wondered if he always reacted to me this way. When I was focused on my human soul, I couldn't tell what was happening here. How many times had I disappointed Alex by coming up to him without really being here? It seemed like I was disappointing everyone these days.

Arianna reached for Melodie's hand, not paying much attention to me, probably because she didn't know I was fully here. "Thanks, Ari."

She did a double take before throwing her arms around me. "It's so good to see you. Are you okay? Is everything going all right up there?" She looked up, not that we could see anything but black sky.

"I'm fine. Things are going slowly, but I'm meeting Mason again soon." How soon? How long had I been down here? "I need to get back there so I don't miss our appointment."

"Can you stay for a minute?" Alex asked.

Arianna released her grip on me and put her arm around Melodie. "Come, dear. I'll show you where you're supposed to be."

"That's just it, Ari. She shouldn't be here." I turned to Alex. "Do you remember Melodie?"

He nodded. "Hades." The word said it all. Alex knew he'd taken Melodie.

"It's so unfair. I don't know what to do to make this stop."

A gust of wind blew all around us. We shielded our eyes as it stirred up the ashes that paved the way to the Fields. Without opening my eyes, I knew Hades was here.

"Did I hear you say you don't know how to make this stop?" He touched down in front of me, and his swirling black smoke performed a trick I hadn't seen yet. It didn't just dissolve. It became a black suit jacket.

"You're all dressed up with nowhere to go." I wasn't in the mood for niceties. I was majorly pissed.

"On the contrary. I'm dressed for dear Melodie's funeral." His hand grazed Melodie's cheek, and she pulled away. Her face was bright red where he'd touched her, where he'd burned her.

"Don't touch her!" I stepped toward him, grabbing Melodie and pulling her behind me. "You killed her. She wasn't supposed to die. Are you so pathetic that you have to stoop to killing innocent people to lure me back here?"

He smirked and leaned down so he was right in my face. "Are you so inhuman that you are willing to allow me to kill so many of your former loved ones while you continue to plot against me? Why don't you tell Melodie how the lives of the Ophi mean more to you than hers?"

Melodie gasped behind me.

"Don't listen to him, Mel. He's just trying to make you hate me. Remember, he's the one who killed you. This is his sick game."

"No, Jodi Marshall. It's yours. You started it when you raised your human soul." He walked around Alex, invading his personal space and running his fingers across Alex's shoulder and back, finally resting on his other shoulder. He clamped down, and his hand burst into flame. Alex collapsed under the pain, falling to his knees.

"Stop!" I reached for Hades, willing my blood to mix. When our hands met, the heat was intensified. Hades let go of Alex and laced his fingers through mine.

"You have some fire power of your own, I see." My hand burned against his. Most of the heat was coming from him, but he was right. I could make myself hot to the touch when I mixed my blood. "Very interesting." The flames on his hand doubled, and I yanked out of his grip. "Still no match for me, though." He blew on his hand, extinguishing it.

I held my hand, palm up, examining the blisters on my skin. Damn, that hurt.

"Tell me, Jodi Marshall. Will you choose to stay in exchange for Melodie's life?" He turned and held his hand out like he was asking me if I wanted the prize behind door number one. "Or do I need to kill your mother next?"

"Don't touch my mother!" My blood hadn't even simmered down before it was raging once again.

"If that's what you wish, then simply release the human half of your soul, and your mother will remain safe." He walked over to Melodie. "But I think, because of your outburst, I'll keep this soul for myself." He gently patted Melodie's hair.

"You're always changing the rules, and you make sure every deal you make has you come out the winner, no matter what."

He held his hands behind his back, looking totally at ease. "When you made the deal with me that night in the cemetery, you thought you'd outsmarted me. And if you want to be technical, *you* were the one who breached that deal. You raised souls that were off-limits to you."

"I didn't mean to. My powers were out of control thanks to you and Chase. You sent him after me. How was that playing by the rules?"

"Easy," Alex whispered, standing at my side, still holding his burned shoulder.

"I never said I wouldn't try to tempt you with more power." He said it so matter-of-factly, like he believed he'd done nothing wrong. Maybe that was the problem. Hades was unaccountable for his actions. He didn't answer to anyone.

"You're basing your argument on a technicality? Is that the best you can do?" I stopped mixing my blood. Instead, I pushed all the poisoned blood to one corner of my body and focused on the life-restoring part of my power. I touched Alex's shoulder. At first, his face scrunched in pain, but then it eased. He smiled at me.

"Thanks." I'd healed his burn. I did the same thing to my left hand, healing the blisters.

"Impressive. I was under the impression only Medusa could heal the Ophi." Something in those words made my brain spin into overdrive. Medusa. Hades hated that we had her soul. She was so powerful, and when she died, that power should've been turned over to him. Only we kept it, with her soul, locked in the statue. The statue. I was right. Medusa had the answers I needed. She *was* the answer.

"I'm a lot like Medusa. But you already know that, don't you?" I narrowed my eyes at him. "That's why you've been gunning for me. After we made our initial deal, you found out about my special connection to Medusa. You realized that I could give you what she never did. That's the real reason you want me here. To drain my powers and keep them for yourself."

"And the prize goes to…" He laughed. "Just because you figured out why I want you dead doesn't mean you can stop me from getting what I want." He waved his hand, and Melodie shot backward. The gate to the Fields of Asphodel flew open, and she was hurled inside. It was terrible to watch, but even worse to hear. Instead of screaming, she yelled my name. She wanted me to help her, but I just watched her go.

"You know, Jodi Marshall, I could make this worth your while." Hades circled me, stopping directly behind me on the second time around. With a wave of his hand, Matt's image appeared next to Alex. Hades leaned toward my right ear and whispered. "Which one of them do you truly love? Are you happy with Matt right now?" His hot breath sent chills down my neck and spine. "I could make Matt human again in his own body, and you could stay human, too. All you'd need to do is relinquish your Ophi soul to me. This would all end. No more torture. You'd have the normal life you've always wanted."

I did want a normal life. I wanted the pain and suffering to end. This war with Hades couldn't go on. We'd all end up dead. I'd already lost so much. My blood tingled in my veins, almost as if it was speaking to me, begging me not to give in to Hades, to what was easy.

"I'll give you until tomorrow night to decide. After that, it's all-out war." He walked around me so we were face to face again. "I've been going easy on you, but if you don't agree to this offer, you'll see a different side of me. And rest assured, I will get what I want, one way or another." He waved his hand, and his suit jacket once again swirled around him in a cloud of smoke until he was gone. Matt's image was also gone.

Alex rushed to me, taking my hands. "What did he whisper to you? And what was with the image of Matt?"

"He wants to make a deal with me."

Alex's eyebrows rose. "Another deal?"

"I know. I'm getting really sick of them."

Alex's face hardened as he pieced together what the deal was. "He wants you to choose Matt and stay human." He nodded. "Maybe you should do it."

"What? No!" I cupped his face in my hands. "Alex, I won't leave you here."

"You do know that's not the same as telling me you love me." He was questioning my feelings for him. He thought my human emotions had taken control of me. That I wanted Matt now.

Arianna turned away, giving us a little privacy.

"I do love you. Nothing is going to change that." Change it, no, but it wasn't exactly that simple, either. I'd been kissing Matt before I came here. I couldn't deny I had feelings for him. Even though it was my human soul acting on those emotions, I'd still technically cheated on Alex. After the whole thing with Chase, I didn't know if Alex could handle this too.

"Alex, there's something I have to tell you. It's been eating me up inside." I wasn't sure which shook more, my voice or my hands. Alex laced his fingers through mine, giving me the strength to continue.

"When I'm focused on my human soul, it's like I'm a different person. The person I would've been if I hadn't come into my powers."

He stared at me, letting me get this out in my own time.

I felt my blood bubbling under my skin. God, how could I ever give up that feeling? The power? Alex? All of this? "I'm like two people. When I'm here with you, I want nothing but you. I want to be Ophi for the rest of my life." Tears trickled down my cheek, and Alex raised our hands to wipe them away. "But when I'm human, I can't help having human emotions. I feel what I felt before all this happened."

"You feel what you felt for Matt." His voice was soft and full of hurt.

He knew? "How did you—?"

"Tony told me. He said all your feelings for Matt would resurface. That the longer you two were together, the more you'd remember how you used to love him. And when he saw you with Matt's sister…"

"I didn't love him, at least not like that. I think I could have. No. I know I could have if I hadn't met you. But I *did* meet you, and I love you, Alex."

"It's okay, Jodi. I'm not mad. That's not who you are anymore. This is you. Right here, with me." He leaned forward and pressed his lips to mine. I melted into him. This was what I wanted. I deepened the kiss, wanting to lose myself in him.

He gently pulled away, looking off into the distance. "Unless you want to take Hades up on his offer. You'd be free from all of this. He'd leave you alone."

"No. I don't ever want to be free from you. Not having you would be worse than being in Hell."

He pulled me to him again, wrapping his arms around me. "You're running out of time. The longer you're away, the more pissed-off Hades gets."

"I know. I'm going to Mason and then straight to Medusa. I'll have an answer tonight." I had to. Otherwise, Mom was dead. Hades would take her, and I'd be parentless.

"I wish there was something I could do to help you. Do you think there's any way you could raise me? I mean, I've died before."

"No way. It would probably kill you, and in a way I wouldn't be able to fix." I rubbed his arms. "I refuse to lose you, too."

"I can't imagine Matt's really been a help to you."

No, it was more like I was helping him, and he was confusing the hell out of me. "He's trying to get used to being human in someone else's body. While I'm waiting to hear back from Mason, I'm getting Matt set up for his new life."

"Does he understand you won't be in it?" That was the million-dollar question.

I lowered my eyes. I couldn't lie to him.

"That's what I thought. Even the nice guy can become *that* guy when the girl he loves is on the line." He sighed, trying to stay calm.

"He feels lost right now. He's scared, and I understand that. He's going to outlive everyone around him. It's depressing. I can't help wondering if I made a mistake bringing him back. Maybe he doesn't want this for himself. Maybe I'm just torturing him more."

Guilt welled up inside me. Here I was in the underworld, where Alex and my friends—no, my *family*—were suffering. They were in real pain, and I was worried about making my former human boyfriend immortal.

Alex didn't say anything. He was trying to handle my feelings for Matt the best he could, but it was tearing him up inside. Once again, I was hurting him.

I leaned into him and pressed my cheek to his chest. "This will all be over soon, and then we'll be together again."

I wasn't sure if he believed me. He didn't agree or disagree. He didn't stroke my hair or try to kiss me.

I stepped back, studying his face, trying to judge what he was feeling.

He nodded over my shoulder. "Chase is coming this way with a soul. You should go."

I knew he meant back to my human soul. Tune out everything here and return to my plan to free us all. Of course, that meant returning to Matt and all those feelings, too.

# Chapter 25

I wasn't in any condition to deal with Chase right now, so as I stared at Alex, I let myself slip out of my Ophi soul and back into my human one. Back into Liz's body.

"Jodi?" Matt shook my shoulders. "Can you hear me?"

I opened my eyes and sat up. The sun was lower in the sky. How long had I been gone? "What time is it?"

"Six-thirty. I was getting really worried. You haven't moved in hours. Were you back there…with him?"

"Six-thirty?" I jumped to my feet. "We have to go. We're late. Mason is waiting for me, and I have to figure this all out tonight."

"Slow down." Matt was on his feet now. He grabbed my hand, holding me back. "Tell me what happened."

"I'll explain in the car. Come on. We need to go!" I ran for the car, willing my legs to move faster than they wanted to. Luckily, Liz was in good shape. I flung the door open the second I heard the car unlock. I was in my seat with my seatbelt on before Matt even got his door open. "Seriously, step on it!"

I started the car and peeled out of the parking lot. We raced to Serpentarius and I prayed we didn't run into any cops along the way. For once, luck was on my side.

"Now tell me what happened." Matt flashed me a stern look.

"Hades took Melodie, and he's going after my mom if I don't agree to his latest deal by tomorrow night."

"Melodie?" Matt choked out.

"I know. It was awful. I brought her to the Fields of Asphodel, and I told her the truth about me. She blames me for everything, and she should. She died because of me."

"Don't do that. This isn't your fault."

I really wished people would stop sticking up for me. This *was* my fault. "Please, don't defend me."

He shook his head, not happy that I wasn't taking his word for it. "What was the new deal?"

God, I really didn't want to tell him. "He wants me to give him my Ophi powers and go back to being human for good."

Matt's eyes widened, and a hint of a smile crossed his lips.

"Don't." I turned away from him. "I'm not discussing it. I can't let Hades take all those Ophi just to save myself. I won't do it. And if you ask me to, I'll only end up resenting you for it. Besides, I still have to go back to get Amber out of Tartarus." I knew he wouldn't argue with that last part.

He stayed quiet for the rest of the drive. I pulled into the club's designated lot around the back, and I jumped out of the car as soon as it was parked. I ran for the back door and knocked, hoping that was where I'd find Mason. The door had to be outside his office.

I pounded on the door, yelling, "Mason, it's Jodi! Open up!"

Matt had caught up when Mason opened the door. "You're late. I thought…never mind. You're here now." He stepped aside and ushered us in.

We headed straight to his office so we could talk without a bunch of Ophi ears listening in on the conversation. Mason had recruited a new group of Ophi after the others came to the school with me. I didn't even sit. I stood at his desk with my arms crossed.

"What did you find out? I'm on a serious time crunch."

Mason's eyes flew to mine. "Did he threaten Carol? Is she hurt?"

"She's okay. Hades killed my best friend—my human best friend, and he's going after my mom if I don't end this by tomorrow night."

Relief washed over Mason's face. He sat down and formed a triangle with his hands. "The only way out of this war is to make another deal with Hades. But you need to come up with something so huge and airtight that he can't get out of it. There can't be loopholes."

"What could I possibly offer him that he'd want badly enough to give up the other Ophi souls and promise to stop coming after me?" It seemed impossible. I needed something solid, not more cryptic Ophi garbage.

"I don't know. No one's been able to come up with anything big enough. But we all did come to the same conclusion."

"What's that?"

"You have to connect to the Medusa statue."

I had to suppress the urge to scream at Mason. Why had I given him a day, when he hadn't come up with anything I didn't already know?

"I'm going to Medusa right after we're finished, which I guess we are because you haven't told me anything I don't know."

"I'm sorry, Jodi. I did the best I could." He held up a finger. "I did find something that will help you, though."

"What?" Was he holding out on me? I didn't have time for this.

"Medusa will recognize your soul, even in human form." There was more. I could tell.

"But?"

"She will attack you until that recognition is made." He looked down at me. "You may not survive the initial contact."

"May not? You're not sure?"

"No. You are a direct descendent of hers, which means you have a better chance of her sensing your soul, even in human form."

"What about in someone else's human form?" I motioned to Liz's body.

"Yes, that does add to the complication."

"Still, I don't have a choice. I have to go see her."

"No way," Matt said. "You can't be serious. You might die, and then everyone is screwed. You're the last hope your people have—that *I* have—and you're willing to throw that all away?" His eyes pleaded with me, but I held strong.

"If I don't try this, everyone *will* die. There's no 'if' about it." I looked back and forth between Matt and Mason. "I'm the Chosen One. Even if it kills me, I have to do this. I'm the only one who can."

Mason nodded. He understood, but Matt was a different story.

"I'm not letting you. I'm sorry, Jodi. I won't let you sacrifice yourself."

"You don't have a choice, son." Mason was out of his seat and standing next to Matt, threatening him with his poisonous blood.

"Mason, no!" I stared at him in horror. The Ophi from Serpentarius didn't believe in actively using their powers. They even worked with humans, keeping their distance of course, but still. And yet, here was Mason, ready to kill Matt to save our kind. More specifically, to save Carol.

"Don't hurt him, please." I reached toward Mason. "He doesn't understand. That's all. But I'll make him see this is necessary."

"No, you won't," Mason and Matt both said.

Matt crossed his arms. "You may as well let him kill me because I'm not letting you do this."

Mason held his hand out over Matt's shoulder, and his other hand reached for the letter opener on his desk. He was ready to shed his blood and end Matt's life.

"Matt, please. I don't want you to die. I brought you back to give you the shot at life you were supposed to have. Don't make all that be for nothing."

"I don't want all that. I don't want to be here. I'm not supposed to be. I died kissing you. Yeah, it sucked that we couldn't be together and that I missed out on college and finding out who or what I'd become. But *this*," he patted his chest, "isn't me. I wasn't meant to be immortal. It's obvious you love Alex. You're willing to do anything to save him. The few moments we've had together have been amazing, but they aren't who you really are. I've felt that." He ran his fingers through his hair. "I mean, you went back to Alex *while* we were kissing. If that doesn't say it all, then I don't know what does. You've made your choice, and if you're going to go through with it, then you're going to have to end my life now."

My body shook, and since I didn't have Gorgon blood running through Liz's veins, I knew it was from the pain of knowing Matt was right. I'd basically turned him into a monster. I couldn't blame him for not wanting this life.

"I'm so sorry." I stepped closer to him and took his hands in mine. "I thought I was doing the right thing bringing you back. I wanted to make up for—"

He pressed his finger to my lips. "You don't have to apologize or try to explain. I know you, Jodi. You have a good heart, and I've always loved you for it. I don't blame you for any of this."

"Is this really what you want?"

"I want you to be happy."

I choked back the tears that burned my throat. He really was perfect.

I met Mason's eyes, and we silently agreed that Matt deserved better than this existence.

I squeezed Matt's hands. "I want you to know that I do love you. The human in me will always love you." I didn't let him respond. I pressed my lips to his, and when I did, Mason cut his hand and gently touched Matt's shoulder.

His body slumped forward, and I held him up for a second before crumpling to the floor with him. He was dead. For good this time. I cried on his shoulder for several minutes, and Mason stepped out of the office to give me some privacy. This wasn't just goodbye to Matt. It was goodbye to my human life. I knew now that I couldn't go back home to see Mom. I didn't trust Hades enough to believe he wouldn't take her early if he found me with her.

I let my tears speak for me as I cried for everything I'd lost. The people I loved and would never see again. I could've cried all night, but I somehow managed to find the strength to stand, and when I did, Mason was there to help me up.

He held me by the shoulders and stared deep into my eyes. I couldn't help noticing his hand was already bandaged. "I'll take care of the body. You go to Medusa and end this thing once and for all."

"I'll bring Carol back to you. I won't let you feel like I feel now. I won't let you lose someone you love."

He nodded and let go of me. I turned for the door, but he called my name. "Jodi, don't forget that, once you stop being human, you have someone who loves you more than anything."

"I know. Alex is a huge part of why I'm doing this."

Mason gave me a weak smile, and I left. I had been in such a hurry that I'd left the keys in the ignition. Good thing, too, because I wouldn't have been able to go back in there and see Matt's body on the floor of Mason's office. I drove out of the parking lot and across town.

Finding the school was going to be a little tough. I'd only driven directly to it once with Alex. When I stole Melodie's car, I'd tried to find the dirt road leading to the school, but it turned out it wasn't a road at all, and I'd crashed the car into a tree.

When I knew I was close, I slowed down, peering through every opening in the woods, looking for the road. I passed several trails and almost turned onto one, but at the last second, I straightened out the wheel and kept driving. I was going on instinct, which felt more than a little odd since I wasn't an Ophi right now. Still, I waited until I got a feeling. It happened about half a mile down the road. I felt a tightness in my chest. When I looked toward the trees, there was a road, barely visible. I slowed even more and turned down it.

The bumpiness was familiar. This had to be it. My poor mom's car bounced and protested against the rough terrain. I hoped I wasn't doing any major damage to it. Finally, I saw the cemetery. This was it. I pulled up behind the row of cars. The first two belonged to Ethan and Carson. The third was Chase's red sports car. As I got out of Mom's car and sprinted past the others, I resisted the urge to stop and key Chase's hot little number. I didn't have time.

I ran up the steps to the front doors and yanked them open. Since Hades had taken us all while we were here, the doors were still unlocked. I stopped when I saw the golden statue. Even though I knew it well, I was still in awe of it. If it wasn't for the serpents on Medusa's head, the statue would've been gorgeous. Every time I'd been near the statue in the past, I'd felt drawn to it. My blood recognized Medusa's soul inside, and I felt a pull. Now, I felt nothing, and it made my heart ache.

If I couldn't feel Medusa, maybe it meant she couldn't feel me now, either. And what would she do when I touched the statue? She'd killed Abby when Abby insulted her by joining both hands with her. If she thought a human was touching her sacred statue…I couldn't even think about how she might end my life. For a moment, I wondered if I should try holding just one of the statue's hands first. Kind of test the waters. Her right hand had life-restoring power. But Medusa knew me by the special connection we had. The way I could hold both her hands instead of one at a time.

I had to do everything exactly as I had when I was an Ophi. That was my only hope of her recognizing my soul. No, wait! There was something else I could do. I ran past the statue and up the stairs, straight to my bedroom. I'd left the locket here. Medusa's locket. I'd been so angry about everything that happened between Chase and me, and I'd blamed the locket—or at least the moment when I let Chase put it on me. I searched my dresser drawers, not remembering where I'd put it. How had I lost track of something so important?

Chase had done a number on me. He'd made me question everything about myself. The only good part about this situation now was that I wasn't around him. I hated him for making me hurt Alex, for making me become so consumed by power that I'd lost sight of Medusa for a while.

I ransacked my bed next, remembering that, in my state of sobbing, I'd taken it off there. I flung the sheets and blankets to the floor and even checked in between the mattress and box spring. Nothing. Where was it? I picked up each blanket, shaking them in case the locket was tangled up inside. When I reached the bedspread, something fell to the floor with a small tinkling sound.

I looked down to see my locket. The beautiful bloodstone, which no longer had blood in it, was now mostly green. If only Medusa's blood was still inside. Maybe I could've drunk it and made her recognize me before she stopped my heart. But then again, I didn't have Gorgon blood in my veins right now, and that meant the locket wouldn't open for me, no matter how hard I tried. I had to hope wearing the locket would be enough. I put it on, making sure the clasp was tight. I couldn't take any chances. My life would depend on Medusa sensing her own power lingering in this necklace.

I looked down at the bloodstone, wishing I felt something, anything, now that it was around my neck. But I didn't.

I walked back downstairs very slowly, gathering my courage. The stairs seemed to go on forever, and the statue looked bigger than ever as I approached it. My heart raced, and my hands shook. It was surreal that I was nervous about talking to Medusa. She was my ancestor, my family.

I stood in front of her and spoke aloud, clutching the locket in my right hand. "Medusa, if you can hear me, it's Jodi. I know I look a little different right now, but this was the only way I could come see you. I need your help to save the others. I need to connect to your statue so we can talk and figure out how to defeat Hades once and for all. If you could avoid…killing me, I'd really appreciate it. I'm sort of counting on you recognizing my soul quickly, which is why I'm wearing your locket. *Our* locket. We are one and the same now. Even in this body, you must be able to see me."

I let go of the locket and inched my hands toward the statue. This was it. I might die. "Please, Medusa," I pleaded as my hands slipped into hers.

At first, nothing happened. I thought maybe Medusa's soul had no effect on humans. I opened my mouth to talk to her, but an intense pain shot through my hands, up my arms, and into my chest. My lungs and heart clenched as if they were being shocked. The pain traveled up my neck and to my brain.

My eyes rolled back into my head, and I blacked out.

# Chapter 26

Silence. That's all there was. The air around me was completely still. I couldn't feel my body, and all I saw was darkness. Was I dead? Had Medusa killed me? I couldn't move, so I spoke with my mind. It was how Medusa and I had always communicated when we were connected by the statue.

"Medusa?"

No answer.

"Hades?" I wondered if I was back in the underworld. If Medusa had killed me, that was where I'd end up.

"No, child." Medusa's voice filled my mind. Peace washed over me. She was here. Even if I was dead, it was okay because Medusa was with me. She'd make sure I moved on safely.

"You aren't dead, Jodi."

"You know who I am. You recognized me."

"Yes, but not before I hurt you very badly. This body will no longer be able to serve as a host to you."

What? Where was I if I wasn't in Liz's body?

Through the connection, Medusa read my mind. "You are still inside your host body, but you won't be able to remain there. You need to reach out to another body nearby and put your human soul into it."

Oh, God. She'd destroyed Liz's body, made it so I couldn't use it anymore. And now that I was human, I couldn't raise my own soul. "I can't. I don't have any powers."

"I know you are weak, but I can help you."

"Help me? I won't be able to do anything at all. You'll have to do it for me. My Ophi soul is in the underworld. I can't access it without going back there."

"No, you can't do that. I'm keeping your soul in this shell. If you return your focus to the underworld, I won't be able to hold your human soul here. It will move on." She shook her head, making the snakes hiss. "I can't raise a body for you, either. Not from inside this statue."

What else was there?

"You are tethered to the statue right now."

Tethered to the statue. Trapped like she was.

"Yes. In a way, that is true."

"If my human soul passes on, I'll be forced back into the underworld."

"Yes."

"I can't go yet. I don't know how to defeat Hades. That's why I'm here. Mason said I'd have to make a deal with him. One big enough to end all of this for good."

"I agree." Medusa lowered her head, giving me a good view of the snakes wriggling around.

The question was, what did Hades want?

"Me," Medusa answered my unspoken question.

"What do you mean you?"

"You know the deal the Ophi made with Hades for my soul."

I nodded. "Yes, they freed you from him. He can't touch you."

"Not while I'm locked in this statue." She held our hands out to the sides, and I could feel an unseen force keeping our arms from extending any further.

"Medusa, I don't understand. What are you saying?" She spoke in riddles most of the time. I needed answers, real answers, and fast.

"You must free me. Break the statue."

She couldn't be serious. The second I did, Hades would take her.

"Not if I'm inside another."

All this mind-reading was really making it difficult to think. "Inside another. How?"

"Think about it, Jodi. It's what you do, right?"

She wanted me to free her soul and then place it inside another body.

"Not just any body." She stared into my eyes, looking into my soul. "Your body, Jodi."

"*I'm* not even in my own body."

"But you could be." She gave me a brave smile. "You'd have to say goodbye to your human soul forever."

"Won't Hades torture it for all eternity? I'll have this double vision thing forever. I can't. It will drive me insane. You have no idea the torture I've gone through living in both souls."

"We can bury your human soul under your Ophi one, but for good this time. Deeper than before. You won't be able to access it ever again. It won't be easy."

Nothing I ever did was easy. "Okay, let's say I can do that, get my human soul back in my body and bury it there. How do you expect me to get you free?"

"I can give this body—"

"Her name was Liz." I didn't want to treat Liz's body like an empty shell or an old coat I was borrowing. Liz had helped me get to Medusa. Her body deserved to be taken care of and treated fairly. I hadn't done a good job of protecting it. The least I could do now was speak properly, respectfully, about it.

Medusa nodded. "I can give Liz's body enough power for you to remain inside it long enough to break the statue. Once my soul escapes, you'll need to let go. That's all. Liz's body doesn't want to hold you inside, and my power will wear off from the exertion. We'll go to the underworld together."

And Hades would sense Medusa's soul like a big, blinking, red light flashing the words "Come and get me!"

"You'll need to act quickly. Rebury your human soul and then find me. Call me to your own body. Force me inside. I will try not to resist you, no matter how unpleasant the experience is for me."

I knew what it felt like to be forced into the wrong body. It was painful and…well, I didn't want to think about putting Medusa through that.

"Don't worry about me. It won't be pleasant for you, either. You'll have both our souls fighting for control of your body."

"Fighting? Why would we fight?"

"Perhaps fighting isn't the right word. We'll be at odds with one another. You'll have to unite us."

My head wanted to explode. How was I supposed to unite two souls inside my body?

"Think about how you split your soul. This will be the exact opposite."

Great. That cleared things up...not at all.

"What will all of this do? Why put your soul inside my body?" She was leaving me out of half the plan, maybe more.

"Hades will recognize my soul inside you. He'll also know you are too powerful for him to threaten. You'll have the upper hand."

"To make another deal?"

"Yes. And this is where you need to be very clear. The deal must be my soul for the safety of all Ophi for all time. You must make him understand that, if he should break his end of the deal in any way—*as deemed by you*—that you will regain control of my soul once again, and we'd be more powerful than he wants to deal with."

Could I do that? Could I make demands of a god? I was only one Ophi—well, two with Medusa sharing my body.

"I wouldn't ask you to do this if it wasn't possible."

Okay, maybe it was possible. Difficult but possible. There was still one major problem, though. "Medusa, I can't let you sacrifice yourself for us. The Ophi need you. They wouldn't have made that deal with Hades ages ago if you weren't important to our survival."

"That was before you came along, Jodi. My blood is in your veins. You can be what I used to be to the Ophi. I'm no longer needed."

"No. I can't let you do this. You're like a mother to me." I was already losing my mom again. Now that Liz's body was destroyed—or would be after Medusa's power wore off it—I couldn't even say goodbye to her. How could I give up Medusa, too?

Medusa smiled warmly. "Your loyalty and affection are much appreciated, my child. But you will come to learn that, when you lead, you must make sacrifices. I believe you've already had to make sacrifices of your own."

Definitely. I'd sacrificed Matt, Melodie, and my entire former life, including Mom.

"See, you know why I have to do this, and you must also know that I *want* to do this. You are the future, Jodi. I see that. I'm grateful for the time I was given with you and the other Ophi, but that time has come to an end. My power lies in your veins. You can provide the connection my statue once did."

Have the Ophi connect powers with me? Become the next Medusa? This was crazy. I was nowhere near what Medusa was.

"Yes, you are, Jodi. Why do you think everyone around you wants to protect you? Why do you think Matt, Alex, and Chase all fell in love with you?"

"Chase?" My voice squeaked. "He hates me. He tortured me."

"Because Hades made him. You saw glimpses of the way he used to be. Against my advice, you held on to those rare moments. He showed them to you, alone, because he loved you. My guess is he still does, whether he is showing it or not."

Now I really felt sick. I couldn't forgive Chase for what he'd done to me, Alex, and the others.

"Sometimes punishment is necessary. Hades is not wrong about that."

"Why would you say that? You make him seem like he's justified for torturing souls."

"It's about consequences. Every action has a consequence. Hades used to make those consequences become a reality. If you make this deal with him, he will do that once again."

"You think he's a fair god?" He was anything but in my mind.

"I think he once was, before he became threatened by the Ophi. Much of that was my fault. By keeping my soul here, the Ophi were disrupting the power balance. Hades felt threatened. His reaction may not have been fair, but it was a consequence we brought forth."

"What will he do with your soul if I agree to this?"

Medusa was quiet, which meant I wasn't going to be happy with her answer. Hades hated the Ophi. He wouldn't go easy on Medusa.

"He's wanted my soul for a very long time. It will give him a lot of power."

"What if that power is enough to undo the deal I make with him?"

"You'll have to make sure that's not possible. The deal must be solid. No loopholes."

This was too risky. I could lose Medusa in addition to losing everyone else I loved. "I can't. Hades would want us to do this. He wants to get his hands on you."

"That may be true, but we are out of options. We must join forces. If we don't, Hades will kill your mother and then all your friends."

She was right. I couldn't let everyone die—even if it meant giving up the one person who had given me my powers.

Medusa tilted her head to the side and looked at me the same way Mom did when she was proud of me. "You said goodbye to your mother. You found the strength to stay away from her to keep her safe. You can do this, too."

"How do you have so much faith in me?"

"Because you are one of mine. I wouldn't ask you to do this if I thought you'd fail."

Failure wasn't an option. Hades would get all our souls if that happened.

I took a deep breath, which isn't at all necessary when you're just a soul stuck inside a reanimated body. "Tell me what to do."

Medusa smiled. "You make me proud, Jodi Marshall."

"Before we do this, I just want you to know that I'll never forget all you've done for me. I can't thank you enough."

"You don't need to. You are saving my people. Even after Hades claims me, I will live on in each and every one of you. Mostly in you."

If souls could cry, I'd have been bawling by that point.

"Now." She squeezed my hands, sending a burst of life-restoring power to Liz's body. "This should give your host body enough strength to break the statue."

"Which brings me to the big question. How do I break solid gold?"

"The statue isn't solid. If it was, my soul wouldn't be able to exist inside it."

Well, that helped, but I was still confused as to how to do it.

"You only need to make a crack in the statue, and I'll do the rest of the work. Find some pliers, and break one of the fingers off the statue. I should be able to squeeze out of the opening."

I nodded, but my insides twisted at the thought of destroying any part of the statue I'd grown to love.

"Be quick about it, Jodi. My power won't sustain Liz's body for long. If your soul releases before you free me, I won't be able to help you."

"Got it."

She sent one more wave of power to Liz's body before smiling and saying, "Good luck."

This felt too much like a goodbye. There was an enormous chance that I'd fail miserably. Still, I had to try.

"Thanks," I said, as her grip released from mine. Liz's body slumped to the floor, and for a moment, I thought Medusa's power hadn't been enough to sustain her. I looked at the statue and forced myself to my feet. I wasn't giving up. I'd drag the body if I had to. I used the walls to make my way to the closet in the hallway. Arianna kept tools in there. I found the pliers in the toolbox on the bottom shelf.

I hobbled—the quickest pace I could manage—back to the statue. The mirror on the wall caught my eye, and I gasped. Liz's hair was fried, hanging off her scalp in huge chunks. Her skin was spotted with black, charred from Medusa's touch. I tore my eyes away from the mirror and moved toward the statue.

I held the pliers up to Medusa's right hand, opening them up and positioning her index finger between the pinchers. "Hurry, Medusa," I said, but then I choked. The power was draining from Liz's body. I used both hands to squeeze the pliers, but I couldn't hold on. My soul was trying to escape the decaying body.

My soul released, and I saw Liz's body slump forward onto the statue. As I spiraled through the air and to the underworld, I heard the pliers clatter to the floor.

# Chapter 27

I'd failed. My soul had released too soon, and Medusa was still trapped inside the statue. It was over. I had nothing left to bargain with Hades. He'd never let us out of the underworld. All of this had been for nothing. Matt was dead again. Melodie was dead. Everything was worse than it had been before. I cursed myself as the human half of my soul found its way back to the underworld.

I saw the River Styx beneath me. Most likely my body was in the palace. Either there or in Tartarus. I hoped I wasn't coming back in time for my daily torture. I'd had enough after I'd ruined the lives of so many people. Even Mom wasn't safe. Yes, coming back meant Hades wouldn't take her soul, but she had no idea that Matt was gone again. She had no idea that I wouldn't see her ever again. I'd stupidly allowed myself to think that Mom and I would be able to see each other on occasion, now that she knew the truth about me. I'd been stupid about a lot of things.

My soul soared over Cerberus' heads, which barked repeatedly at me. I felt myself being pulled toward the palace, toward my body, which was waiting to escort the next soul to the afterlife. Being able to move through the air like this was a lot like flying. I was more swirling white smoke than anything else; I could see what was happening around me, but I had no form. I wasn't like the other souls that came here, probably because my soul was split in half. It was hard to have any form at all when you weren't complete.

The palace doors opened as if they were expecting me. I tried to tell myself it was only coincidence, but the sinking feeling I had told me otherwise. Hades knew I was coming. I saw myself standing off to the side of the thrones, looking like a zombie, a shell of my former self. It was odd, considering that was my real body and my Ophi soul, yet I seemed more alive as a floating half-soul than the person I was staring at. What had happened to me?

Instead of rejoining my Ophi soul in my body, my human soul stopped in front of the judges. I hovered there, unable to move.

"What's going on?" My voice was like a faint echo. My soul was slowly taking on a human form being around my body, but I was transparent like a ghost.

The judges on the ends sat back in their chairs, while the one in the middle leaned forward. "Jodi Marshall, you are here to be judged. Await our decision."

"What? I'm not here to be judged. I had to return to my body. Right there." I tried to point, but my limbs weren't fully visible.

"Await your judgment," the middle judge repeated, only much louder this time.

Laughter behind the judges made me look up. Hades was seated in his throne and staring right at me. A young woman sat by his side. Persephone. It had to be her. I'd never seen her before, and even though I'd heard stories about her beauty, I was shocked at how stunning she truly was. Her hair, the color of grain, cascaded down to her shoulders, and she wore a crown of asphodels on her head. Chase was standing next to my body, practically drooling over Persephone. But how was she here? Mason had said this was her allotted time with Demeter. She should've been free from this hell.

"Welcome, Jodi Marshall." Hades' voice filled the palace. "You're earlier than I was expecting. Did things not go quite according to your plan?" He tapped his fingertips together, looking very pleased with himself.

He must have known what I had been doing before I came here. He knew I'd failed miserably, and now he was going to rub it in.

"Be careful, Hades. Your wife may think you missed me or something. Don't want to upset the Mrs., especially when she's not very fond of you as it is."

Hades gripped his armrests and glared at me. "Careful, soul. You are in no position to get me angry. I'm showing mercy by allowing my three judges to decide your fate."

"No one should be deciding my afterlife, because I'm not dead. This isn't me. Not all of me. You can't send half a soul to the afterlife." I directed my words to the judges. "Do you hear me? I'm not a full soul like this. You can't judge me. I need to get back inside my body, which is very much alive."

"'Very much' might be a stretch." Hades smiled again. "Victoria went kind of hard on you today. You look rather beaten and burned."

I studied my body again, wondering what would happen if I focused on my Ophi soul. Would this soul simply return to my body? It was worth a try. At this point, I was defenseless. Who knew? Maybe this plan was desperate enough to save me.

"Don't even think about it, Jodi." Hades was out of his seat and standing by my body. "I'm not allowing your human soul to return. You've owed me this half of your soul for months. I'm collecting what is due to me."

So that was it. The judges were allowing Hades to force my human soul to move on because, technically, I'd killed my human self. I was getting really tired of technicalities. If only I'd been able to get Medusa free. Maybe this would all have changed. Maybe I'd have a fighting chance.

The palace doors opened behind me, making me jump. I hadn't even realized they'd closed after I came here, and now an intense black cloud was sweeping into the palace and coming to rest in front of the judges. The smoke settled, and I saw the faces of my friends. All the Ophi from the school. Alex.

If only I could run to him, throw my arms around him, press my lips to his. But I was barely able to keep from falling through the palace floor.

"Welcome, my Ophi friends." Hades raised his arms wide in greeting. The gesture was full of sarcasm, as were the words. We weren't friends. We were sworn enemies now.

"What's going on, Hades? What game are you playing now?" I wasn't sure I was ready for his answer.

"Game?" He raised one hand to his chest and pretended to be offended. "Why, Jodi Marshall, I don't know what you mean. I just thought you'd like to see your friends one last time. Consider this my going-away present. A send-off party of sorts."

This was fun for him. He was going to torture me and make my friends watch. I eyed Persephone. She looked bored by all of this, as if it was an everyday event that didn't concern her in the least. She wasn't going to be any help to me. At least not in fighting Hades. When I first saw her there, I thought maybe I'd be able to use her hatred for Hades and how he'd kidnapped her to my advantage. I was wrong. She didn't want to be here at all, and she wasn't helping a single one of us.

"This must be really old for you, Persephone," I said. She looked up at me, surprised that anyone had addressed her.

"Don't talk to her!" Hades' voice shook the palace, and if I'd had any control over my soul or if I'd been inside my body, I would've had to steady myself like everyone else. But the one perk to being a floating, transparent soul was that I couldn't fall over. At least not from the ground shaking.

"Touchy subject." I nodded. "It's interesting how nothing in *our* lives is off-limits to you, but no one here is allowed to even mention Persephone. How'd you get her here, anyway? She's not supposed to be with you in the summer months."

Hades' face had surpassed being red and had reached purple. He was full of rage, and it was all directed at me. "Rhadamanthus, Minos, Aeacus, call down her judgment now! I want her out of here and in Tartarus, suffering for eternity like she deserves."

My God! If the judges sent me to Tartarus, I'd never have enough focus to return to my body and Ophi soul. The pain would be too intense to tune out. My human soul wasn't strong enough to block it. Even when my Ophi soul had been shielding this half of me from the torture going on here while I was back in the real world, I'd been sucked back here by it. My human soul wouldn't stand a chance. I stared at my body, all robotic and lifeless. It would stay that way forever.

More than anything, I wished I could get back inside my body, but Hades was keeping me frozen here. I wished I'd succeeded in freeing Medusa. I wished I could rip Hades' head off and feed it to Cerberus.

Everyone was yelling around me, but I heard Alex's voice above the others. "You can't send her to Tartarus. She hasn't done anything to deserve that kind of punishment."

Hades burst out laughing. "Now, that is the funniest thing I've heard in a long time. She's a necromancer."

"We have reached our decision," the middle judge said, leaning forward in his seat again.

If a soul could gulp, I would have. This was it. They were sentencing me. Would I really go to Tartarus?

"Jodi Marshall, we have reviewed your life and you will be sentenced to an afterlife in the Elysian Fields."

"What?" Hades and I both said, only he was on his feet and flames were sprouting from his dark hair and hands, sending plumes of black smoke into the air.

"This is impossible! She's done terrible things. She's tortured souls. She's killed humans. She belongs in Tartarus, being punished for her wrongdoings!" The flames on his head soared higher.

Persephone shook her head. "You are thinking of her Ophi soul. This is her human soul being judged. I'm not even here all the time, and I can see that." She turned away, resting her head on her hand on the armrest. "Idiot," she mumbled.

Hades' flames went out. He really did love her. She was awful to him, yet he loved her.

"That's your punishment," I said. "You kidnapped her, forced her to come here and leave her mother, so while you love her, she despises you."

He glared at me. "No one is free from punishment."

"Consequences." I used the word Medusa had. "Our actions have consequences."

"As unorthodox as this sounds," the middle judge said, "you may escort your human soul to the Elysian Fields."

"No!" Hades roared. "She will not be rewarded for her life, not even her human life."

"It is a fair judgment," the middle judge asserted. He waved his hand and an image of me floated in the air. "Watch and you will see." It showed me standing up for my mom when kids at the bus stop were making comments about how young she was to have a baby. I hadn't known it then, but Mom had witnessed the entire thing. Her face was streaked with tears, but she was smiling. She was proud of me. The image changed to Mom telling me she'd decided to homeschool me. I didn't argue. I hugged her, knowing it was best for her.

The next image surprised everyone. It was me in Liz's body. Hades slammed his fist down on his throne, most likely because he hadn't guessed what body I'd taken over. Had he been paying attention, he would've guessed it was Liz and her boyfriend. But he'd been too preoccupied with getting Persephone back here, however he'd managed to pull that off.

In Liz's body, I told Mom the truth about me. I put her mind at ease, explaining that I was okay. I'd given her peace of mind. The last image nearly tore me apart. I was in Mason's office with Matt. I turned to Alex. His face fell as he watched me say goodbye to Matt. As he watched me grant Matt's request to let him go. As he watched me give Matt the last thing he wanted from me—a kiss.

The image dissolved, and the middle judge spoke again. "Jodi put her own feelings aside for those she loved. She sacrificed herself when she thought she could help others. She deserves an afterlife in the Elysian Fields."

Alex didn't look at me. His eyes were glued to his shoes. Maybe the judges thought I'd acted admirably, but I'd definitely hurt Alex.

Hades stood. "I won't have it. You are missing one big part of Jodi's life. Her human soul is only half of her."

"Then allow her to return her human soul to her body, and we shall judge all of her when her time comes." The middle judge sat back as if that was the end of it. I knew differently.

"That soul is mine. She took it from me months ago. I will claim it now."

"Then our judgment stands." The judges fell silent. They were done. They couldn't overrule Hades. They'd given their judgment, but Hades didn't have to follow it.

"Chase, throw her in Tartarus!" Hades yelled.

Chase faltered. He looked at me, and I saw a glimpse of his former self again. Had Medusa been right? Did that part of him actually love me?

"Send her to the Fields of Asphodel," Alex said, stepping forward. I stared at him, wondering what he was doing. "If the judges believe she should be rewarded, and you think she should be punished, then compromise. Send her to the Fields of Asphodel. She'll soon forget who she is, and you won't have to worry about her anymore." Was that what Alex wanted, to not have to worry about me anymore? He didn't meet my eyes. "I'll take her there myself."

Hades stepped forward and stared into Alex's eyes. "You expect me to believe you don't have a plan in the works here? You're in love with her."

"Did you see that last image?" Alex's voice was full of rage.

"Alex, I—"

He held his hand up. "Don't. Just don't. It's over."

Hades smiled. "Well, isn't this interesting?" He rubbed the five o'clock shadow on his chin. "You know, I think I'm going to allow this. I'm feeling suddenly amused. You may escort your former girlfriend to the Fields of Asphodel."

"The human half of her was never my girlfriend." He emphasized the word *never*, and the full impact of it hit me like a knife to my chest.

Hades laughed. "I love it. I have to say this is probably the best punishment after all. Being sentenced by the one you love—no, no, being denied and condemned to losing all sense of *yourself* by the one you love."

There was nothing left for me to do. I turned to Persephone. "I'm sorry you're stuck with him. Your consequence for eating food while you were here was way too harsh. If he wasn't such a selfish prick, he'd let you go. Maybe one day he'll learn that when you love someone, you have to put your own feelings aside and do what's best for that person."

Persephone met my eyes and smiled. She agreed.

"Don't talk to her!" Hades threw his fist forward and grabbed my human soul. The palace door flew open. He leaned in close and said, "For your information, Persephone came here willingly." With that, he flung me out of the palace. As I soared through the air, I saw Alex following, ready to escort me to the afterlife he'd sentenced me to.

# Chapter 28

Hades had thrown me with enough force to send me straight to the gates of the Fields of Asphodel. If I wasn't so upset that Alex had seen me with Matt, I would've hated Hades even more for denying me the time with Alex on the walk to my afterlife. But as it was, I was grateful that I didn't have to see the hurt on his face or figure out what to say to make things better.

My soul stopped at the gate, and I stared out over the fields, wondering how long it would take for me to forget everything. Being Ophi, seeing Mom again, getting tortured in Tartarus. But most of all, I wondered how long it would take to forget Alex. Somehow I knew that would take the most time.

At the sound of Alex's footsteps, I placed my transparent hands on the gate.

"Don't go yet." His voice wasn't angry or hurt. It was pleading.

I turned to see him smile at me. "You're not mad?"

"No. I had to make Hades think I was, though." He moved toward me, reaching his hands out to touch me, but that was impossible thanks to my lack of form. "I couldn't let him send your human soul to Tartarus. You'd never be able to reunite with your body from there."

"I don't think I *can* go back to my body. Hades is blocking it or something. I couldn't get close to it."

Alex shook his head. "He wasn't doing anything. You were."

This was too weird. First Alex wasn't upset with me for kissing Matt, and now he was telling me I was stopping my soul from going back to my body. "What do you mean *I* was doing it?"

"Only your Ophi soul can put your human soul back in your body. You have to put your focus back on your Ophi soul and call this," he waved his hand in front of me, running it the length of my ghostly form, "back to you."

Of course! Why didn't I think of that? "I'm such an idiot. I could've called my soul back to me right away."

"It's better you didn't." Alex looked around, making sure no one was coming our way. "Now Hades will think your human soul is here. You can catch him by surprise."

"And do what?" I raised my phantom arms out to my sides. "I failed, Alex. Medusa told me I had to break the statue and free her spirit. She wanted to bargain her soul for ours. Only, the body I borrowed didn't hold out long enough for me to break the statue."

Alex sighed and put his hands on his hips. "That's what she told you to do? We can't lose her. Do you realize what that would mean for us, for the Ophi? Connecting to her statue—her soul—is what gives us full access to our powers. It's why the Ophi at the school have always been stronger than the others."

"That's not entirely true. Chase was pretty damn strong before he came to the school."

"Yeah, but he had Hades fueling his powers, *and* he was the other Ophi in the prophecy. He's a special case." He waved his hand, dismissing the topic of Chase. I was sure he'd noticed Chase's reaction in the palace when Hades told him to take me to Tartarus.

"Besides," I said, shifting the focus off Chase, "Medusa said that, since her blood is in my veins, I could do the same thing for the other Ophi that she did."

"You'd become the next Medusa." He said it more as a statement than a question.

"Crazy, right?"

He smiled at me. "Not at all. I've felt your power." Yes, he had. Some of our makeout sessions had gotten a little intense, and I'd given him some of my power. He'd loved the feeling. "Of course,

I'm not sure I want you making that same kind of connection with other Ophi."

I swore my cheeks blushed, even in my ghostly, bodiless state. "No, not like that. Nothing like that. Certain things are reserved just for you." My mind wandered back to Matt and how Alex had seen me kiss him. "Listen, about what you saw—"

"You don't have to say anything. He wanted to move on, right?"

"He said outliving everyone he loved would've been torture."

Alex nodded. "He was probably right." He cocked his head to the side. "He told you he wasn't upset with you for how he died the first time, didn't he? That's why you kissed him while Mason released his soul."

Alex knew me well, but apparently he knew people, too. "Yes."

"The judges were right. You do put other people's needs above your own. You tried to do right by him because you didn't want him to suffer anymore. You cared about him. Loved him."

How was he getting this out? I wasn't even saying the words, and they were slicing through me, making me feel so guilty for loving two people at once.

"Alex, I told him I love you. I chose you."

"I know that. Even in your human form with all those leftover feelings for Matt, you chose me in the end."

I moved closer to him, and even though I couldn't actually touch him, I traced the air around his face. "There was something about you from the moment we met. Even when I was scared of you, I was drawn to you. I think I always knew we were supposed to be together."

"Then let's get you back into your body so we can be together."

"Okay." I closed my eyes, focusing on my Ophi self.

"Jodi, wait!"

It was too late. I was already tuning out, but I heard Alex's voice faintly in the background. "You can't let Hades know…" What couldn't he know? I couldn't hear the rest. I was already becoming aware of new sounds. Yelling. I blinked. The judges were arguing with Hades. Chase was cowering on the floor in the corner, most likely because Hades had punished him in some way for not following orders earlier when I was sentenced to Tartarus.

No one was paying attention to my body because they thought it was virtually empty. Persephone got up from her throne and walked out of the room. I felt sorry for her. She was stuck with Hades for all eternity. She'd definitely drawn the short stick. I tried to keep very still. Alex had been trying to warn me of something. The only thing I could think of was that he didn't want Hades to know I was going to call my human soul to me. I couldn't do it here. Hades would see my soul, or at the very least sense it. I had to get out of the palace and to the Fields of Asphodel. But how?

My eyes searched the room. I was too scared to move any other part of my body, in fear of drawing attention to myself. Chase was staring at Hades and cringing every time Hades raised his voice. What had Hades done to him while I was gone? As much as I hated Chase, I felt bad for him now. I knew what Hades was capable of. I wiggled one finger, hoping Chase would see it, but he was too focused on Hades.

*Damn it, Chase! Look at me!* I wiggled my finger more, but it was useless. I kept my eyes glued on the others as I slid my right foot back a little. No one noticed, so I slid my left foot back to meet it. Chase's head jerked in my direction. He'd seen me move. I waved my fingers slightly, motioning him over to me. His eyes widened, but he stayed on the ground. He was petrified. I hated that I needed his help, but Chase had always loved it when I needed him for anything. I hoped, if I kept insisting he move toward me, he'd finally give in.

I inched back again and gave another small wave. This time Chase moved toward me a little, but Hades' voice boomed, rendering Chase useless again. Who would've thought Chase would crumple like a baby after all the terrible things he'd managed to pull off? I kept inching backward until my hand was near Chase's shoulder. I sent a small wave of life-restoring power to him, and he straightened up under my touch. His eyes rose to meet mine. I wasn't sure if I could trust that he'd actually help me, but I didn't have any other options.

He stood up and took me by the arm. "Keep your stare as vacant as possible," he whispered. "I'm going to get us out of here. Just follow my lead." He walked me over to the palace doors.

"I don't remember saying you could leave." Hades slammed the doors in Chase's face.

Chase closed his eyes and took a deep breath before turning to Hades. "I wanted to check up on Alex. I'm not sure we can trust that guy." Of course he'd throw Alex under the bus. Even if it was a good excuse, he'd jumped at the chance to question my boyfriend.

"What about her?" Hades pointed to me. I tried to keep my eyes focused straight off into the distance, but I could see him in my peripheral vision. Part of me wanted to make eye contact with Tony or Arianna, let them know I was okay, but I was too afraid of doing anything that might screw up my plan.

"You guys seemed...busy. I didn't want to leave her here unguarded."

Hades wrinkled his brow as he thought for a moment. "Fine, but be quick about it."

"Yes, sir." Chase opened the door again and pulled me through it before Hades could get a good look at me.

I waited until we were halfway to the Fields before I said a word. "Thank you for that. I couldn't have gotten out of there on my own."

"I'm assuming you and Alex have a plan." He gave me a sideways glance.

"Yeah." I wasn't about to tell him what the plan was. Sure, he'd helped me get out of the palace, but that didn't mean I trusted him with information.

"You aren't going to tell me, are you?"

"Can you really blame me? You haven't earned a shred of my trust. You've been a monster to me."

He lowered his head. "I don't want to stay here. I'm guessing you guys are trying to find a way out. I want to come with you."

Come with me? Was he serious? "You think helping me once is enough to make up for all you've done?"

"No. I know you still hate me. I guess I'm trying to appeal to your humanity."

"Yeah, well, right now it's at the Fields of Asphodel."

He nodded his head, probably expecting as much. "Can't blame me for trying."

"I can blame you for a lot of other things, though. Like all of us being stuck here in the first place."

"Are you saying I was your downfall?" He finally let go of my arm and shoved his hands in his pockets.

"That's putting it mildly." I glared at him as the memories of all the ways he used me flooded my mind. The good thing about my time in Liz's body was that I could almost forget the events of the past few months. All but Alex. Now everything was back. All those feelings. All that pain.

"Should I be prepared for a dose of poison to keep me under control until you go through with your plan?"

"Not unless you make me resort to that."

"Then you do trust me."

"As far as I can throw you."

He reached for my bicep and gently squeezed it. "Hmm, doesn't look good."

He was being that guy again. The almost-human one. "Don't do that."

He lowered his hand and shoved it back into his pocket. "Sorry."

"No, I didn't mean touching my arm." I moved away, knowing he'd take that as an invitation to touch me again. That was just the way he was. "Not that I want you doing that again, either. I just meant don't try to act nice. You only do that when you want something. You play people like that, and I'm not in the mood. I have too much on my mind."

"Are you telling me you want me to be a jerk to you?"

Ugh! He was so frustrating. "How about we don't talk? That seems like the best solution."

He shrugged, and to my surprise he didn't say another word.

Alex ran up to me when he saw me approaching with Chase in tow. "What's he doing here?"

"He was my way out of there without looking suspicious."

Alex glared at him. "You can leave now."

"No, I can't. If I go back without Jodi, Hades will come looking for her."

"He's right." I reached for Alex. His touch felt incredible. He pulled me to him, wrapping me tightly in his arms.

"We should do this quickly before anything goes wrong."

"I don't trust him," Alex whispered in my ear. "He might go running back to Hades."

"He's scared. He doesn't want to be here any more than we do."

"What are you saying?" He let go of me, studying my face for answers. "You're not thinking of—" He looked past me at Chase. "Please, don't let him play you like that again."

"I haven't made up my mind either way yet. All I'm worried about right now is getting my human soul back in my body before Hades figures out what I'm doing." I kept my voice low, hoping Chase wouldn't hear. I turned to face him. "You'll need to go wait over there." I pointed off toward Tartarus.

"Why?"

"Do I really need to answer that?" Our lack-of-trust issue was obvious.

"Fine." He turned and walked off. "Far enough for you?" he yelled back.

"Turn around."

He rolled his eyes, but he did as I asked.

"Okay, here's the plan. After I call my soul back to me, we'll tell Chase that I wanted to see it off before it wandered deep into the Fields. It was a closure thing. He'll buy that."

Alex nodded. "Sounds good. But what's our next move after that?"

"I have no idea." I sounded like a complete failure as a leader, but I wasn't going to lie to Alex and pretend I had this great plan to free us all. I had nothing.

I stood in front of my human soul and reached my fingers for the ghostly hands. I willed my blood to mix. I spoke only with my mind. "Come back to me. Find a place beneath the Ophi half of my soul." I watched the soul shimmer and enter my body. It was like seeing a ghost walk straight through my chest. I felt its presence as it struggled to find a place to settle. My blood pushed it down, burying it deep inside me.

The soul didn't resist at all. It knew its place inside me, and maybe it was even relieved not to be sent to the Fields, where it would lose itself entirely. Once the process was complete, I no longer felt like two separate people. I was whole again. Even with the human side of me dead, I needed that half of my soul to be fully me.

"Everything okay?" Alex asked.

"Yeah. Good as new." I threw my arms around him and pressed my lips to his. I could've stayed like that forever, but a mist of white soared through the air, landing next to us. The second it took shape, my heart nearly stopped.

"Medusa?"

# Chapter 29

It couldn't be possible. I'd seen Liz's body fall when my soul released. How had Medusa gotten free? As I stared at her, I wondered if I'd completely lost my mind and was seeing things. After all that had happened, it wouldn't be so unbelievable.

"Yes, Jodi. It's me." Her soul smiled at me, looking motherly as usual. Well, except for the snakes on her head, which were slithering about freely after being trapped in the statue for so long. No matter how much I loved Medusa, those snakes would *always* freak me out.

"How? My soul released before I could free you. I tried to hold on, but I couldn't."

"When your soul released, Liz's body was still gripping the pliers. The force of her fall snapped the tip of the statue's finger off. It was a small hole, and it took some time to get my soul out of it. But I'm here now, and I'm ready to move forward with our plan."

I swallowed hard. Something had actually gone right. It hadn't just been the pliers I'd heard hit the floor. A small part of Medusa's finger had come off. And now she was here, which meant we might get out of here.

Alex stared in awe. "Wow, is this how she appeared to you when you connected to the statue?" He quickly covered his eyes. "I'm not going to turn to stone or anything, am I?"

I was the only living Ophi who'd ever seen Medusa. They could feel her power when they touched the statue, but that was the extent of the connection they had to her.

"Yes, and no, you won't turn to stone." Even though Medusa never told me, I knew her curse didn't affect the Ophi. We were immune to it. "She's beautiful, isn't she?"

Medusa smiled at us both. "I could see you all along, Alex. You've done well, protecting Jodi. I can't tell you how much I appreciate that." Her snakes reached out to him, almost lovingly. Almost. They were still snakes, after all.

Alex blushed. "It was my pleasure."

"Medusa, how are you here? Why didn't your soul go to the palace to be judged?"

"My blood is in your veins. Part of me truly lies in you. My soul was drawn to you because of it." I smiled, thankful that I didn't have to rescue Medusa from Hades. "As much as I'd love to catch up, we must move quickly. It won't be long before Hades senses the presence of my soul. This much power won't go unnoticed."

She was right. We had to move quickly. "How do we do this? How do we get your soul into my body?"

"Much the same as when you reunited your human soul with your Ophi soul." She could see that just by looking at me. Amazing! "Call me to you, but be prepared."

She'd warned me that this wouldn't be pretty for either one of us, but we had to be strong and make it work. "Will you be able to talk through me? I mean, which one of us will be controlling my body? The two-soul thing must be confusing."

"I will let you control your own body. I'll only talk through you when necessary, and we will be able to communicate in your mind, just like we did when I was in the statue." That didn't seem so bad. "I'll have to present myself to Hades to let him know I'm here. He won't make the final deal with you without having proof of my presence in your body."

That was true. I was planning to put Hades in a corner, tie his hands where the Ophi were concerned. He'd never take my word for Medusa's presence inside me. "I'm ready when you are."

Medusa looked over my shoulder at Chase. I hoped he was still facing the other direction like I'd told him to. "It's not safe here. You'll need full concentration, and if you cry out,"—in pain is what she meant—"he'll see what's happening. You can't trust him, Jodi. Don't be fooled by his feelings for you. Not every Ophi is good."

I wasn't going to let Chase ruin anything for me again. I hated having to write off any Ophi, but Medusa was right. Not all of them were good. Victoria and Troy sure weren't. But what about Bristol? She was helping me by taking care of Amber. She was worth saving.

"I can't read your mind anymore. We aren't connected, but I know you are thinking about saving some of the others you originally banished here." She was good. "We'll get to that in time. For now, let's focus on joining together." She reached for my hand and led me into the Fields of Asphodel, closing the gate behind us. "Alex, guard that gate. Don't let anyone in. And no matter what happens, don't touch Jodi." That meant I was going to be in pain, enough pain that Alex would want to help me.

I gave him a brave smile. "I'll be okay. It's not going to be comfortable, but we both know Medusa won't intentionally hurt me."

He nodded, but the fear was written all over his face. He reached for my free hand through an opening in the gate. "I love you, and I'll be right here."

I squeezed his hand before letting go and turning back to Medusa. "Okay, let's do this."

She took both my hands in hers. "If we have a connection to start, it should make this easier. And just remember that, once I'm inside you, it won't hurt anymore. It's only the initial forcing of my soul into an unfamiliar body that will be painful for us both."

I gathered all my strength as I mixed my blood. This was it. I couldn't put it off any longer, or Hades would find Medusa's soul and stop us. I reached forward with the power surging through my veins. "Come to me. Join me, and we will work as one." I said the words in my mind and aloud, hoping they would be more powerful that way. Commanding a soul as powerful as Medusa's was going to take major strength.

Even though she wanted to do this as much as I did, her soul fought me. I remembered how painful it was to enter Liz's body. This was ten times worse. Having another soul invade your own body while you were still using it felt like trying to shove a sumo wrestler into your skin with you. I fell to my knees the second her soul entered my body. My screams were loud enough to...well, wake the dead. Hades would no doubt be here soon. My arms and legs shook uncontrollably, and my blood made my skin bubble. I must have looked like I was possessed, which I sort of was.

Alex screamed—not the scream of someone who was watching his girlfriend writhe in pain. It was the scream of someone being tortured. Despite the torment I was in, I forced my eyes to him. Hades had him by his neck, and his hands were aglow with flames. He was burning Alex to get my attention.

"I'd stop right now before he dies."

Medusa would want me to keep going, but I couldn't sacrifice Alex. Not Alex. I gathered all my strength and pushed Medusa's soul back out of me. She appeared on the ground next to me, staring at me in horror, her snakes biting at the air.

"Jodi, what have you done?"

"I'm sorry. I couldn't let him die."

Hades released Alex, who slumped to the ground. His neck was burned and peeling.

"Alex? Are you okay?"

He choked in response. He'd be all right.

Hades waved his hand, and the gates to the Fields burst open. "Medusa, my dear, how lovely to see you." His voice was laced with hatred. The kind that sounded sweet enough to kill. "I've waited a long time for you." He turned to me. "I guess I owe you some thanks, Jodi Marshall. You've brought me the one thing I've wanted more than anything else. The origin of the Ophi line."

"Don't touch her!" I blocked Medusa's soul with my body, but Hades waved his arm, sending me flying into a row of asphodels. He advanced on Medusa. "I'm going to enjoy stripping you of your powers and torturing your soul for eternity."

"No!" God, I'd screwed up. I'd ruined everything. By saving Alex, I'd sentenced Medusa to eternal hell.

"What are you waiting for, Hades?" Medusa's voice was strong, not intimidated in the least. How did she manage that?

"I like to enjoy my triumphs, savor every moment."

"Hades, you can't touch her. The Ophi sacrificed so much to protect her soul from you. You swore to it."

He turned to me, glaring like I was a pesky little bug that wouldn't stop buzzing around him. "That deal is over." He stepped toward Medusa, towering above her. "You broke it the moment you stepped out of that statue."

"No. Our deal was that I remain inside the statue as long as it was there to hold me. It broke, and my soul could no longer be held inside. I didn't break any part of our deal."

"And that means you can't touch her, Hades."

A smile crept across Hades' lips. It didn't look like it was ever going to stop widening. "You'd think that, wouldn't you? But the way I see it, the deal was contingent upon your soul being trapped inside that statue. Look where you are. Even your soul recognizes that this is where it belongs. You came right to me."

"No, she came to *me*." I stood up, finding courage I didn't know I had.

"That's laughable." Hades crossed his arms. "How do you think you can protect her?"

I wasn't going to tell him. I'd show him instead. I willed my blood to mix, but he knocked me down again with a flick of his finger. "I don't think so. You aren't putting her soul inside you. Though I see you've managed to restore your human soul to its former place." He glared at me, like he was looking deep inside me. I felt violated by the stare.

Alex was still trapped on the other side of the gate. He looked better now, but he couldn't get to us. He pulled on the gate, but Hades had it locked firmly. Alex wasn't even a threat to him. Hell, I wasn't a threat, either. Medusa was the only one strong enough to fight him—maybe, and if I hadn't thrown away the entire plan to protect Alex, we might be on our way back to the school right now.

"Rethinking things?" Hades asked, enjoying the moment. "If you've found a way to defeat me, please do tell. I'm very interested to hear what you've come up with." He laughed like it was the most absurd notion. Maybe it was.

"What are you planning to do with her?" I had to keep him talking. Maybe he'd get overly confident and say more than he should.

He tapped his finger against his elbow as he stood there with his arms crossed. "You *would* like to know my plans, wouldn't you?"

"What I'd like is for you to leave us all alone." I said it before I had time to even think about the words coming out of my mouth. Medusa was in trouble, and it was my fault. Anger was fueling my actions. Of course, it might get us all killed, too.

Hades laughed. "See, that's the thing about the underworld. I rule. I get what I want. Everyone else, well, let's just say if you aren't in the Elysian Fields..." He waited for me to fill in my own ending. I wasn't going to give him the satisfaction.

"What do you want? Enlighten us." I stood up again, tempting him to put me back on my ass for the third time.

"You have spunk. I have to give you that. If we weren't enemies, I might actually like you."

I doubted that. "No, I think Chase was always more your style." Chase. Was he still out there? I doubted he'd be of any help if he was. He was petrified of Hades, even more than the rest of us were. I was sure it had to do with Hades taking his mom. That, and the fact that Chase was a power-crazed idiot.

"I bet there's something you didn't know about Chase."

Great. More surprises. "What's that?"

"I have access to all his thoughts."

"What?" How could that be possible?

"You and Chase have more in common than you think. You were both missing part of your souls at one point. I've had a piece of his since he got here. I took it. It allows me to see what he sees."

No wonder Chase was terrified. He was a spy for Hades, and he knew it. That also meant he didn't want to be. Damn it. When was I going to stop feeling sorry for that creep?

"Why? If you wanted answers, you should've taken a piece of *my* soul."

"Because I needed a willing participant."

Willing. So Chase had agreed to this. My guess was that he'd thought it was a good idea, but Hades' control over him became too much. Maybe this would teach him something about letting power go to his head.

"You heard everything Chase and I said on the way here, didn't you?" I stepped closer to Medusa, hoping to get close enough to call her soul to me without Hades noticing.

"Actually, no. I wasn't watching. But when I felt Medusa's soul enter the underworld, I tuned in. Convinced Chase to look for the both of you. What a happy coincidence he was still nearby."

Alex let out a guttural cry and lunged at Chase. A whoosh of air left Chase's lungs as Alex slammed him into the ground. The sickening sound of breaking bone followed.

"Alex!" I rushed for the gate, not caring about Hades or what he might do to me. "Stop! He isn't worth it."

Chase had blood running down his face, and his nose was bent to the left.

Alex shoved himself off Chase and started toward the gate. I reached my hand through and touched his cheek. "Don't become like them." I couldn't help worrying that Alex would wind up like his parents—evil. He was a great guy, despite their terrible influence, but when situations like this came around, I worried he'd lose it and give in to that darkness that seemed to overtake so many Ophi.

He pressed his hand against mine. "What are we going to do? He's been spying on us, Jodi. We have to get rid of him."

"But not like that. Not by beating him to death." I swallowed hard. "I won't lose you just to get rid of him."

His jaw clenched. "I'll be okay. I won't become either of my parents, and I definitely won't stoop to *his* level." He glanced back at Chase, who was holding the bridge of his nose and cringing.

"Good, because we have bigger problems right now." I nodded back over my shoulder.

Alex peered around me, and his breath caught in his throat. I yanked my hand back through the gate and whipped around.

Hades was gone, and he'd taken Medusa with him.

# Chapter 30

I ran back through the fields to where they'd been standing. There was no sign of either of them or that they'd ever been here.

"Damn it! He used Chase as a distraction and took her." I fell to my knees and pounded the asphodels. Twice my feelings for Alex had put us all at risk. Maybe I wasn't meant to be in a relationship. Maybe as leader, I had to sever my personal connections and put the needs of the group first. Only I couldn't. I wasn't human anymore, but my emotions still felt human. I loved Alex. I couldn't see how that could be a bad thing.

He banged on the gates until they finally opened. Hades wasn't keeping them locked now that he'd gotten away with Medusa's soul. Alex rushed to me and pulled me to my feet. "We have to find her. My guess is, once Hades has her under control, he'll come back for us. We aren't going to sit here and wait for him."

I nodded and wiped my tears with the backs of my hands. "I can't believe I suck this bad as a leader."

He gripped my shoulders. "Don't do that. Don't sit there and feel sorry for yourself. Medusa wanted you to become like her. To take her place. She wouldn't have asked you to do that if she didn't believe in you. You're her only hope right now. So push whatever feeling of helplessness you have aside, and do your job."

That was another reason why I loved him. He called me out when I was acting stupid. Medusa believed in me. Alex believed in me. Out of the people I still had in my life, they mattered the most. I wasn't going to stop until I fixed this—for them.

"I'm going to try to communicate with her. She used to be able to appear in my mind. We're both here, so maybe we still can." Unless Hades was torturing her. Then she wouldn't have the strength to make the connection.

Alex let go of me, and I closed my eyes. "Medusa? Can you hear me?" I waited, listening for even the smallest sound. "I'm going to find you and join your soul with mine, but I need help. Can you give me any sign of where you are?" I wasn't even sure she could hear me, let alone answer or give me a sign, but I had to try. Still nothing.

Alex gently grazed my arm with his hand. "Anything?"

I shook my head. "Wherever he has her, she can't hear me. Either that, or she's in so much pain that she can't respond."

"You think she's in Tartarus?"

It was a good bet. I nodded.

"Let's go."

We had no plan other than finding her. If Victoria had her, I'd have to use my powers to knock out Victoria. My blood was already boiling under my skin. I had enough emotion running through me to wipe out every Ophi here with my poison. Chase was lucky he wasn't around anymore.

Chase! "Alex." I grabbed his arm, stopping him just outside the gate. "Chase might know where Medusa is. He must have seen something."

"I don't know. He was on the ground and in a lot of pain. Besides, Hades didn't go by us, so how would Chase have seen him? Hades may have part of Chase's soul, but that doesn't mean Chase has access to it or that he knows what Hades is up to."

That was true. Hades had hurt Chase in the palace, too. If Chase had any insight into what Hades was going to do, he might have avoided that.

"All right. We'll check Tartarus and hope for the best."

Finding strength in each other, we walked hand in hand, an army of two. We were almost to the entrance to Tartarus when Bristol came walking up behind us.

"Jodi!" Her voice was a loud whisper.

I turned to see the fear on her face. "What is it? Did something happen? Did you see Medusa?"

"Medusa?" Bristol's head jerked back. "She's here?" Even she knew that wasn't good.

"Yes, and we have to find her soon."

"She's not in there." There was more. "The others are. All of them. Hades said he wants us to torture them until there's nothing left."

"You don't mean…"

"Until they're dead."

No. My hands shook. Alex yanked his hand from mine.

"Jodi, you're on fire."

My power was out of control.

"What's going on? What are we going to do?" Bristol's eyes pleaded with me. "I don't want to kill anyone. I've been taking care of that girl Amber for you. I've been doing everything you asked. I just want to get out of here. I don't belong here. I'm not evil."

Now *she* was losing it. I reached for her but thought twice about it. I didn't want to burn her with my touch. "Calm down. I'm going to figure this out."

"You better do it soon. They can't hold on much longer."

"What is Hades having you do to them exactly?" They couldn't have been in Tartarus for that long. Hades had only left us moments ago.

Her body shook as she took a deep breath. "He's making them relive every death and raising they ever caused, all at once."

That was how Hades killed an Ophi. It was supposedly the worst way you could die. He wanted to end this quickly. No savoring the moment this time. He was done playing around.

"Please, Bristol, do whatever you can to slow things down. I need to find Medusa. Once I do, I can save us all. I'll get you out of here, but I need your help right now."

Her eyes teared. "But how? I don't know what to do."

"Create some sort of distraction. Anything. Get the focus off the others. Pretend you're hurt, in pain."

I calmed my blood for a moment, focusing on the life-restoring power alone. I gently touched Bristol's arm and sent a wave of the energy to her.

"What is that?" Her eyes widened, and she smiled. "That's amazing."

"Think you can handle this now? I gave you a power boost."

She nodded. "Yeah. I can do it."

"Good. Go!" I pushed her toward the entrance, and she ran in.

"Great," Alex said, "but we still don't know where Medusa is."

"Yes, we do." There was only one place she could be. "In the palace. She's with Persephone." I took off running toward the palace.

Alex easily kept up with me. The guy always had been fast. "Why do you think she's there?"

"Because it's the one place that has been off-limits to us. Hades keeps Persephone guarded from everyone and everything."

"You're right, but then how are we going to get to her?"

I pictured the look Persephone had on her face when we were all in the palace. She hated Hades. "Hades told me Persephone came here on her own, but I don't believe it. Something is up. Persephone will help us because she'll do anything to get back at Hades for imprisoning her here."

Alex smiled. "That's crazy enough to actually work."

"Yeah, but we need to find Persephone's chambers in the palace first. I think I know where to go. I saw her walk away during the argument earlier."

We raced the rest of the way. The palace entrance was quiet. Hades was gone, which wasn't good for us. That probably meant he was with Persephone, guarding Medusa.

"What now?" Alex asked, catching his breath.

I pulled him off to the side and out of view of the judges, not that they really cared that we were there. Their only concern was judging new souls. Still, we ducked behind a pillar. "We need to find Persephone and see if Hades is really with her. He might be somewhere else. We have to know for sure because we don't have time to waste."

"I know what you could do," Chase said, walking around the pillar and facing us. His nose was still crooked, and he had dried blood caked on his face.

"Get out of here!" Alex yelled, shoving Chase in the chest and sending him slamming into the pillar.

"Would you two stop it?" I grabbed Alex's arm. "We can't afford to draw attention to ourselves right now."

"He's a spy. Hades can see everything he can." Alex was fuming, and he jabbed his finger in Chase's chest.

Chase held up his hands, showing he wasn't going to fight back. That was different for him. "Hades can only see through my eyes when he's tuned in. He's not right now."

"How do you know?" I asked him.

"I can feel it. It's like he takes control of me."

I wondered how many things Chase had done since we'd gotten here that weren't actually his actions, that were Hades'.

Chase focused on me, pleading with me to listen. "You need a power boost. You didn't fail last time just because you were worried about Alex. You were weak. Splitting your soul took a lot out of you, whether you feel it or not."

That made sense. Still, this was Chase talking. I couldn't exactly trust him.

"Take my power. All of it."

I narrowed my eyes at him. "That would kill you."

"I know." His voice was soft and low. "I can't live this way. I was supposed to die a long time ago. If my mom hadn't bargained for my life, I wouldn't be alive. She's dead because of me. Hades took her, and he isn't going to give her back." He shrugged. "Let me do this. I owe you all a lot for what I've put you through. Let me make up for it—at least some of it."

This wasn't just sacrificing himself for the good of the Ophi. He *wanted* to die. "You'd get to be with your mom again." That was his real endgame.

He smiled. "I can't fool you. Yes, I do get something out of this. You had to know I would."

Yes, because he was Chase. He never did anything without getting something in return. "You're really ready to die?"

"Can you call being Hades' puppet living? I died a long time ago. I'm just not at peace."

"What makes you think you will be after the judges get through with you?" Alex asked.

"I guess I don't know for sure, but I think they might go easy on me, considering my actions weren't all my own."

Maybe. Maybe not. I knew the judges were fair. They'd know what to do with Chase. Still, could I go through with this? Could I kill Chase to save Medusa? If I didn't save her, the rest of us would be dead in no time. I didn't know how long Bristol could hold off the punishment that was killing my friends.

I looked to Alex, who shook his head. "I'm not making this decision for you. This is your call. I'll support whatever decision you make."

He didn't have to tell me what he wanted me to do. I knew already. He wanted me to take Chase's power. Alex didn't care about Chase. No, that wasn't entirely true. He had very strong feelings for Chase. They just weren't good feelings.

"Come on, Jodi." Chase tapped my elbow, which got him a stern look from Alex. "What's there to think about?"

"A lot. You're asking me to kill you."

Chase shrugged. "No big loss, right? You hate me."

"I don't—" I stopped myself. Alex would never understand my crazy screwed-up feelings for Chase. Yes, I hated him, but I felt sorry for him, too. It was so screwed up *I* didn't even understand it. "I don't want to kill anyone."

"Hades isn't with Persephone," Chase said. Either he had a really good poker face, or he was giving me the reason I needed to go through with this plan.

"Are you sure, or is this just a tactic to get me to end your life for you?"

"You can go check first if you want, but Hades was on his way to Tartarus last I saw him. He wanted to see your friends die."

Damn it! Bristol would never be able to stall if Hades was overseeing things. I couldn't go check Persephone's room. I had to take Chase's word for it.

Alex ran his hand down my arm. "This is our last chance."

I nodded and walked over to Chase. "This is what you want? Really? Because there's no coming back from this."

"Trust me, you'll be saving me along with everyone else—if you succeed, that is." He smirked. Even moments from death, he was taking a little dig at me. Yes, I could still fail, even with Chase's power. Unless...

"The prophecy."

Chase and Alex both cocked their heads at me. "What about it?" they both asked, giving each other horrified looks for thinking the same thing.

"Chase, the prophecy about us, we thought it meant we were supposed to destroy the Ophi line, but we were wrong. Medusa told me that prophecies didn't always mean what we thought they did. They're tricky. I think this is the true meaning. We're supposed to join powers to save everyone."

Chase smiled. "Are you trying to make me go out a hero?"

Alex scoffed. "Not likely."

No one could call Chase a hero after all he'd done, but he was definitely helping us. "Let's just say you're doing a good thing, going out on a high note."

"Good enough for me." He reached for my hands, but Alex stepped between us.

"What are you doing?" I widened my eyes at him. "I thought you wanted me to do this."

"I do, but how do you know he won't dose you with poison? This could be a trick."

Chase put his hands behind his back. "Fine. I won't touch her. She can place her hands on my chest and take my power all on her own."

That was barbaric. "Alex, please. He's helping us. I'm not going to end his life without his consent."

"He already gave his consent. This was his idea."

I sighed and reached for Chase's hands. Alex shook his head and stepped aside, but not before saying, "Try anything, and I'll kill you myself."

"You *would* sacrifice everyone else's freedom just to get back at me," Chase said.

"Enough! Let's do this." Time was ticking. I took Chase's hands, and he started to transfer his power to me. I let it fill me. Before it took over, I looked Chase in the eyes and said, "Thank you."

He didn't answer. He just smiled. I watched the life drain out of him as his power left his body and filled mine.

# Chapter 31

By the end, he was too weak to give me any more power, so I had to take it from him. I pulled those last traces of Ophi blood to me. I lowered to the ground with Chase. Alex supported his shoulders to keep him from slumping forward on me or accidentally breaking our connection. When it was over, I let go of Chase and nodded to Alex. He eased Chase's body to the floor. I was proud of Alex for not just letting him fall in a heap. He must have found some sympathy for Chase after all.

"How do you feel?" he asked me.

"Amazing." I felt guilty for saying it. I'd just taken Chase's life, but his power was inside me, and I was ready to find Medusa.

"Lead the way." Alex held his arm out, motioning for me to go first.

I walked out of the entryway and off to the left. That's where I'd seen Persephone go earlier.

"It has to be around here somewhere." We passed a few locked doors, but none of them seemed right. Hades loved Persephone, even if she didn't love him in return. He'd give her the most beautiful room in the palace. We came to a door with a gorgeous, shiny embellishment. It was a swirly design that reflected the light in a way that almost looked like the sun. On instinct, I traced the design. It was an elaborate letter P. "This is it." I raised my hand to knock.

"Wait! Are you just going to trust what Chase said? Hades could be in there."

"I killed Chase. I owe him this." I knocked.

Soft footsteps sounded on the other side of the door. I held my breath, and Alex and I exchanged a look while the doorknob turned. Persephone stared back at us, her long, white gown trailing behind her.

"Are you lost?"

"I don't think so. We're looking for Medusa." I tried to peer around her into the room, but she was blocking my view.

"What do you want with her?"

"Honestly, I want to put her soul inside my body, so we can put your tyrant of a husband in his place."

She smiled and raised an eyebrow. "Then come in." She stepped aside, and I saw Medusa's soul sitting on the edge of the bed.

I rushed to her. "Are you okay? Did he hurt you?"

"No, my child. I'm fine. Persephone has been a very gracious host." Medusa looked comfortable, like she'd been visiting with an old friend instead of being held against her will. Even her snakes looked peaceful.

"Did they do something to you? You seem awfully calm."

"Nothing of the sort. But I find Persephone to be very good company. For the moment, I'm almost content. And now that you're here, I suspect we can move forward with our plan."

I swallowed my guilt and told her about Chase.

"I suspected the prophecy about you two wasn't what everyone thought. That it wasn't even as Hades interpreted it. But this, I did not see." She placed a hand on my shoulder. "You did the right thing. Do you not know that?"

"I do, but it doesn't make me feel any better. I killed him."

Persephone walked over to us with her arms crossed. "Hades was using that boy as a slave. It was awful. I don't blame him for preferring death over that kind of existence. I'll see to it that he is fairly judged and receives an afterlife that suits him."

"You can do that?"

"Sweetie, I'm queen of the underworld. I can do whatever I want. Hades won't go against me."

A nervous giggle escaped my lips. "I don't suppose you want to demand that he free us and leave us alone for good."

"I rarely get involved in the lives of mortals. Souls are another story."

"Fair enough. Thank you." But I couldn't help wondering if she *wasn't* getting involved in our lives. "Why aren't you with your mother? You don't have to be down here now."

"My father asked me to come." Zeus? "He thought I'd be a good distraction. Hades didn't question it. He was just happy to have extra time with me."

"But why would you do that? You hate him."

"Yes, but I'm not like him. I couldn't stand how he attacked you. The judges weren't wrong. You're a good person, Jodi, human or Ophi. Just because Hades hates the Ophi doesn't mean the other gods feel the same way."

Not all the gods were against us? I couldn't believe it.

"Jodi." Alex tapped his wrist, even though he wasn't wearing a watch. "We need to move a little quicker."

"You must be trying to save your friends, the ones in Tartarus," Persephone said.

"Yes." I hated to ask, but I had to. "You don't think you could buy us some time, do you? I'm not asking you to save us. I just need a little time to unite with Medusa before I—we—can go after him."

She bit her bottom lip as she thought. "I might have an idea. Let me see what I can do." She walked toward the door and then disappeared in a silver swirl of smoke.

I immediately turned to Medusa. "Ready?"

She stood. "Ready."

I knew this would still be painful, even with Chase's power inside me, but I also knew I could handle it. I wouldn't let Chase's death be in vain. I took a deep breath and called Medusa's spirit to me. Like last time, she fought me as I brought her into my body. I didn't want to be forceful, but the gentler I was, the more her soul fought.

"Jodi, you have the power in you. Use it," Alex said. "I can tell you're holding back. Medusa will understand, and you'll end the pain for both of you sooner if you just get it over with."

I hadn't thought of it that way. I allowed the power to take over and shove Medusa's soul inside me. It was like being suckerpunched by a giant. All the air escaped my lungs. I fell backward into the dresser, but I kept pushing her soul down. It wanted to find a way out—that or take over. I had to show it I was in control. I pushed it down, sandwiching it between my Ophi soul and my human soul. Finally, it settled in.

Alex reached for me as I pushed off the dresser and stood up tall. "Is she—?"

"Yes. I feel her." Medusa had said she'd be able to hear my thoughts, so I spoke to her in my mind.

*Medusa, are you okay? In any pain at all?*

*I'm fine. Thank you for making that as quick as possible.*

*Thank Alex for that. I was trying to do it slowly until he pointed out I was only causing us both more pain.*

*I'll thank him later. For now, let's go save the others.*

"Let's go." I took Alex's hand in mine. Part of me wanted to tell him to stay here. I might be all juiced up on the power of not one but three Ophi right now, but Alex was still himself. If Hades attacked him…

"I can handle myself, Jodi." Damn him for knowing me so well.

"I know." Total lie.

"Then quit gripping my hand so hard."

I eased up as we passed the judges. They stared at us knowingly, but they didn't say a word or try to stop us. Maybe they weren't exactly happy with how Hades had been running things either.

I really wished I had a swirling cloud of silver or black smoke to carry us to Tartarus right then. Running was too slow. Hopefully Persephone had bought us the time we needed.

"What's the plan? Run in there and…" Alex waited for an answer.

"Save the others. That's as far as I got."

*You can stop Victoria's group from torturing your friends.* Medusa's voice in my head made me jump. It wasn't like when she appeared in my mind. I couldn't see her at all. I only felt her presence, and when she spoke, it was like I was thinking in her voice.

*What if Hades is there? I mean, he must be, right? He won't stand there and do nothing while we save the others.*

Medusa was silent, devising a plan. It was odd that I couldn't hear her thoughts. We were nearing the entrance to Tartarus, and she still hadn't said a word.

*Medusa, do you have a plan? What do we do about Hades?*

Still nothing. I stopped running and looked down at my body. I hadn't felt Medusa leave me. She must still be inside my body, but why couldn't I sense her?

"What's wrong?" Alex reached for my arm. "Did something happen?"

"I don't know. I can't hear Medusa in my mind anymore. I'm not sure she's still here."

"Have you tried calling to her?"

I raised an eyebrow. Of course I'd tried that.

"Do you think her soul escaped?"

"I didn't feel anything. I would know if it had, wouldn't I?"

Alex shrugged. "I've never had another soul sharing my body, so I have no clue what that would feel like."

"I can't go in there without her. Even with Chase's power, I won't be strong enough."

"You don't know that, and we can't just stand here while the others are in there suffering."

"What if I fail?" I couldn't bear the thought, not after all I'd gone through to get here.

"Then we'll figure something else out."

I stepped forward, determined to do something—even something stupid—but my head swam with shrieks and screams. I pressed my palms to my ears to block them out, but that didn't help. "Ahh!"

"Jodi!" Alex grabbed me by my arms before I fell to the ground. "What is it? What's happening?"

I could barely hear him over the screams. "I don't know. The screams, they're awful. So much pain."

*I'm sorry, Jodi. I tried to focus on their pain to block it from you, but there's too much. I couldn't shield you from it all.*

Medusa was back—or really, she'd never left.

*You mean there's more? You're experiencing some of this, too?*

*Yes. I tried to take it all so you could focus better on stopping Victoria and her followers, but I couldn't hold it all.*

How was I supposed to save everyone with this mind-numbing shrieking in my head?

"Hey, can you hear me?" Alex asked, gently touching my cheek.

"Yeah, sorry. Medusa, she's back." I struggled to form sentences with everything going on inside my head.

"That's good, right?"

"Yes, but she can hear the screams, too. They're hindering both of us. I don't know if we'll be strong enough to push through them."

Alex lifted my chin, raising my eyes to his. "Listen to me. I know how strong you are. You were able to block the sounds of the tortured souls from your mind when you learned to raise them. Remember?"

Yes. When I'd first arrived at the school, I'd felt every emotion and physical pain the souls went through when I raised them. I'd learned to block that out. I'd have to do the same now. "But this is so much more than one soul. It's all our friends, Alex."

"Then you have even more reason to do this." I'd always wondered how Alex could go from caring to serious and disciplined so quickly, but now I was grateful for it. He was keeping me grounded, pushing me to do what I had to.

*Medusa, are you ready?*

*Ready when you are.*

*Then we're going in.*

I nodded to Alex, and he kissed my cheek. I closed my eyes and pushed the pain and screams out of my head. I forced them away. Once I could think straight again, I stepped into Tartarus. I kept myself positioned in front of Alex, hoping he wouldn't notice that I was acting as an Ophi shield. Alex's hands flew to his ears as we got closer to the others. The screams were eardrum-shattering.

His face scrunched up in pain. "That was in your head?"

"Not so easy to tune out, but I'm doing all right."

I heard Hades' laughter echoing off the walls. He was enjoying every moment of this. I wasn't surprised. If only Medusa and I were strong enough to overthrow a god. I would've loved to torture *him* for the rest of eternity. Hades stood in the middle of the group. All my friends were on the ground, writhing in pain. Smoke was actually coming from their mouths, eyes, and ears. They were burning from the inside out.

*Don't focus on Hades,* Medusa said. *Go for Victoria and the others doing the torturing.*

Easier said than done. My blood was boiling, more than it ever had before. My skin was taking on a reddish tone, and it shimmered.

Alex pointed to my arms. "What's happening to you?"

*Tell him not to touch you. You'll burn him.*

"Don't touch me. My blood is making me hotter than fire right now."

"Can you handle all this power?"

"We're about to find out." I reached my hands forward in Victoria's direction. I wanted to take her down first. She'd pretended to be like a mother to me. She'd lied to me and stolen Medusa's locket from my room. She'd ruined Alex's life and treated him like a worthless stranger. I let my hatred for her fuel me.

*I'm with you, Jodi. Simply command your blood to reach her soul.*

*But she's alive. I can only reach souls of the dead.*

*All you need is to touch her. Your power will take her down instantly.*

*How do I get to her without alerting the others that Alex and I are here?* The only thing I could think of was charging at her like a linebacker. Did linebackers charge?

*The element of surprise is never a bad thing. Try commanding some souls first. Get them to attack Victoria and bring her down. Then you can charge her like you just pictured.* Of course she could read my mind. Hers was a mystery to me, but being Medusa and having her blood in my veins gave her access to all my thoughts.

*Got it.* I focused on reaching out to the other tortured souls in Tartarus. I commanded them to listen to me alone, to disconnect from the pain they were feeling and come to me. One by one, they stood and walked toward me. Bristol was the first to notice them—and me. She met my eyes, and a small glimmer of hope flashed across her face. She pretended everything was as it should be, and I realized she wasn't torturing Amber or anyone else. She was faking the entire thing. Tony was on the ground like the others, but he wasn't in pain.

*We will save her, too,* Medusa said. *She's worth saving.*

Yes, she was, and I hoped that, once I started attacking Victoria and her followers, Bristol and Tony would do what they could to help.

The souls were getting closer and drawing everyone's attention. Abby turned first, doing a double take. Then Hades narrowed his eyes. He didn't turn toward the souls, though. He was searching—for me. He knew I was here.

"Come here, Jodi Marshall." A smile crossed his lips. "Let me see you. I'm sure we can find a place for you among your friends."

I stayed in the shadows until the souls reached Victoria, who had stopped torturing Arianna and was backing away. She tried commanding them, but they wouldn't listen. They were obeying me alone.

Hades flung his arm out to the side, sending the souls flying into the black abyss behind them. So much for taking out Victoria. I was on my own.

# Chapter 32

Now what? I may have had the power of three Ophi inside me, but I was up against Hades and a bunch of pissed-off Ophi who would love to see me dead.

Hades laughed. "Is that the best you can do?"

Alex stared at me, waiting for my next move.

*Now what, Medusa?*

*I have to make my presence known.*

*You want to talk to Hades?* He didn't seem like he was in a talking mood. More like a "rip-the-head-off-the-Ophi" mood.

*No, I want to show him what we can do. Go for Victoria.*

Football-player tactics—that was what we were left with. I felt my body temperature lower and my blood calm, like it was preparing for the biggest battle of all. "Stay here," I told Alex. "This is going to be crazy, and I need you playing backup, okay?"

"You mean you want me staying out of harm's way."

Exactly, but his male ego wouldn't be able to handle that. "If I fail, our hope rests on you. That's hardly staying out of harm's way."

He grabbed the back of my head and pressed his lips to mine. "Just don't die, okay?" It was his attempt to lighten the mood.

"What do you think, mac and cheese for dinner?"

"Nah, I'm swearing off the stuff." His eyes fell on Victoria. "I don't need any reminders of her."

I placed my hand on his chest. "Wish me luck." Without waiting, I turned and sprinted toward Victoria. She saw me and tried to move out of the way, but I had youth on my side. Not that she was that old. I bet she wished she was my mom's age right then, though. I pressed my left hand to her throat and sent a jolt of poison her way. She fell backward onto the ground, and I went down with her, not wanting to break the connection. After about five seconds, she was unconscious. I stood up and looked around. Everyone was watching me. Hades could've stopped me, but he stared, and I couldn't help wondering if he wanted to see just what I was capable of. For once, I didn't want to disappoint him.

I lunged at Troy next. "This is for killing your own son, you bastard." I went for his neck too, but he slapped my arm away. He fought me, swinging his arms and landing a punch to my stomach. I felt Medusa's soul recoil, but not in fear. She was angry. My blood boiled, bubbling under my skin. Now, it was her anger making me burning hot. I smiled at Troy for a second. He gritted his teeth and swung at me again. This time, I grabbed his wrist. He cried out in pain as my touch burned his skin. Smoke sizzled under my hand.

"You think that's bad?" I asked him. "Try this." I sent poison to him in such a concentrated dose that he went down immediately. I turned to see Tony trying to gather everyone, probably preparing to escape.

Hades smirked and raised an eyebrow. "Interesting. I have to say those two were becoming my favorites. They really threw themselves into their work here."

"Yeah, well, that's because they're sadistic—" I stopped, realizing Alex could hear every word I said. Sure he hated them, but they were his parents. He didn't need me announcing my true thoughts about them right now.

"Go on." Hades laced his fingers in front of him.

"Gladly." I walked over to Abby, ready to take her down next, but Arianna looked up at me.

"Jodi, she's my daughter." It was the first time Arianna had spoken that way about Abby. Every time the subject had come up before, Arianna just seemed disappointed and even ashamed of the Ophi Abby had become. But she still loved her daughter—still wished Abby would change.

Abby's eyes widened, and she swallowed hard, not because she was afraid of what I'd do to her but because she was touched that Arianna wanted to protect her.

"See that human weakness?" Hades said. "That's why you never should've returned your human soul to your body. You'd be better off without it."

I turned to him, stepping closer and challenging him to stop me. I was definitely more confident with Medusa's soul inside me. "You know, there was a time when I thought you were right. But both of us couldn't have been more wrong. Emotions fuel our power. My human emotions are purer than my Ophi ones. They give my power something extra. I need my human soul."

Hades laughed. "You think I didn't know that?" He crossed his arms. "You forget, knowing souls is my business. Why do you think I wanted your human soul so badly? If it was in Tartarus or even the Fields of Asphodel, you wouldn't have been able to access those emotions. You would've been weaker."

Damn it! When was I going to stop underestimating this guy? "Then I guess you know what else I've done." I looked around for Persephone, realizing for the first time that she wasn't here. She'd said she was going to help buy me some time while I brought Medusa's soul into my body. Had she set me up? Had she warned Hades I was coming and left?

"Looking for someone?" Hades smiled, but it quickly faded. "I sent her away."

"You sent your wife away? Why?"

"I think you know the answer to that."

Because she'd helped me. Because Hades realized that Persephone was more than willing to stab him in the back.

"I'll have to remember to thank her when I see her again."

"You won't ever see her again. I'll see to that. Your soul will stay in Tartarus forever."

"No, it won't." I stepped closer to him and stared into his eyes. "I saw the way you watched what I did to Victoria and Troy. That was actually a trick Chase taught me, and believe it or not, he helped me with it this time, too."

"Chase." Hades balled his fists. "I'm going to—" He lifted his head in the air. "He's dead? How?" Hades' eyes lowered to me again, but he still wasn't really seeing me. Anger clouded his vision.

"He's with the judges. They're going to see to it that he receives the afterlife he deserves." Whatever that may be, I still wasn't sure, and I didn't think I really wanted to know.

"You killed him?" Hades cocked his head to the side. "You hated him that much?"

"No, he asked me to take his powers. He didn't want to be your puppet anymore."

"So you forgave him for everything? You're dumber than you look."

"I didn't forgive him for everything. I'm not naïve enough to think he was innocent in all of this. He played his part. But he didn't deserve to suffer for all eternity as your puppet either, and I needed his power."

"Why? You think, now that you have his power, you're strong enough to defeat me?"

"No, I needed his power for another reason." I moved even closer, and Hades narrowed his eyes, unsure of why I kept invading his personal space. "Look at me. Really look at me."

Hades' lips started to curl into a smile. I knew he was thinking he'd burn me with his stare.

I rolled my eyes. "If you do that, you'll miss what I'm trying to show you, and believe me, you're going to want to see it."

He sighed, blowing his hot breath right in my face. If he wasn't so freaking hot—like underwear-model hot—I would've been totally grossed out. He lowered his head so we were almost at eye level.

*Get ready, Medusa. He'll be able to see you inside me.*

*I'll be sure to smile.* It was the first time I'd heard her crack a joke, and the fact that it was coming now when we were standing off against Hades just made it that much funnier.

"What?" Hades jerked his head back. At first I thought he was questioning how I'd gotten Medusa's soul inside me, but then I realized I was laughing. "Is something amusing to you?"

"Sorry. You'll see what it is in a minute." I tried to keep my composure, but truthfully, Medusa's humor was keeping me from losing it and crumpling in front of Hades.

He leaned forward again, slower this time, making sure I wasn't about to burst out laughing again or try anything else, either. I held perfectly still. He needed to see this. Otherwise he wouldn't fear me, and then we'd all be screwed.

Recognition flashed across his face. "Medusa?" His voice was soft and low. He stood up and whirled around. "Persephone!" His voice shook the entire underworld, and everyone covered their ears. I was the only one still standing—other than Hades.

We all waited, but Persephone didn't come. Hades screamed her name over and over again. It was kind of pathetic. Here he was, the king of the underworld, and Persephone was really the one calling the shots. And she didn't answer to him. My mouth curved into a smile. I thought about how much time had passed since we'd come here.

"She's gone," I said.

Hades whirled around. "What did you do with her?" He grabbed the front of my shirt, and Alex was by my side in seconds.

"Let go of her!"

"Alex, stay back. He's not hurting me." Yet.

Alex's chest heaved, and he didn't move away.

"Boy, I could kill you with one flick of my finger. Don't be an idiot."

"Alex, please!" I pleaded with him. I couldn't lose him now. We were so close to getting the hell out of here. "For me."

Alex met my eyes and stepped back.

"Smart move," Hades said. "Although taking orders from a girl is so—"

"Like what you do with Persephone." The words tumbled out of my mouth.

*Jodi, now is not the time to anger Hades,* Medusa said.

I hadn't meant to say it out loud.

Hades let go of my shirt and raised his hand to me.

"She's gone, you know. Persephone. You thought she'd come back because she was developing feelings for you, but you were wrong. She played you, and she won't be back until fall, when you force her to be here."

Hades let out a sound that was almost a roar. His hands burst into flames.

"See what dealing with us has done to you. It's not worth it."

"You're right." Hades calmed. The flames disappeared. "You've just given me all the reason I could ever need to end your lives right now."

No! That wasn't my point at all!

Hades looked around. "As much as I'd love to start with you, Jodi Marshall, I think I'll save you for last. I want you to watch your friends die. I want you to witness their pain. I want to see you suffer."

*Medusa, what do we do?*

Before she could answer, Hades disappeared. That wasn't what I was expecting. We looked around, trying to find him before he snuck up on us. Alex reached for my hand. I squeezed it. If this was the end, I wanted to be with him.

Even Victoria and Troy's followers looked scared. They may not have been with us right now, but they were still Ophi. And now that Victoria and Troy were unconscious on the ground, they had no one to protect them—not that Victoria or Troy would sacrifice their own lives to save anyone else.

*He's toying with you all, Jodi. He'll go for the easiest target first.* I was so on edge wondering where Hades was and when he'd pop out that I jumped at the sound of Medusa's voice in my head.

*Why? He has the element of surprise. He could take down any one of us.*

*He could, but he won't. He'll start small and make each death worse until he gets to you.*

"Anyone see him?" I asked.

Everyone shook their heads, even Abby. Look who was suddenly jumping the Hades ship. If she wasn't Arianna's daughter, I'd have taken her down by then.

*Medusa, who is the weakest one here?*

*I think you already know.*

McKenzie? She was the sweetest girl I'd ever met, but she wasn't exactly helpless. Her powers had been coming along before we got here. Leticia? She'd still been struggling to get hold of her Ophi abilities. It must be her. I walked over to Leticia, still on the ground by Quinn. He'd hurt her so much, Tony hadn't been able to get her up. I remembered how much I'd hated training with Quinn. He couldn't stand any weakness. No wonder he'd chosen to punish Leticia.

Alex let go of my hand, but he stayed no more than two feet away from me. He even bent down to Leticia with me. "Stay by me, okay, Leticia?"

She looked around, and the color drained from her face. "You think he's coming for me first?"

I couldn't lie to her. "Yes, but I'm here and so is Alex. We'll protect you."

She nodded, but her lip trembled. I helped her to her feet, and Alex stood on the other side of her. We were shielding her with our bodies. I turned around, keeping my back to Leticia, and Alex did the same.

"Eyes open, everyone. Yell the second you see anything." I was leading again, and this time, it felt right.

"We're not going to see him until he's right on top of us," Jared said. "The best we can hope for is to scream, but most likely, it will just be the agonizing cry of the life leaving our bodies."

I shook my head. As much as that was probably true, I had to hope Medusa and I could stop Hades before he killed anyone. Hope was all I had right then.

It was silent for a moment, and then I heard Hades laugh. He appeared right behind Jared and waved at me. I lunged for them, but Hades touched his finger to Jared's shoulder. Jared's eyes rolled back, and he slumped to the ground.

He was dead.

# Chapter 33

I froze, staring at Jared's lifeless body. Instead of his face, I saw Matt's. Jared was like family to Matt, and now he'd be in the afterlife with him. I'd killed Matt and so many people he loved.

*Jodi, you need to get a hold of yourself. Jared is gone, and the others will be too if you don't do something.* Medusa was the voice of reason as usual. I had to get past Matt, and now Jared, too. *We need to join our powers to show him he can't do this. If we don't do something big soon, he'll keep killing everyone.*

I could only think of one thing that would get his attention and keep him from killing anyone else. *Let's raise every soul in Tartarus.*

*We can't raise every soul. The Titans are in the pit of Tartarus. Believe me, you don't want them here.*

No, and neither did Hades. *We'll keep them in our back pockets.* Threaten *to raise them if need be.* Hell, I'd raise anyone or anything to end this once and for all.

I willed my blood to mix, and I felt Medusa channeling her power as well.

*Focus on mixing our powers together. We have to blend them so you'll have total control over them.*

*You're giving me total control over your powers? I thought we were in this together.*

*I'm right here, but only one of us can use the power. It's your body. I won't take it over on you.* She didn't say it, but there was an implied "unless I need to" attached to that sentence.

I was so focused on Medusa and joining our powers that I'd lost sight of Hades again. I turned from Jared and searched for Hades' smug smile. He had vanished again. He was going to sneak-attack someone else, the coward.

"Alex, stay with Leticia. Everyone be ready to run. The second you see swirling smoke, get out of here."

"Why don't we just run for it now?" McKenzie asked.

"It's too risky. We wouldn't get far before Hades attacked one of us."

"Jodi, what are you doing?" Alex sounded out of breath. He must have been freaking out. "What's the plan?"

"You'll see." I wasn't about to verbalize it, not without knowing where Hades was or if he was listening in.

*Let's do this,* I said to Medusa. I reached out to the souls that were in Tartarus with us, the ones in this section at least. I'd leave the pit as a last resort. For the first time, the raising was easy and painless. The souls knew I was trying to free them. Most of them had seen me here with them. They willing latched on to Medusa's and my power, hitching a ride out of Hell.

"No!" Hades appeared in front of me this time.

"Jodi, look out!" Alex rushed to me.

Hades reached for me, but my skin was literally on fire now. As he was able to produce flame himself, I doubted it would burn him, but he pulled away. I'd at least succeeded in shocking the hell out of him. Hades changed tactics as I raised more souls. They swirled around us and out of Tartarus. Hades looked up at them before glaring at me.

"You think I can't stop you?" He grabbed Alex, wrapping one arm around his neck.

"Keep going, Jodi," Alex choked out. "Let him kill me. As long you beat him, I don't care what he does to me."

Hades laughed. "How brave and incredibly stupid of you. She can't beat me. I'm a god."

My focus wavered.

*Jodi, concentrate. I don't want Alex getting hurt either, but if you stop now, Hades will win.*

Oh, God. She wanted me to forget that Alex was being strangled to death. Forget that his life was in Hades' hands.

*You are the Ophi leader. You must do what's right for the group. Alex would want you to.*

*I can't lose him.* I was still pulling souls from Tartarus, but my pace slowed. *Please, Medusa. I can't.*

"That's right, Jodi," Hades said. "Back off or your precious boyfriend is mine."

I turned to face Hades.

*Jodi, no!*

I wasn't giving up, but I wasn't letting Alex die, either. I continued to pull souls, but this time, I sent them after Hades. Slowly. I held them back while I locked eyes with Hades.

"Let him go, and I'll call them off." I gestured to the souls walking his way.

"This trick again? I stopped them earlier. Why would you try to send them after me now? Desperate, perhaps?"

"Let go of Alex or they will attack."

Hades smiled. Apparently, he found me quite amusing. He sure laughed at me enough. "Oh, Jodi Marshall. I kind of hoped you'd go out on a better note. This is...well, pathetic."

"Then let go of Alex and take me on yourself." My voice was strong, and there was a faint echo to it. No, not an echo. It was Medusa's voice mixed in with mine. How was that possible?

*Medusa, are you doing that?*

*We are one.*

*But you didn't want me to stop raising the souls.*

*I trust you know what you're doing. I'll follow your lead.*

Hades squinted, and the full weight of his anger bore down on me. He pushed Alex to the side. "Have it your way. We'll fight to the end. *Your* end."

"For once, you're right. I intend to fight to the end, but it's going to be the ending *I* want." The one that freed the Ophi for good. My blood reached out to the souls, giving them the command to attack. They seemed happy to get the chance for revenge because I didn't need to tell them twice. They lunged for Hades. At first, Hades fought them off with no problem, but I continued to call more souls. And this time, I wasn't stopping with Tartarus. I pulled from the Fields of Asphodel, too. I wasn't touching the Elysian Fields. The souls in there deserved the peace they'd found. I wouldn't deny any of them that.

Hades was getting angrier, and a small amount of fear shone in his eyes. He knocked the souls down repeatedly, but they wouldn't stop coming back. It was unending. The others just watched, not sure who was going to win in the end. I had to admit it didn't look like either of us would come out victorious. We were too evenly matched.

Hades tried to disappear in a swirl of smoke, but the souls latched onto him. He only succeeded in moving about a foot, and they came with him. My dad was gripping Hades' neck, trying to protect the daughter he'd been denied the chance to know. "Enough!" Hades bellowed, but I didn't listen. I wasn't going to be the girl who fell for such an obvious tactic. "Figure it out. You can't win."

"Wrong." My voice was a blend of mine and Medusa's again. "*You* can't win."

This time Hades noticed the change. "Do you plan to live the rest of your life with Medusa's soul inside you?" He sent another group of souls back to where I'd summoned them. "Better ask Alex if he's okay with dating both of you. It's going to be like a twenty-four-seven chaperone. Very romantic." He was trying to get to me, make me question what I was doing.

"That would scare you, wouldn't it? Knowing we were joined against you? Do you really want us as an enemy?"

"We aren't getting anywhere here. How long can you really keep this up before your body collapses under all that power? Did she tell you what could happen to you?"

*Don't listen to him*, Medusa said in my mind. *He's trying to make you doubt me. He's desperate. He knows we are too strong to fight.*

*He's too strong to fight, too. We aren't winning. We're struggling just as much as he is. He's not wrong. We can't keep this up forever. I'm sending the others out while Hades is under our control.*

*They won't be able to get out, Jodi. Only Hades can send you all back to the mortal plane now.*

Crap! This really wasn't going to work.

"Are you ready to deal?" I asked Hades, sending a new wave of souls to pound on his body.

"Deal? You're really looking to make a deal after all the others you made failed so miserably?" He laughed again as he sent the souls flying backward, my dad included.

I raised them again and sent the souls in rows like an army. As one row fell, the next attacked. It would've been a great strategy against anyone who wasn't a god. I couldn't kill him. I could only annoy him until he was willing to listen. I wondered how long that would take. I was getting tired of this.

"Well? Are you debating your answer, or is this all taking too much of your energy?"

"We could go on all night," Medusa and I said together. "Now, the question is, are you ready to deal?"

"Fine." He belted back a few more souls. "Here are the conditions—"

"No." I cut him off. "I'm making the conditions this time. You don't get a say in this."

"I don't deal like that."

"Sure you do. You've made unfair deals with me from the start."

"You were the one to set the first deal, Jodi Marshall. I simply agreed to it."

As if that was how it had really happened. "You set me up to fail. You took my deal, knowing you could work around it and come out on top."

"I don't make deals I can't win."

"I don't either, anymore. So, let's make a deal we'll both benefit from. And this time, no loopholes or ways to manipulate your way out of it. We do it fairly."

"Call off your souls, and we'll talk. I'm not dealing like this. Not while I have to beat back souls every two seconds." He pushed his hands forward, sending the souls toppling into Abby and Quinn.

I had to make sure this wasn't on his terms. I wasn't putting myself into a position to get played again.

"We'll go to the palace. All of us. The judges will determine if the deal is fair."

Hades smirked. "You're going to let them decide the deal? You may as well hand your souls over to me now. They work for me."

"Like I said, I'll decide the deal. The judges will confirm its fairness. That's all." I'd stopped saying we. Medusa's voice was no longer mixed with mine.

*Medusa, why aren't you talking with me anymore?*

*Because you don't need me. You are handling this on your own. I'll still be here if you need me, but I'm stepping back.*

"You need to call the souls off if we are going to move to the palace."

"No. I think my friends and I will go first. The souls will keep you company until we're in the palace. Then I'll call them off so you can join us." Wow, I was actually calling the shots. This was either going to go really well, or Hades was going to be so pissed off he was going to kill me the second he got the chance.

"Angering me more isn't the best idea right now," Hades said through gritted teeth.

"I'd say the same to you, and since I don't trust you to let us go peacefully, I'm going to have to insist on my plan. See you at the palace." I motioned for the others to head out of Tartarus. Abby, Quinn, and the other Victoria and Troy followers stared after us. Damn it. "Any of you who want to stop being Victoria's and Troy's little lapdogs and start acting like real Ophi are free to join us."

Alex touched my shoulder gently. I could tell he didn't want to distract me from raising the souls and keeping Hades under control. "Are you sure about this?"

I looked at Arianna, who was staring hopefully at Abby. "Yes, I'm sure."

I waited for the others to leave before I followed behind them. I didn't need to see Hades or the souls. I could sense what was happening here. I waited for Abby to come with us. She stared at Lexi and Arianna, not moving. Finally, I turned and motioned for her.

"Come on, Abby. This isn't you. Your mom and sister know it. Drop the tough girl act and get over here with us."

She walked past me, barely looking at me. "Fine. But I'm only doing this to get out of this hellhole. It has nothing to do with you or anyone else." Liar. The way she said "anyone else" gave her true feelings away. She wanted her family back, and though she'd never admit it, she was grateful I was giving her the chance to have that again.

We headed to the palace, one big group of Ophi. The old and the new mixed. Tensions were high, especially since these were the people who had tortured us for countless hours. Well, all except Victoria and Troy. They were still unconscious in Tartarus. As much as I wished I could give Alex his parents back, I couldn't. Medusa had told me that some Ophi just aren't good. Victoria and Troy were proof of that. They wouldn't change.

"You okay?" Alex asked. "Controlling the souls still?"

"Yeah. Medusa and I have this under control."

"Thanks for letting the others come back," Lexi said, coming up on the other side of me. "That was pretty cool of you."

"It was the right thing to do."

We walked up to the palace doors and paused as a group. We all looked at one another for a moment.

"Understand that, by coming with us now, you are swearing to be on our side. We're family from here on out. Whatever's happened before now is done. We move on together. That's the only way to keep Hades from doing this again."

Everyone nodded, but I wasn't satisfied yet. "Anyone have any hesitations?"

Not even Abby spoke up. Arianna took her hand and squeezed it. Abby's bottom lip trembled.

"Good. Then let's do this and get the hell out of here." Seriously, the Hell jokes had to stop, but they were our only source of comic relief in this place.

I opened the doors and stepped inside. The judges were sitting at their thrones, but they weren't alone. Another god was standing in front of them, and judging by the lightning bolt he held in his hands, I knew it was Zeus.

It always came back to Zeus.

# Chapter 34

Why hadn't I paid more attention in lit class when Tony—or Mr. Quimby as I'd called him then—was talking about Zeus? I racked my brain for anything I could remember. He was like the head honcho of the big Greek gods. He was the one who'd placed Ophiuchus in the sky as a constellation to appease Hades, who didn't want all his souls being taken from the underworld. Oh, crap! I was still using Medusa and my powers to send souls after Hades. Was that why Zeus was here? Had Hades called him to do something about me? Was I about to earn a spot next to Ophiuchus in the sky?

I let my blood calm and stopped commanding the souls. Maybe I could still talk my way out of this. Zeus was supposed to be the god of justice or something like that. He might listen to reason. Zeus slammed his lightning bolt downward, hitting the ground with enough force to shake the entire underworld. I bet even the Titans in the pit felt it. His long, blond hair flew up in response to the gesture.

"I take it you are Jodi Marshall," Zeus said, his sky-blue eyes staring directly at me. Somehow I didn't think it was a good thing that he'd already singled me out.

"Um, yes, sir." I debated bowing. He was the king of the gods, but I'd never been a huge fan of Zeus. I hoped he wasn't aware of that little fact.

"You've been causing a great deal of trouble for me."

I braced myself for what was coming next.

"Those souls you raised are wreaking havoc in the mortal plane."

How could I have forgotten about them? I'd raised them to get Hades' attention. To show him what Medusa and I could do together—how miserable we could make his existence if he didn't strike a deal with us. I never stopped to think about what hundreds of zombies would do when they rose from their graves.

"I'm sorry. I had to get Hades to listen to me. To stop torturing me and my friends. I'll release them now."

Zeus put his hand up. "No need. I've already taken care of it. They are once again under my brother's control."

His brother. The way he said it sent chills down my spine. Zeus was Hades' brother, and he was here to help him.

"Zeus, I never meant to cause a problem for you. Hades has been—"

"A jackass?" Zeus raised one eyebrow at me. "Yes, I'm well aware of what my brother is like." He paced in front of the judges. "Why do you think I let him rule down here? He has the least impact on the mortal plane this way. It keeps him out of my hair…most of the time. But then you came along and stirred up all sorts of trouble for me." He stopped and stared at me. Compared to Zeus, Hades looked like a puppy dog. Zeus was downright frightening. "I can't have you disturbing the balance of things like this. When my brother is upset…well, it's never good."

"Are you here to take me away? Put me in the heavens with Ophiuchus?"

Alex grabbed my hand. Obviously the thought hadn't crossed his mind.

"No." Zeus walked toward me, stopping only two feet from me. "I'm here to moderate a deal between you and Hades. I won't allow this sort of thing to happen again."

Moderate a deal. Maybe this wouldn't be so bad. I'd chosen to come to the palace hoping the judges would help us come to a fair arrangement. Zeus could help me make Hades agree to a deal that I liked. Or Zeus, being Hades' brother, might screw the Ophi over completely. But Persephone had said Zeus asked her to go to the underworld to distract Hades. That had to mean he was on my side, or at least not on Hades' side, which was good enough for me.

"Ah," Zeus said. "Speak of the devil."

A cloud of black smoke swirled in the palace doorway. Hades had arrived. He looked at Zeus, and his eyes widened. "Brother. Did we have a meeting set up for today? Perhaps it slipped my mind with all I had going on here."

"No. No meeting scheduled, but my presence is necessary." Zeus motioned to me and the other Ophi. "We have a situation. One I don't feel you can handle on your own." He looked around. "I take it Persephone has gone."

Hades gritted his teeth. Great, Zeus had to remind him that, thanks to me, he'd missed saying goodbye to his wife. "For the time being."

"Then I was right to come." Zeus walked past the judges and sat in Hades' throne. Wow, what a slap in the face. He was asserting his position over Hades.

Hades' fist clenched. "I believe that is *my* seat, brother."

Zeus rested his lightning bolt on Persephone's throne. "As you are, in a way, being judged here too, I feel your place is down there with the Ophi you've created such an unpleasant feud with."

Did Zeus just say Hades had created the feud? Maybe he *didn't* blame me.

"You can't be serious," Hades yelled.

"Have you ever known me to joke?" Zeus' face showed no emotion.

I raised my hand like a little schoolgirl. "Excuse me, Zeus. I have a deal I think would be fair for all involved."

He sat forward in his chair, lacing his fingers in his lap. "Go on. However, unless the deal includes Medusa's soul, which I can clearly see resting inside you, you should consider revising it."

He'd sensed Medusa's presence immediately. He really was more powerful than Hades.

"Actually, it does." My voice wasn't my own at all. It was Medusa's. *What are you doing?* I asked her.

*What needs to be done. The gods have wanted my soul for a long time. I need to show them I'm willing to give them what they want in exchange for your freedom.*

*Medusa.* Even my mental voice was shaking with emotion. *I'm not ready to say goodbye to you.*

*I know, my child. I don't want to say goodbye to you, either, but we must do what is best for our people.*

What was best for the Ophi was having Medusa with us. *Medusa, do you trust me?*

*You know I do.*

*Then let me make the deal.*

*It is your body. I will not speak through you again.*

*Thank you, Medusa.*

I hoped this would work. "Zeus," I paused, waiting for him to allow me to continue. He nodded. "I know you and the other gods want Medusa's soul to move on to the afterlife where you feel she should be. I've discussed this with Medusa, and she wants me to take her place. To lead the Ophi and be the one to give them power. I agreed, but now I see I was wrong. I can't become the next Medusa. There is no such thing."

"Then there will be no deal!" Hades yelled behind me. He rushed to the throne. "Brother, she doesn't want to give up Medusa's soul, which means we do not have to go along with whatever she wants. Put an end to this now."

"Wait!" I held my hand up. "I'm not finished. Please, hear me out." Again, I waited for Zeus, ignoring Hades completely.

"Go on," Zeus said, dismissing Hades with a wave.

"Hades has trouble ruling the underworld alone. That's why he took Persephone. Only, she doesn't stay here all year long." I hoped reminding Zeus that Hades had kidnapped his daughter would work in my favor. "What I'm proposing is that Medusa's soul will fill the gap Persephone creates when she leaves. She'll help Hades rule—not as his wife, though, but as his partner. Who better to help souls move on than Medusa?"

Zeus wrinkled his forehead, thinking about my offer. Hades turned and glared at me.

*Jodi, may I?*

*Go right ahead.*

"Hades," Medusa said, her voice coming from my lips once again. "You've seen what Jodi and I are capable of together. You don't want an enemy, and neither do we. Jodi's powers are now under control. As long as you promise not to interfere with the Ophi, and allow her to teach them the right way to be necromancers in their own world, then I will assist you for all eternity in Persephone's absence. I will be nothing but helpful to you. Not as a servant, but as a partner."

"I wouldn't get your powers," Hades said. "How does this benefit me?"

"You would not need my powers. I'd use them myself to help you rule here."

Hades could pretend he wasn't happy with the deal, but he knew as well as I did that having Medusa's help was definitely going to benefit him.

Zeus nodded. "The deal sounds more than reasonable to me."

"Hang on!" I said, regaining control of my voice again. "There's one more thing. No, two more things. First, Medusa shouldn't have to be locked inside some statue at the school when she's on the mortal plane. Can you return her body to her? And second, if Hades should break his end of the deal, I want you to promise you'll stop him."

Zeus drummed his fingers on his knee. "As for Medusa's body, I cannot produce it. As you know, she was beheaded. Her head was a prize of sorts, and I will not take that away from its victor. However, she can exist as a soul, much like she'd look here, fully in form."

"Without the snakes?" I asked. "She was beautiful before Athena cursed her. Will you allow her to take that form again?"

"You're asking me to go against my daughter now? Isn't it enough that I am making my brother adhere to a deal with you?"

"Honestly…no. Hades brought this on himself. He came after me and tried to make me break our deal. If he hadn't done that, I would've upheld my end of it."

Zeus glared at Hades. "By your lack of comment, I'll assume that's true. However, Medusa betrayed Athena, and I cannot deny my daughter the curse she placed on Medusa as a result. She will remain as she is."

I felt a tugging sensation. *Medusa, what's happening?*

*Zeus is trying to take me out of your body. It would be wise to assist him.*

Even though I wasn't happy with Zeus' decision, I mixed my blood and released Medusa's soul from my body. She appeared next to me, beautiful—except for her snakes—and wearing her locket, which once again contained her blood.

"How?" I looked at Zeus, who shook his head at me like I was an ignorant mortal. He was king of the gods. Restoring the locket and returning it to Medusa was nothing compared to what he was capable of.

Medusa removed her locket and held it out to me. "This is yours now. Lead them well."

I took it, surprised that it was exactly as it had been the first time I'd seen it. Alex helped me put it on. My fingers rose to touch the precious bloodstone. I was never taking it off again.

I faced Zeus. "Thank you."

He nodded. "Now, as for your second condition. If either you *or* Hades breaks your end of this deal, I will intervene. As I said earlier, I won't have this sort of thing happen again. Balance will be restored, and it will remain. You know the rules, Jodi Marshall. And, Hades, you know them as well. Consider yourselves warned."

I smiled, happy to agree. Hades, on the other hand, scowled. His hands had been tied.

"Now," Zeus said, "seeing as Persephone is with Demeter, I believe this throne belongs to you, Medusa."

She gave my hand a gentle squeeze. "I couldn't be more proud of you, Jodi."

My eyes teared as she let go of me and took her place on the throne.

"Hades, are we in agreement?" Zeus stood and moved away, motioning for Hades to take his place.

"What can I say? You've won, brother." Scowling, he stepped up to the throne and sat next to Medusa. They were the strangest pair, but I knew they'd work together. Zeus would make sure of it.

"There's only one thing left before I go," Zeus said.

"Wait!" This wasn't over yet. "Zeus, Hades took a friend of mine. Two, actually. Melodie is human. He killed her to hurt me. I'd like her back."

Zeus nodded. "I have already returned her to her mortal life. She will have no memory of being here." Maybe I hadn't given Zeus enough credit. He was a decent god after all.

"And Jared. Hades killed him."

"Jared was an Ophi casualty. I cannot reverse that." He said it matter-of-factly and with no feeling whatsoever. That brought him down a notch in my book.

McKenzie sniffled behind me. We'd be having another memorial when we got back to the school.

"Jared will be with Matt and Amber in the afterlife," Zeus said.

"But Amber is in Tartarus and Matt's—"

"They've been moved to the Elysian Fields. I have restored all the souls to the places the judges have deemed suitable." Zeus smirked at Hades, exerting his power over him and the underworld. I could've hugged him if he didn't scare the living dead out of me.

At least Matt would be happy now, and he wouldn't be alone. I'd rest easier knowing that. But I'd still lost my dad. I knew better than to ask for him back. Zeus would never allow it. But maybe there was something I could still do for him. "Zeus."

He cocked his head. "You are about to ask me for yet another favor?" His tone implied he thought that would be unwise but, well, I didn't give a damn what was wise. I wanted to do what was right.

"My father, Derek Colgan. I can't believe he was meant to be in Tartarus."

"He was not," the middle judge said. "We reviewed his life and determined he should be placed in the Fields of Asphodel."

The Fields were better than Tartarus, but my dad would lose all sense of himself there. "Then I want to appeal to you all. My father was manipulated by Victoria and Troy. He wasn't a bad person. He left my mother and me to keep us safe."

Zeus raised his hand. "I can tell that you will not allow your father's soul to remain in the underworld. You'll raise him every chance you get."

I started to lower my head but stopped myself. "He's my father, Zeus. Wouldn't you want Persephone to do the same for you if she were in my position?"

Zeus sighed. "Your father will serve my brother here in the underworld during the time that Medusa is at the school with you." He turned to Hades. "Serve, not be tortured in Tartarus." I was about to thank Zeus when he added, "And when Medusa is here, your father's soul will return to the school to help you train the others. I suspect he'll be a willing soul to work with."

Tears streamed down my cheeks. I knew that was the best offer I could've hoped for. And while I also knew Zeus was only doing this to ensure Hades and the Ophi didn't go to war again, I was more than grateful. "I can't thank you enough."

"You will thank me by ensuring this never happens again." His eyes bored into mine so intensely that I knew pissing him off would be ten times worse than feuding with Hades. "Now, I need to get going, but first, Hades, you need to return them to the mortal plane."

I didn't even look at Hades. Instead, my eyes found Medusa.

"I'll see you in a few months, my child." She smiled at me the way a mother smiles at her daughter.

I nodded. "I'm looking forward to it."

Hades waved his hand, and a swirl of black smoke wrapped around us, lifting us in the air. Just like when he'd brought us here, we couldn't see a thing through the smoke. But soon enough, we were brought down to rest in the cemetery of the school. We were home.

There were hugs all around. Even Abby hugged her mom and sister. Things were going to be okay. We'd find a way to use our powers to help people. To save innocents who weren't meant to die. We'd still have to raise souls from the underworld to train, but we'd return them. And best of all, we were going to have Medusa with us for part of the year. Not as a statue that only *I* could talk to, but as a soul we all could see and communicate with. The Ophi were going to be okay. Better than okay.

Tony approached me with open arms. "I've always regretted that I never had a daughter of my own, but I'd like to make up for it by being the best second father to you—when your father is serving Hades in the underworld, that is. Of course, it's completely up to you. I understand if—"

I hugged him tightly, because he was the closest to a father I'd ever had, and I knew Tony would do his best to fill the hole in my heart each time my dad had to return to the underworld to serve Hades. Over Tony's shoulder, my dad's soul nodded to me. I smiled back at him, knowing he was glad Tony would look after me when he couldn't.

Carol was already on her cell calling Mason. Her smile and the happy tears streaking her face said it all. Our lives were getting back to normal. She walked over to me and placed a hand on my shoulder. "Mason said he wants to work with you to show you how you can be around your mom without putting her in danger. It will take a while before you get to that point, but in time you can do it. It's his way of saying thank you for all you've done."

It was my turn to cry. Being able to see my mom again meant the world to me. I threw my arms around her and cried on her shoulder. When I finally pulled away, Alex was waiting for me.

He wrapped one arm around my waist. "You did it."

I wiped my tears away. "I didn't think I was going to pull it off."

"I knew you would. You're incredible, Jodi. The Chosen One." He smiled. "You've earned yourself anything you want to do. What's it going to be?"

I reached up, draping my arms around his neck. "Anything?" Before he could answer, I pressed my lips to his. Being with him was Heaven to me, and I could stay this way forever.

# Acknowledgements

I'm not sure how to even begin expressing my gratitude to Kate Kaynak and Spencer Hill Press. I'll never forget the night I got the call saying Spencer Hill Press had offered on my series. The tears of joy, relief, and disbelief I cried that night are forever burned in my memory. Every step along the way has been an absolute dream come true. I'm truly blessed to work with such a close group of people who make me feel like family every time I talk to them or see them in person. Trisha Wooldridge, I feel like you are just as much a part of Jodi's story as I am. You made the editorial process fun, which is saying a lot. And all the Tony fans out there have you to thank for his role in this series. Thank you for being someone that I absolutely love to work with, and for understanding the way my brain works. Thank you to my team of copy editors, Rich Storrs, Keshia Swaim, N. Apythia Morges, and Shira Lipkin for polishing my books and making them ready for readers. To Kendra Saunders, Jennifer Allis Provost, and Kayleigh-Marie Gore, thank you for all your hard work in getting this book into the hands of book bloggers and readers everywhere. Marie Romero, you are a master at making the inside of a book just as gorgeous as the outside. Many thanks to you.

Lauren Hammond, my agent of awesome, I don't really know how to thank you for always being in my corner, for taking my panicked phone calls, for texting back and forth on weekends, and for the countless other things you do. I hope Hammond and Hashway are together forever. And to my agency sisters, writer friends, YA Bound sisters, and critique partners, your support keeps me sane. I'm so glad I have you all to share this journey with me.

To my daughter, Ayla, who has come to hate my computer and the amount of time I have to spend on it, I love you for thinking you have a famous mom. As long as I'm famous in your eyes, I'm happy. To my husband, Ryan, thank you for always offering to help me work, even though we both know you aren't a reader or a writer. Your support means so much to me. To my mom, Patricia Bradley, thank you for reading every word I write and then not being afraid to tell me when I can do better. You do more than support me. You push me to be better. To my father, Martin Bradley, who tells everyone he meets that his daughter is a writer, thank you for always letting me know you're proud of me. My sister, Heather DeRobertis, you keep me sane when I'm feeling overwhelmed, so thank you for that. Thanks to my friends and family for always asking how my writing is going and understanding when I hibernate in my writing cave.

Thank you to Donna Rosenblum for not only reviewing my books in the *School Library Journal* but also coming to see me at BEA. As always, many thanks and cyber-hugs to the book bloggers who have supported this series. Keren Hughes, Kayleigh-Marie Gore, Brooke Delvecchio, Meg and Kassiah at Swoony Boys Podcast, Ida Keranen, and Beth Consugar, you all have been so incredible from the very start of this series. And to everyone who reads my books, thank you for taking the time to step into my world.

The moment seventeen-year-old Samantha Thompson
crawls out of her grave, her second chance at life
begins... Only Sam came back wrong.

**SPENCER HILL PRESS** · spencerhillpress.com

# "I am...forever watching..."

COLLEEN BOYD

SWAMP
Angel

## December 2013

SPENCER HILL PRESS · spencerhillpress.com

# Guilty until proven innocent...

River Daniels lives an ordinary life as a high school junior growing up in the confines of rural Texas until her boyfriend's brutal attack leaves her both a murderer and a fugitive. When River's closest girlfriends come to her aid, they make a hasty decision to not only help her, but leave their own troubled lives behind and join in her escape.

Tulip Teen • tulipromance.com

What if **you** let someone precious slip **away?**

LISA AMOWITZ

BREAKING GLASS

When the girl Jeremy loves disappears,
he tries to call her back from beyond
the grave to solve her murder.

How **far** would **you** go to get them **back?**

# #1 NYT and USA Today Bestselling Author of the Covenant & the Lux series.

## Some Rules Are Made To Be Broken... But Breaking the Ultimate Rule Can Change Everything.

HEATHER McCOLLUM

SIREN'S SONG

Jule Welsh can sing. She enthralls people
with her bel canto voice. But it takes
more than practice to reach her level of
exquisite song; it takes siren's blood
running through her veins.

**SPENCER HILL PRESS** · spencerhillpress.com

Kelly Hashway is a former language arts teacher who now works as a full-time writer, freelance editor, and mother to an adorable little girl. In addition to writing YA novels, Kelly writes middle grade books, picture books, and short stories. When she's not writing or digging her way out from under her enormous To Be Read pile, she's running and playing with her daughter. She resides in Pennsylvania with her husband, daughter, and two pets.

www.kellyhashway.com